Illusions of Lust

by Kylie Doyle

1

To all the unhinged women who ever secretly thought

'I could totally run a cult...'

Yes you could baby girl, this one's for you.

Trigger Warnings

This is an extremely dark romance that is not for everyone between two toxic people in a relationship that should be in no way emulated or strived for. Please take care of your mental health first and foremost.

Gaslighting, Emotional manipulation, Knife Play, Manipulation and coercion, Religious/spiritual indoctrination, Cult dynamics, Dubious consent / power imbalance, Vigilante justice (off-page and on-page), Graphic violence and death, Blood rituals/sacrificial themes, Branding and body markings, Self-harm (branding and blood for ritual purposes), Threats of violence and sexual violence, Stalking (from MMC to FMC romanticized within genre context), Explicit sexual scene, Consensual non-consent (CNC) / powerplay, Rough sex and dominance/submission dynamics, Obsession and possessiveness, Potential dubious consent in early scene, Manipulation under the guise of healing/spirituality, Fire / arson, Blood imagery and oaths, Implied substance use (herbal, ritualistic), Attempted suicide of FMC (MMC saves her)

Table of Contents

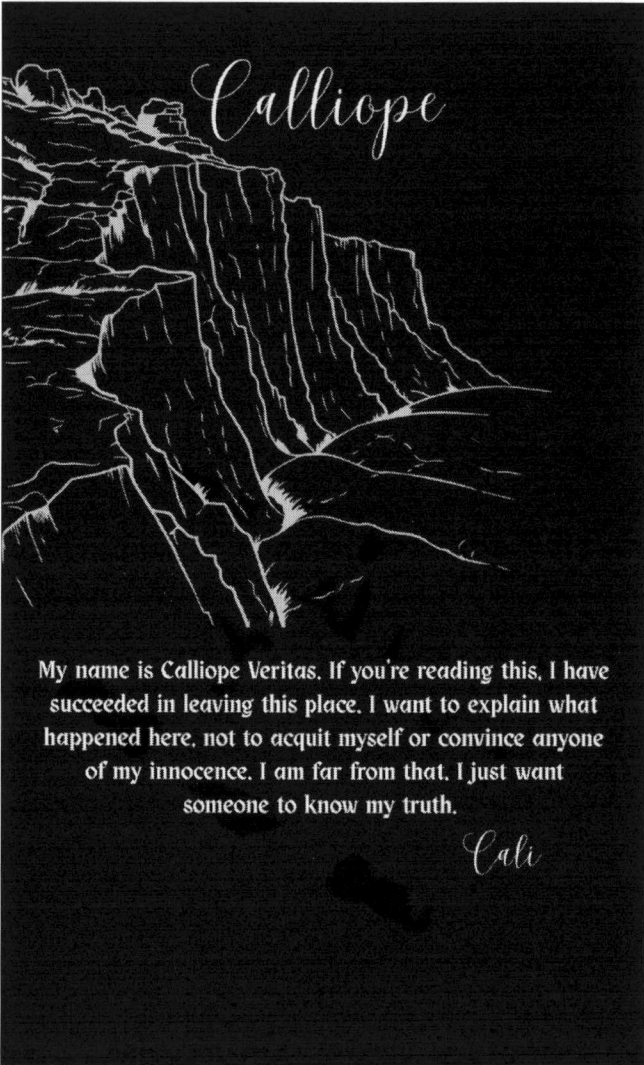

Calliope

My name is Calliope Veritas. If you're reading this, I have succeeded in leaving this place. I want to explain what happened here, not to acquit myself or convince anyone of my innocence. I am far from that. I just want someone to know my truth.

Cali

Chapter One

My head is already pounding, and it's not even noon. I can't stand the sun lately, so I'm still hiding in my chambers. It's my favorite place on the compound if we're not counting the cliffs. This room is my little sanctuary from everything that haunts me here. Its modern Gothic style, with over-the-top opulence, has my name all over it. I had the walls painted a custom black glitter, and most of my accessories such as my bamboo bed linens are also black. It's like living inside the void, with my reflection fractured across every angle by the mirrors scattered throughout the room.

The wall directly across from my bed is floor to ceiling books, complete with a rolling ladder. It's a book girl's dream. The wall that faces the ocean is all glass, and in the center is a set of custom French doors with red stained glass that reflects tiny rainbows across my dark grey hardwood floors. Although, as of late, that wall has been covered by my heavy midnight velvet curtains more often than not.

I've been spending more time here, hiding from everyone's prying eyes and whispering voices. It's the only place in the world where I can find any peace anymore. I flop down on the bed with my current read in my hands. A tragic romance I've read a thousand times. Love cut short by death. A tale as old as time.

I don't know why I read romances to begin with. I've never fallen in love with anything but power. I've had plenty of boyfriends, but they all had something I could gain from them—some kind of influence they wielded. I always enjoyed sucking the life out of them and discarding them like accessories I no longer cared to adorn myself with. Men don't know how to wield true power. Most are overgrown babies looking for the perfect wife to take their mother's place. Then they find me. Someone to stroke their egos, explore all their wildest fantasies with, actually fuck them.

Even the rich and the mighty fall to their knees with the right motivation. The more powerful the man the more I revel in watching them fall at my feet. The second they're willing to give me the world at their expense, to leave their wives and children behind, or go into debt just to pay for my attention is the very moment I lose interest. Then the hush money comes, so I don't, you know, ruin their fucking lives. They just make it so easy. Men are so malleable, so driven by their instinct to rut. If they were being honest, none of them loved me either. I've always curated my personality especially for them, they never even knew me. Like a siren, they would all drown themselves for me even now, given half the chance. I'd just have to say the word. I'm almost at the part of my book that actually makes me cry when a knock interrupts my only emotional outlet.

"Cali, you can't hide in your black hole all day."

Not if you keep interrupting me.

I throw the book down and quickly walk from my king-sized bed to the door, ripping it open. "What do you want? I'm busy."

My publicist and university friend, Vivianne Belmont, stands in front of me. Her face twists at my curt greeting, but she doesn't cower. I admire that about her. She's stunning. Her reddish copper hair against her alabaster skin is striking, and her emerald eyes are always sparkling as if she knows something you don't. Which she most likely does, she's one of the smartest women I know.

"Good afternoon to you as well," she says, pushing past me so I have no choice but to hear her out. "You can't keep avoiding the initiations."

I return to my book, ignoring her until she snatches it away.

"You can have this back when you've done your part to keep this place running."

From the smile on her face, I take it she thinks she's won this one.

"I have plenty more where that came from!" I yell before the door closes behind her—both of us knowing full well that I can't start another book before I finish the one in her hands.

Viv is correct, as much as I hate to admit I am wrong. I can't keep avoiding initiation night. I used to look forward to these evenings: the drugs, the sex, the sin. I no longer participate in any of it. Instead, I oversee the events like some kind of twisted monarch. Vivianne and her twin brother Zander, could perform the ceremonies without me, but people expect my presence. It somehow comforts them. It makes them feel like they are safe to surrender. All I do now is say a few words and then watch the heathens give in to the desires they don't dare admit to themselves outside of that room. At one time, it was entertaining, and even I gave in to my own dark desires. Now, it just feels like a noose and every dark sin I commit tightens the rope around my neck a little more.

I sigh dramatically before dragging myself out of bed with a groan and letting my burgundy silk robe fall to the floor. I admire my form in one of my full-length mirrors. I never was one of those girls who poked and prodded at her body. Even as curvy as my hourglass figure is, I always felt like a goddess. If I'm being honest, I watch my own body during sex more than I watch my partners or the actual act. Call me self-obsessed, but I think that's better than the alternative.

I'd rather spend my day naked while I read one handed but I decide to get dressed, seeing as Vivianne happens to be holding my current read hostage. My black knee length sundress with the pockets begs me to wear it, and I top off my look with my most giant pair of sunglasses and floppiest floppy hat: no makeup and no panties. No bra either for that matter. As I close the heavy door I 'salvaged' from an old abandoned church, I smile softly, impressed with my dramatic sense of style. My small moment of bliss is rudely interrupted by Zander's sarcasm.

"She rises from the dead!" His voice is like an old Hollywood movie narrator as he teases me.

"Why are you here?" I don't even stop walking down the hall to look at him.

"Why are you dressed like a mistress at a funeral?" he says, following me like an annoying younger sibling.

11

"If you don't watch your tone, it will be your funeral I am dressed for." I begin to walk a little faster as I attempt to put distance between us.

He catches up and gently stops me by grabbing my arm and turning me to face him.

"I'm worried about you, Cali. You can't keep isolating yourself like this. It's not healthy."

I rip my arm out of his hand.

"Do not psychoanalyze me, Zander. This whole place is enough to make anyone lose their mind. We're all fucking crazy for even being here. Let me be crazy in peace, for Christ's sake."

My feet start moving again, and I do not wait for his response. Everyone's so scared I might do something crazy like kill myself, and it's exhausting. Not unfounded though. I did tell everyone, 'the only way any of us will ever escape here is in a body bag,' at the last meeting I physically attended. Nobody here can take a fucking joke. It doesn't help that Zander majored in psych, which honestly makes this hellscape all the crazier.

I sigh heavily. I shouldn't be so abrasive to Zander. He does care about me in his twisted way. He sometimes gets jealous of my admirers and previous sexual conquests. He also gives mind-blowing head and impressive dick.

Actually, both the twins are magnificent in their own right. Even Vivianne has her wiles. I have experienced both. There are no feelings involved, not for me anyway. We have an understanding. What happens in ritual stays there, respectively. I love them in my warped way. If I were to say I consider them the siblings I never had, I would be incredibly fucked up, but there is a bond I can't deny. We've built this depraved world together. They are my right hands and my only friends. I have never fully trusted anyone but my mother, may the gods rest her perfect soul. If I did lean toward trust with anyone, it would be the twins.

I need to stop giving them such a hard time. I'm drowning in my misery right now, and I bite every hand they reach out to me with. I love what we have built together, strange as that is. It was beautiful and pure once, before I committed the ultimate sin. Borderline justified or not, I don't think the Sky Daddy would appreciate my leniency with the commandments.

Religion is so subjective. To my people, I am more than a sovereign leader; I am a deity, godlike in my stature. The adoration is wild, and if I am being honest, I used to delight in their worship and praise. Now, it sickens me to the point where I toss the contents of my meals regularly due to the stress of it all. I clutch my stomach in anticipation of this as I walk down the hallways to the only place I have

13

to drown these chaotic and intrusive thoughts, willing myself to keep myself stitched together.

●

A part of the gardens and cliffs is public for anyone in the compound to enjoy. I of course, have a restricted secret garden with a private overlook of the cliffs. It is my little paradise. It is the very part of the island that gave me that little tingle in my chest when the Realtor showed us around the property. I stride confidently to my pavilion on the edge of the tropical botanicas overlooking my favorite view. I close my eyes and breathe in the scent of salty florals— peonies, freesias, and hibiscus high notes and bursts of lavender, rose, and various herbs mixing with the earthy grounds and salty air. The sound of the waves crashing against the bluffs eases my nervous system into safety. I take another deep breath, holding it at the top before breathing out completely.

Sitting here I can almost imagine I have a different life than the one I live. I imagine myself with an apron on, sweating in front of an oven, and children fighting in the background while I say something pathetically domestic like, 'You kids, wait till your father gets home.' I chuckle to myself because even if I had lived a different life, that one is the furthest from any reality I could conjure.

I've never met anyone who gave me the desire to procreate. Children complicate what is already a complicated dance. People change or stop being who they were pretending to be in the beginning, and kids are a noose around freedom's neck. Breakups are messy enough as it is. Divorce is worse and kids just add another layer of complexity. I sound like a child of divorce not over the trauma, but I am an orphan. Death got the jump on my parents.

Honestly, at least they will never see the monster I have become or maybe they do. I just prefer to believe there is nothing after death. It is more comforting than facing the chains that will bind me and the faces I have disappointed. My mother was a trust-fund kid turned hippy, where most of my original wealth came from. My father was a military man listed as MIA ten days after my birth. My mother died when I was sixteen much too young for a girl to lose her mother. I'm thirty-one now, so I have lived half my life without her. The U.S. military paid for my university education, and I invested everything left to me by my mother, tripling my net worth and making myself a mogul before I was even twenty-one, which gave me plenty of time to scam men into falling in love with the idea of me and then bounce with even more money to invest and spend as I pleased.

I am sitting on the bench in the Gothic gazebo specifically designed for me to be in the sun. I have this habit of feeling faint in the heat, but I truly love the outdoors and feeling the rays kiss my skin. So, the shades block the harsh heat and I can sit to my heart's content. My feet swing absentmindedly and then immediately stop. There is a figure silhouetted against my private skyline. I rise from my seat and begin walking toward the figure. Sometimes the members can get lost in the gardens, but no one has ever ventured onto my side. Bile rises in my throat because I am fully aware of the spies among my loyal followers all with their specific and unique agenda or hired to care about someone else's interests. The latter I can usually pay off, but the former has to be discreetly disposed of.

My inner circle of heathens and staff are highly vetted by my resident hackers and security team, of which Viv happens to be in charge. Nothing gets by them and the intruders always push too hard or ask too many questions and are found out long before they ever get a chance to play out their plan. I have eyes everywhere, my own agents hidden among the common. Some have had orders to assassinate me, some to report on the inner workings and substantiate the crazy but true rumors. By the time I reach the figure, I feel a little faint.

"You are not supposed to be here. This is a restricted area," I address the figure, who I can now see is a man facing away from me.

The figure turns. His wavy chestnut hair is blown across his face by the wind, revealing his dark blue eyes that meet mine in pure defiance. His sharp jaw ticks as if he's annoyed with me, as he looks me over head to toe in a way that does something to my insides before responding.

"Says who?"

"I just did," I gesture to myself dramatically.

"And you are?" His eyes sparkle with amusement and his mouth forms a smirk.

"Calliope Veritas, but you already know who I am. If you're here, it would be impossible not to." I am starting to wobble a little. I want to wrap this up quickly. "You can leave of your own accord, or I can have you removed from the premises."

I turn to walk away, not caring who he is. There is no one here whose authority rivals my own. Who he is doesn't matter. I hear his footsteps falling into step behind mine.

"Problem is Calliope, I'm unsure how to get out of here. See, I got all turned around…"

I can hear the bait in his voice, but I don't bite.

"Clever, but not clever enough. Back the way you came is the way out," I point toward the gardens without stopping, because if I do, I will undoubtedly faint.

It's much hotter out on the cliffs where the sun feels closer. When I reach my gazebo, I turn to face the footsteps, but he has already slipped out of sight just as quickly as he came into view which is impressive. I am perplexed by his mere presence, as this part of the property is entry by an old-school lock and key, and I am the only one in possession of the said key. He would have had to climb the maze hedges without being caught on camera or by security, and that's unbelievable even to meet me.

I can feel an instant migraine approaching. I must have gotten overheated confronting my stranger and now I have minimal time to get to my cooling pool in my private gardens. I walk as fast as possible and get there just in time to collapse in the azure waters before I faint. I close my eyes and take a deep breath as I wiggle my toes and kick my feet. My dress is soaked, but it helps me regulate my temperature faster.

"You really shouldn't be out there on days this hot Cali," Vivianne's honey voice floats.

"Sucker for punishment, I guess." I don't open my eyes but I flash her a smirk.

"Must have been pretty bad if you're sitting in the pool in your funeral clothes."

"You and your brother have the same sense of humor… I do not share it." This time, I do open my eyes to stare blankly at her. She clutches my book in her hands, and my eyes settle there.

"If you ever want to see this book alive, you'll follow me." She turns on her heel, waving my book as she walks.

"I'm soaked Viv. Can't I change first?" I yell after her.

Without turning around, she yells, "At the risk of you settling back into your black hole? I think not. I'll have one of the staff members bring you something."

I sigh to myself. I will never win this argument, but I'll get my book back if I comply. I step out of the pool, my dress dripping wet, and I don't bother with my shoes. I run after Vivianne and catch up to her just as she's rounding the corner to walk through the part of the gardens that my followers have access to. My mind flashes to the stranger with the dark blue eyes. I debated telling Viv about the incident but decided not to. She would lose her marbles knowing I had been exposed and vulnerable like that, and I would most likely lose access to the key of what's left of my sanity. Neither she nor Zander would allow me to risk my safety like that. I may be the leader of this cult, but there are some things even I can get overruled on. I follow behind her silently instead.

♦

Vivianne leads me to my office, where she has already laid a stack of folders on my desk. I groan audibly, and she points to the pile, her lips pursed in annoyance.

"Groan all you want. When you decide on the initiates, you can have your freedom and your book and return to masturbating or doing whatever you do when you read alone in your room."

"Wouldn't you like to know?" I joke, but she is less than amused with me right now.

"Okay, Vivianne, you win."

I leaf through the candidates, pretending I give a fuck about any of this anymore. Viv rambles on about each candidate. Everyone has a reason to be initiated, some kind of justice has been stolen from them that they want to take into their own hands. Only the top followers and contributors get put before me as prospects. Only the worthiest of the revenge they seek. There are no guarantees we can facilitate it, but we do our due diligence. We look over every aspect of their case. If there is insufficient proof, we will never act upon the request.

Cephalonia is a name whispered outside courtrooms and lawyers' offices to victims whose justice fell short or never came. On the outside, we are an elite trauma healing facility. We offer intensive therapeutic in-house treatment. We have community gardens, yoga programs, daily reiki and spa treatments, and top-notch behavioral and trauma-informed therapists. You name it, Cephalonia specializes in it. At one time, that's all there was to us. Now, we just happen to be in the business of facilitating justice.

At some point during our discussion, a staff member whose name I do not know brings me a change of clothes. I strip down my wet dress before he leaves the room.

He's stunned, but Viv just says, "Thank you, that will be all," and he leaves.

I love doing shit like that in front of the followers. Viv shakes her head at me.

"I hate when you do that."

I laugh and continue thumbing through the files of this year's prospects. One option stops me in my tracks, my adventurous blue-eyed stranger. I keep my composure but listen when Viv gives me his background.

Aztyn Diamandis. Thirty-five. Single and never married. He is seeking justice from a high-profile woman who killed his brother. Before coming here, he owned a construction company. That explained the muscular build. He sold the company for nearly two million and donated it to Cephalonia almost six months ago.

"Normally, I wouldn't put someone like this up as a prospect with so little time with us, but he has shown impressive dedication to the movement, and I think he's worth moving along."

I didn't choose him immediately, but I knew I would say yes as soon as I saw his head shot. I pick several others and throw him in the pile like a last-minute consideration.

"Book, please." I put my hand out like a child begging for a snack.

"Pick a date first," she demands, the book clutched against her perfect tits.

"The first phase of the initiation can begin Friday. That gives me some time to prepare myself."

"I'll book the spa for you for the day then."

She hands me the book with one hand while she schedules things on her phone with the other. I leave her to her bliss. My job is done for now, and its only Monday, so I go down the halls with my nose between the pages and saunter by memory and peripheral vision.

When I arrive at my chambers, a small note is tacked to my door. I stare at it while my hand trembles over the knob. A red ribbon and red sealing wax keep the black paper bound. I tuck the book under my arm and look around the halls before reaching for the note. I should call Viv and Zander and have security check it out first, but something inside me screams not to. It could be a bomb although at least that would mean I could escape this place. My hand quivers as it approaches the strange new decoration on my door. My fingers tap the paper quickly, like a child checking to see if the stove is hot. I immediately feel foolish and grab the letter from the door. It feels heavy and almost cold in my hands. The paper stock is thick and expensive between my fingers.

It's the same paper we use for correspondence and invitations within the inner sanctum. I chose it specifically for its ominous and yet intriguing nature. The twins didn't share my enthusiasm at the time, and Viv had just checked off the task on her list and continued to shove more choices for other details she deemed insignificant and trivial in front of me. When building something, nothing is insignificant and every detail matters.

I open my door and lean against it as it shuts. Slinking to the floor, I begin to open the letter. It smells vaguely familiar, but I can't place the tobacco and mahogany scent that lingers on the paper to a face. Beautiful calligraphy is inside, and my breath hitches as I begin to read:

She moves like a damned angel
cast out from the heavens.
Dancing in and out of the shadows she made home.
The light burns
threatening to devour her soul
and yet she craves the sun.
She craves a life she cannot have
a life out of the shadows.
A wish she admits to no one.
Is everything you've built worth burning for
Little Muse?

The letter falls to the ground as a single tear cascades down my cheek. I deeply revere poetry, often moved by the colorful and romantic language. The personal and vaguely threatening flattery surprises me, and the feeling of my stomach twisting is unfamiliar and feral. I do not recognize the beautifully sloping handwriting, and the note is not signed. Only myself and the twins have access to this wing of the compound. Everyone who works on the premises must sign in and out, and the surveillance is state of the art.

I can't tell the twins and certainly can't alert security, or vicious chaos will surely ensue although that might be a trip.

After deciding I don't want anyone else to know, I pick the letter back up, clutch it to my chest, and feel something other than a thirst for an end for the first time in as long as I can remember. It's not hope. Hope is a fool's dream. This world is wicked and I am a violent and dark manifestation of that wickedness. There is no hope here not for me. This emotion is something else.

The letter is still clutched to my chest when I reach the back of my closet to find the switch. My fingers find it and flick it upwards. The wall opens slowly to reveal the panic room I had built in. The panic room that not even the twins know about. I had the builders keep it off the blueprints, and I paid more than enough for them to forget that they had ever built it.

The only things in it are my Bocote desk, a few of my most cherished books, and my diaries. The light flickers on as I pass the sensor. I slip the letter into the drawer of my desk and lock it. I know that no one but me knows about this room, but when you are me, you can't be too careful. There are secrets here, but we hold them as a collective. I have private secrets that I go to extreme lengths to keep to myself. The twins and I have to share nearly everything. It's never really sat right with me, so I write things in journals I

25

would never want anyone to read. All my innermost thoughts and every sin I have committed. The only possessions I cherish are in this room my journals, the signed copies of my favorite authors' books, and now this mysterious letter. As I leave, I flick the switch back down, and the wall swings back into place. My own little Narnia except there's no magical land behind that door. Just everything I hide from the world.

I return to bed after my very eventful day, book still in hand. I close the dark curtains around the four posts and switch my reading light on. It's the big-girl version of reading under the covers and is one of my guilty pleasures. I lie back on my pillows, propping myself up for a good reading session, when his face crosses my mind, and I am so distracted that I cannot continue reading. I hang my head off the edge of the bed, letting the blood flow, the curtains skimming my face ever so gently.

The matter of how he got into my paradise is irrelevant to me now a mere aside. I want to know why. Why did he risk initiation and being kicked out entirely to sneak onto my side of the cliffs? Was he the one who left me the letter? The overwhelming feeling of being hunted creeps into my chest, making it feel heavy and constricted but I am not afraid. I am electrified and more alive than I have been in ages. Every cell in my body vibrates in response to the fight or flight taking over me. Perhaps I was wrong. Who he is likely matters a great deal. I settle back into my dark hole. My book beckons, but I don't reach for it. Instead, I fall asleep dreaming of being chased and the thrill of being caught.

Calliope

I never leave the private grounds any more but today something beckons me out of my black hole. I do not want to admit to myself that I want to see him again, but the part of me that is ever curious wonders, will he be out there seeking me too?

Cali

Chapter Two

I am in the market when I see him. A part of me hoped he would be here, so I dressed the part of a muse before arriving. My black dress is fitted but casual, my shoes are sensible for the occasion today but fashionable, and my wide-brimmed hat completes the look, giving me a certain edge—not unlike the classy Italian women you see in the movies. I look like someone might ask to paint me at any moment. I catch him watching me in my peripherals as I squeeze and evaluate the market's fruit. He is dressed as my counterpart, coincidentally: a white linen shirt, slightly open, revealing the sharp cut of his clavicle, and black linen pants with matching black oxfords on his feet. I pretend not to notice him, sensing that noticing him is exactly what he wants me to do.

"How are the summer crops doing on the farm?" I ask the shopkeeper attending the fruit stand today.

"Oh, just wonderful, Calliope. We fixed that aphid problem with the solution you told us about, and the next day we released the ladybugs. No sign of a second infestation," she responds animatedly.

"I knew it would be fine, and no harm was done to the crops." I smile softly, moving around the stand to keep the handsome stranger in my view.

"We miss you down at the farms. You should come visit us in the next few days—the peaches will be ready."

"I will, thank you. I'm looking forward to it. Have a box each of mangoes, pomegranates, pineapples, passionfruit, and starfruit sent up to the private kitchens for me, please."

"Having a private party up at the cathedral, Miss Veritas?" she leans in to whisper.

I cock my head to the side, my eyebrows knitted together. "Oh, you know me—I always like to pick the week's freshest produce by hand." My voice is tense, slow, and deliberate, my eyes unblinking.

"Of course, I… only wondered…"

"Best we don't do that out loud… isn't it?" After a pause, the smile returns to my face. "Will you have my list sent?"

The shopkeeper nods nervously. I gesture for her to repeat my list to make sure she heard correctly, smile again, and continue through the market. She is only curious if the rumors are true. Some people walk around here with the kind of smile on their face that says, *I know something you do not*, and the rest are unenlightened, so to speak. Curiosity killed the cat… but satisfaction brought it back.

I love the market, but I haven't been down here myself in months. I can draw a small crowd, and the more curiosity eats at those who do not know, the braver and bolder they get in their attempts to find the answers they seek. The walls listen here, and I am exposed in a way that would make Viv and Zand nervous. I didn't even bring a security detail. Despite our supreme efforts, there are people here who would do me harm or hold me ransom. I've made quite a few enemies in my most recent endeavors. I couldn't even tell you why I came down today, but I don't fear death— not when he is currently watching me from across the open space plaza.

The market was an important aspect I believed in when we first founded this retreat center. Nothing here costs anything. It's like an all-inclusive resort. So, the idea of a free working market was born. Ours is based on trade. Everyone can bring their best product to the table, whether that's the furniture they make, the food they grow, the preserves they canned, or the jewelry they smithed, and it can be traded for things they want and need. Even our short-term guests love the market; they do, however, spend real money usually, and the shopkeepers are welcome to keep it. Many of the shopkeepers and artisans have websites through which they ship out their products and receive worldwide revenue for their wares. It's really quite incredible to watch.

Deep down, I know I should be afraid of the man surveilling me from across the square, but I am enjoying his intense observation. His presence is calming, and yet I feel my heart beating as if I am a rabbit being stalked by a fox. I am no rabbit though… I only look like one.

I move between the vendors and follow the path down toward the apiary and the private wildflower garden of the bees. This path is less crowded, and the extra shadow I have acquired will have to make a choice: either he will follow, or his tailing of me will have to end for the day. The path bends around the trees, and I notice him hesitate. After a short deliberation, he chooses to follow me—except there's no longer anywhere for him to hide, because we are the only people on this road, and I am about to take a private walkway through the tropical forest.

I turn on my heel to face him abruptly, and he almost jumps back, recoiling from the sudden change in our game. I surprise him, and from the look of amusement on his face and the twitch in his lip, it doesn't happen often.

"Why are you following me?"

Aztyn chuckles. "Why do you think I'm following you?"

My eyes narrow in annoyance and refusal to play into his sparring match of words. "I'm going to the apiary, which, if you must know, is off-limits to the likes of you."

"The likes of me?" he scoffs, his feathers ruffled slightly before recovering. "Haven't you ever brought a guest? Someone you wanted to impress?" he says arrogantly as he takes a step or two toward me.

"You're thinking of Vivianne. I don't do the impressing." I roll my eyes, my arms crossed in front of me. "Try again."

Aztyn's eyes focus onto mine, and my knees shake from the potency of his demeanor. "Will you allow me to accompany you as your guest to the apiary, Miss Veritas?"

"You're stalking me, and now you want to be my guest?" I spit sarcastically.

He just smiles and takes another few steps forward without taking his eyes off me, the charm radiating so violently I almost feel a little dizzy.

"I'll take you with me instead of calling security on one condition… you answer a few questions of mine."

"Three," he responds nonchalantly. When I do not budge, he elaborates, "A few is three. I'll answer three questions."

"If I knew we were being so literal, I would have started at a higher bargaining point."

Aztyn just shrugs.

"Very well then, you may come along."

I wait for him to close the small distance between us and inhale his scent as he comes to stand beside me. Mahogany, caramel, and tobacco smoke invade my lungs, and I am stunned that this man has this effect on me. I've been around plenty of good-looking and incredible-smelling men, and I have never been this much of a puddle before.

Silence hangs in the air between us as the path bends and twists through dense vegetation, becoming less manicured and wilder as we walk. I resist the urge to make small talk; I don't want to accidentally misuse one of my questions, and something tells me this man is strict with the rules. Instead, he breaks the silence first.

"Why are you going to the apiary?"

I glance at him as we walk, and he just flashes me that wicked smile and looks forward again. I can't help but smile, and in response, I feel my cheeks begin to color slightly.

"If you had ever been there, you wouldn't be asking me that. It's the most magical place on the island."

I see his lip twitch the same way it did when I surprised him earlier. "Are you the one who left that poem?"

Aztyn's eyes brighten when he looks at me. "Most people would ask me why I was following you."

"I did, remember? You answered with another question. Besides, I'm not going to waste my questions if I only get three." I continue walking. We're not far from the apiary now.

"I am the one who left that poem," he says, keeping pace with me. "I'll throw in a bonus answer since you're such a clever girl: I left it because after I met you on the cliffs, I couldn't get you out of my head until I did."

I risk another glance in his direction as he speaks. I watch the way his lips move and his hands gesture, the way his eyes rove over my entire body—the language suggesting he is telling a truth, but not the entirety of it.

"I bet you say that to all the girls who swoon at your brooding and vaguely threatening poetry."

"So, you're saying you swooned then?" He whistles, punctuating the air between us. "Good girl."

I place my finger over his lips, disregarding him entirely and shushing him in the process. He's looking at me like I defied some kind of unwritten protocol, but I ignore his expression and turn his face toward the clearing he has yet to see. Clasping his hand in mine, we walk through the

35

opening of the forest. Before our eyes is a magnificent field of wildflowers and the extraordinary hum of thousands of bees collecting pollen—a droning crescendo amongst the blooms. Aztyn has forgotten all about my previous transgression, and I watch him take it all in for the first time. Even the hardest of hearts is softened by the heartbeat vibration of the bees. His eyes widen like a child's, and the air shimmers with the pulse of sound. I lead him down the service paths to the middle of the field. Soft flowering creeping thyme covers the ground around the middle beehive; I had it planted on the paths because it can handle the foot traffic of the apiary workers, and it makes the perfect place to lay down—which is exactly what I do next, after making sure the bees had moved from beneath me.

Aztyn stares at me for a few moments before joining me, and we lie in silence—no words needed but communicating all the same. I close my eyes and feel the deep hum of the bees in my chest. I like to think the vibration of their wings in the air recalibrates my own vibration.

"We only let the most intensely traumatized members work in the apiary," I say with my eyes still closed, but I feel Aztyn shift beside me, his eyes finding me and burning holes through my skin. "The ones that are resistant to other healing modalities or have been traumatized by therapy itself."

I open my eyes and find his, already boring into mine. I swallow hard before turning onto my side, as if we were sharing a bed together, not a patch of ground.

"Why's that?" he asks me, genuinely curious about my reasoning.

"There's something about the bees that heals them on a foundational and primitive level. The bees speak a language our mouths have forgotten but our souls recognize." I begin grabbing some flowers and twisting them into a flower crown as I speak. "In turn, their trauma allows them to treat the bees with the utmost respect and devotion. The world has broken them, so they need something to nurture in order to heal, and in turn they learn to nurture themselves again—some of them for the very first time."

I reach behind me to the spout attached to the honey hives, turn the handle, and let a few drops of the golden nectar of the gods drip onto my fingers, licking two fingers before offering one golden drop to Aztyn—and only the gods know what possessed me to do so. He leans forward, taking my finger in his mouth, his warm tongue sensually whipping against my flesh, and I start to wonder what it would feel like elsewhere before he removes my finger.

"That's pretty magical," he says before taking a deep breath, as if he wasn't just licking honey from my fingers, and I watch as his chest slowly rises and falls, my heart picking up its pace. "You still have two questions, and they expire at the end of today."

"You drive a tough bargain." I flip back and forth in my mind about what question I want to ask next as I weave my crown of flowers before settling. "Why does it feel like you're hunting me?"

Aztyn laughs, and it sounds predatory. "That's because I am hunting you, Little Muse. I didn't come here to listen to the bees hum."

"And yet here you are." The silence falls heavy between us. "So, what are you here for then?"

"The truth... revenge... justice. Isn't that what everyone is here for?" he responds coldly.

"Some, but not all." Knowing asking another question is a risk, I ask it anyway. "So why bother hunting me then?"

"You already asked your three questions," he says, rising from the ground and brushing off his clothing just as I expected he would.

I sit up in response, watching him carefully. The hairs on the back of my neck stand up, and a shiver dances over my skin.

"Next time you realize I'm watching you, Little Muse, you'd be smart to run," he slowly licks his lips while looking at me as if I was just offered up as his last earthly meal. "I like a chase before a feast," he says as he moves between the wildflowers, away from me.

The weight of his words settles on my chest heavily. If I didn't know better, I'd think he was threatening me, but beneath the sinister tone, a different feeling emerges—one I'm not sure I like the implications of. When I finally stand to leave, there is nothing left in the field except the hum of the bees and the sway of the wildflowers in the wind. I leave the crown on top of the hive, and as I walk back to my chambers, I can't help but think how lovely it was to share the silence with a man I'm fairly certain may be my favorite nightmare—and the end of me.

Calliope

Something is happening to me. I can't explain it. Since
that day in the apiary, I have felt a warmth to the
cold almost like spring. Maybe I want to be hunted.
Maybe I don't care if in the end he takes my life.
Maybe the thrill is worth the risk. This can't be love,
so what is it?

Cali

Chapter Three

I should not leave the private grounds today, not after Aztyn's warning, but the kitchen cannot make my favorite iced chai and I am in desperate need of it this morning because the enemies didn't become lovers until chapter 22 and naturally, I then had to finish the book.

The café will be able to handle my request with ease so I have assembled my cutest outfit in which to adventure: my Renaissance inspired corset, a flowy mid length forest fairy type skirt with a slit up the side, and my scuffed-up Docs. They may be heavy but I won't end up barefoot and bleeding if I do have to run. I top it all off with my darkest sunglasses and another floppy hat.

I know I could just go to the twins, tell them about Aztyn, or at the very least take a security detail with me like I am supposed to, but if I am being truly honest with you, I already know the deal here. If a handsome murderous god from the underworld is to be my grim reaper, then so be it. I dream of escaping this hellscape masquerading as a Garden of Eden. It once tricked me into thinking I had found sanctuary, too.

The island is so alive it almost breathes with you, like you took too much psilocybin, but that's just how pristine and lush everything is here. It's like once you eat the fruit here, you're bound to this place like Persephone to the Underworld.

Now, deciphering whether she was taken, or whether she left of her own free will is a matter of perspective, but maybe it was both. Maybe Persephone didn't mean to be captured; it's just that once she was, maybe she figured it couldn't possibly be worse she was already a prisoner. Maybe the choice in captor is what made all the difference. At least this way she was taking her fate into her own hands, even if she was just handing it over to someone else, or maybe she really did just fall in love with Hades. In small afternoons and clandestine meetings. Somehow, I feel as though I am about to find out.

♦

The cafe and the marketplace are not busy today. I didn't get out of bed until noon and by the time I dressed and made the trek to the marketplace, it was nearly one. There is only one other person in the café, and only about a dozen in the square. Not very easy for anyone to hide amongst and for once I wish the square had been full. I order my iced chai, and when the owner asks for my name, I am relieved he did not recognize me behind the shades and hat. It is also amusing to watch him fumble the cup when he computes what I said.

"I apologize Ms. Veritas, I didn't recognize you," he says as he quickly prepares my drink.

"You can make it up to me by sending all the chai you have up to my private kitchens so I don't have to come down here all incognito again, and we can spare us this little embarrassment." I wink to let him know I'm not actually insulted.

The shopkeeper lets out a breath, and I see him relax. "You can count on it," he says, handing me my chai and heading to the back room.

Some people here fear me because I help run the place, others because of the rumors they've heard. I can have legendary crash outs if my mood sours. Then there are the rumors of the cult hard to keep anything entirely secret for long. Although we take our due precautions, some things can find themselves slipping out of the shadows. Some people are here to find their justice, and they fear me most of all. I suppose I understand. Piss off the goddess and incur her wrath, that sort of thing. A healthy dose of fear is good for them. I don't want anyone thinking they can get too friendly with me just because I'm slumming it down in the public part of the island.

As I turn to leave, I see my flower crown from the apiary on the table behind me, except I didn't hear or see anyone come in. I was too distracted during my encounter with the owner. I look around anxiously, and a bead of sweat trickles down my spine. He wants me to know he's here. Now that I do, what next? I can't stay here all day. I could call security but if I am telling the truth this is the most fun I've had in this place in years. I don't want our little game to end and he's banking on that.

When the owner of the shop comes back to confirm he has set up the shipment, I ask if I can leave through the back and he obliges. The back has a small outside area for the staff and a clear view so I can plan an escape. When the sun hits my skin, I realize it's much hotter than when I arrived and will only continue to be so as the heat of the day peaks. There is a service path through the jungle behind the square, and it leads to the private wing. At this moment in time, it is my only option if I don't want to faint in the middle of my escape. It's longer and less direct but shaded, its biggest downfall being the thick jungle that surrounds the path on either side, but I don't have much of a choice so I walk briskly, keeping my head on a swivel.

I don't see him anywhere but I don't relax. Instead, I walk as rapidly as I can along the path. The greenhouses for the farm come into my view. I hear a crack ring out from behind me and to my left that pricks my ears and I stop dead in my tracks. It doesn't sound like a bird or any of the native creatures we have here. I'm listening so hard I swear I can hear my own heartbeat in my ears, or maybe I'm just imagining it but the next sound I hear, I know I am not imagining. A familiar whistle echoes through the dense vegetation and I spook and take off running like a white-tailed deer, dropping my chai.

"You better run rabbit, RUN!" His deep voice cuts through the sound of my feet on the ground.

My path zippers down the hillside but I don't waste time trying to run the path. I cut through the middle grounds, moving in and out of the vegetation as efficiently as I can. Before I know it, I'm bounding through the farmland. I know the banana fields will be dry, and I head through them for the greenhouse I know best hoping not to meet any snakes along my route.

I slip quietly through the greenhouse door and the smell of peaches envelops my senses. It's so pungent I can almost taste it. I look for a place to hide just to catch my bearings before I take off running on the final leg of my journey to safety. I lean up against the water reservoir. The metal is cool against my skin and I catch my breath hidden behind it. The gardeners are gone for the day so no one is coming to save me, and for some reason the cameras hadn't picked me up or security would have been here already.

The crunch of footsteps on gravel alerts me that I have company, so I quietly lift my own feet up onto the platform of the reservoir and tuck myself in behind it. I hold my breath and will my muscles to stay still in this high stakes game of hide and seek. The creak of the door exhilarates instead of terrifies me. I do not want to be caught because I want to win, but a part of me wants to know what it feels like when a predator gets his teeth into your flesh. I want to know what it feels like to be devoured right down to what's left of my soul by a ravenous monster. Just not today, today I want to win.

"I know you're in here, Little Muse." The sound of the gravel under his feet and the gruffness of his voice gives me butterflies.

I am in the back but middle of both rows, and I have given myself the best hiding place to easy escape route ratio possible, although I will have to risk a run down the aisle when he's distracted. I try to keep my breathing steady and calm and my limbs ready to spring into action. I can see him

46

now, but he can't see me as he saunters confidently down the aisles. I watch him reach up and pluck a peach from the tree. I witness his sharper than most canines glisten in the light before he takes a bite the juice from the luscious fruit drips down his chin a little but he wipes it with the back of his hand and licks the remainder from his lips and hands. Then he grins making me weak in the knees. My clit pulses at the thought of him wiping me off of his lips in a similar manner but I can't afford to get distracted here.

"That farm stand girl lied to you. These peaches are more than ready," he takes another bite but lets the juice drip down his chin while he smirks maliciously, and I have never wanted to be a peach so badly in my life.

Aztyn slowly and confidently walks down the aisle, and the closer he gets, the more my insides clench. Not in anticipation of my escape, but because I have never been more turned on in my life. Something is seriously wrong with me and I need to get a grip but there is something about the way he smells, the broadness of his shoulders, and the thickness of his neck that make me feel like something feral has taken over my body. Some lust filled succubus who wants nothing more than the nightmare hunting her to pin her down and leave her used and filled.

"I worked up quite an appetite chasing you through the jungle. I didn't think you'd make it this far," Aztyn stops right in front of the reservoir as if that's what he's talking to, and my heart starts to pound at the realization that he might know exactly where I am hiding. I can no longer see him and being unsure if my plan is going to work, I am nervous about more than getting caught. "You're thrilling to chase, Little Muse."

I almost moan out loud at the compliment. I should be sick with fear but I guess my extracurricular proclivities have desensitized me or maybe it's because I've never met a man who is this much of a man. He does frighten me but in a deviant way that I want to keep feeling. Aztyn continues moving towards the far aisle, and I let out a breath of relief. If I am going to make my move it needs to be soon, my muscles are screaming at me in protest of the position I've had myself crouched in.

"If I catch you before you make it to the door from behind that reservoir, I'm going to fuck you."

So, he does know where I am. *Fuck*. Wait, did he say fuck me or kill me? I am distracted and accidentally knock over a metal bucket, and it spooks me so I spring into action and run. I am pretty nimble but I do not see the piece of lattice sticking out from under the raised planting bed and I trip, practically landing on my face. I feel Aztyn grab me by the foot and drag me back down the aisle. I kick my legs and try to claw my way back to the entrance but it is all in vain and Aztyn just laughs. I could scream. Someone might hear me, but I do not desire to be saved like a damsel. He picks me up and pins my arms against the peach tree branches securing my wrists with rope so my tiptoes barely touch the ground.

"I don't usually fuck my prey but for you, I think I'll make an exception," he says while doing a test tug on the ropes and moves in until I can feel his breath on my earlobe. "I can smell your arousal, Little Muse."

I whimper in response, and he flashes me that devious smile. "What do you normally do with your prey?" I ask sheepishly.

Aztyn chuckles again. "You'll find out soon enough but not today." He stands back to appraise his work and I struggle against the branch trying to find movement. He doesn't budge from his spot just clicks his teeth and frowns as I dangle a little. "You're not being a very good girl."

My inner walls clench, and I press my thighs together. "I could start screaming or call security." I lie badly. Ending whatever this is, is the furthest thing from my mind.

"If you were going to do any of those things, you would have already. In fact, you would have told the twins about me immediately, but you didn't, so let's not waste time lying."

Aztyn strides towards me and traces my curves from my wrist all the way down to the hollow of my hips all the while looking at me like his hunger can only be satisfied by my flesh. I pretend to struggle against his surprisingly soft touch, but my skin is left littered with goosebumps and I swallow hard. I want to know what it feels like to be consumed but I kick out at him out of spite. I am furious he caught me so quickly and I will not make this easy for him.

"What kind of person gets off chasing a girl through the jungle?" I spit in his direction.

The fire flares behind his eyes as he grabs me with one hand by the bottom jaw, his thumb and pointer finger settling in the hollows of my cheeks. "What kind of girl gets off being chased through the jungle?"

I gasp as he slips his other hand under my skirt and inside of me, and my cheeks redden at the thought of him knowing he is right. He sneers cockily at me while licking his fingers, leaving me to dangle from the branch while he tastes me, and I shudder aching for him to do it again. If this man kneels on the ground and takes me in his mouth, I might just die and go to dark romance heaven.

"You taste so fucking good, Calliope." As if reading my mind he rushes forward again, pushing me back against the trunk of the tree, and the shape of it cradles my ass perfectly, almost putting me in a seated position with my hands still above my head as his fingers enter me for the second time.

I let out a cry of pleasure and this time when he removes them, he places them in my mouth so I can taste myself and my eyes involuntarily roll back as pink peach blossoms fall around us.

"You taste even better than these peaches," he remarks, picking another from the tree and taking a large bite, not bothering to wipe the juice from his chin as he chews and then swallows.

I clench my thighs together, rubbing them back and forth craving some kind of friction and his eyes widen as he watches me. I can see the outline of his erection in his pants and I'm impressed by the size of it. I watch him adjust it for my benefit as he watches me watching him and I look away embarrassed. There is something about this man that intoxicates me and not being in control has made me into a girl I don't even recognize. I get the overwhelming urge to beg him to breed me but I keep my mouth shut.

"Now tell me you want me to fuck you."

My eyes flash to his. "Never. I'd rather die." My voice dripping in defiance. I do want him to fuck me. I want him to fuck me until my eyes roll back and I am screaming his name but I just can't help but defy his commands.

51

"That can be arranged," he growls, growing impatient with me, and deep down I know he means it, but what that does to my insides I cannot explain. I feel a heat prickle over my body and I resist the urge to continue to fight him. "Why keep lying when you could be a good girl, and I'll let you cum all over my cock, messy, loud, and ruined before I release you."

"No man has ever made me cum without my interference. What makes you think you can?"

I mean this to be threatening, but he clearly takes it as a challenge.

"I'm no regular man, Little Muse, and I won't stop until you do," he says self-assured as his eyes light up with possibility.

Aztyn pushes his body into mine. I feel his erection against me and his lips find mine as his hands find my hair. I grind against the bulge in his pants for a moment before remembering I am trying to escape. I take his lip into my mouth and bite down hard, startling him and he pulls away. I taste blood in my mouth and smile spitefully, then so does he, equally as spiteful before his lips crash back into mine.

I can't fight it anymore as I let this stranger take complete control of me like someone else has taken over my body and I moan out of sweet submission into his mouth. He breaks away for a moment to kiss a trail down my neck and collarbone, biting the skin at their meeting with such force I know it's going to leave a mark and I yelp in response. Aztyn pulls another peach down from the tree and crushes it above the spot where he just bit me, alternating between licking the sweet nectar from my skin and biting me as I tip my head back in ecstasy.

Aztyn squeezes the peach over top of the ample cleavage I have spilling out of the corset I am wearing and cleans his mess with his exquisite mouth, untying the back of my corset nimbly with one hand. He throws it to the ground disregarding it completely but leaving my skirt and boots on. He rips the slit in my skirt even higher, tucking it off to the side as he falls to his knees to give himself better access to what he wishes to consume. This time he lets the juice drip between my thighs before discarding the peach behind him and swirling his tongue along the slit of my opening. My toes curl inside my boots and my body shudders.

I know I should be ashamed of myself but I rock my hips against his face moaning, practically begging for more. He slips his fingers inside me in a come-hither motion barely inside my entrance as his tongue finds my clit. I am overcome and overwhelmed with pleasure as he relentlessly keeps time with his fingers and mouth, moaning against me as I moan against the wet sounds coming from between my thighs. I'm so close to coming for him I can hardly believe it when he abruptly stops what he's doing.

I look down to find him frowning at a small device he's seemingly pulled out of nowhere. Looking up at me, he does what every man has done since the beginning of time. He disappoints me.

"Sorry princess, but you're going to want to get moving. We've got company."

Faster than I can comprehend, he unties me, redresses me, and dashes out the exit, all while I am in a haze of unfinished ecstasy and shock. I don't even know what just happened, but before I know it, I hear a familiar voice call out my name.

I run out of the greenhouse exit looking a state by the look in Zander's eyes when he sees me.

"What the fuck happened to you?"

"I got a little dirty in the greenhouse," I say knowing that's not enough of an explanation for the condition I'm in but hoping he buys it anyways.

"Did the plants attack you? You're sticky and full of dirt? You look like…"

"Never mind that, Zander, what do you want?"

Zander snaps out of concern mode and back to business.

"Vivianne wanted to talk to you before the initiation tomorrow."

"Of course, she fucking does." I sigh, sexually frustrated. "Let me clean up. I'll meet her in her office."

As we walk toward our private compound, I glance back at the greenhouse. I don't know what came over me during our game, but I sure as hell know I'll never look at peaches the same way again.

.

Calliope

There is something inebriating about Aztyn. I must have lost my damn mind letting him under my skin like that but the the way his scent mixed with mine overwhelmed me with lust and the desire to surrender to his every whim. What the hell is wrong with me?

Cali

Chapter Four

I'm eating my usual breakfast in bed still yearning for release after Aztyn worked me up and then put me away wet when Vivianne waltzes through my door giving me the itinerary for the day. I will be pampered, waxed, blown out and prepped for tonight's festivities. I must look every bit the goddess they believe me to be, and after the gold leaf has been pressed into my skin, and the jewels have been placed to catch the light just right, and the gown is secured against my body, I will undoubtedly and spectacularly look the part. The dress-up portion has always been my favorite. It's like being on stage during a solo. All eyes are on you, and everyone is in awe of you. It's the night I get to be displayed but untouchable, like the whisper of a dream. I sit and observe, I allow them to worship me. They need it *more* than me. They need to believe in something outside of themselves. To them, I am an angel of mercy, a fallen goddess cast out of heaven, so I created my own in defiance of a god who is stingy with his fair play.

"You're not even listening to me, Cali."

She's right I'm actually thinking about a certain stranger and peaches. "I'm sorry, Vivianne, my mind is on the initiations." I sigh as I rub the mark that the rope made on my wrists in secret under the covers.

"At least for once, your mind is on the task at hand. Hurry up, you're going to be late."

"No such thing when you're the top dog, Viv." I shrug.

"Right, but you know how Lucy feels about rushing your wax."

"Point taken." I push my unfinished food to the side and hop out of bed to grab my robe. Viv's eyes linger on my naked body, but I don't mind; I even move a little slower for her benefit.

◆

My bare feet echo down the hallway, and the breeze beneath my robe gives me the cold shivers. The spa will be warm, but these hallways sometimes have a chill I can't deny. No one else seems to notice. Maybe that's because they wear clothes, but I have always felt a rather sinister inhospitality alone in these passages. I try not to wear clothing if I can help it, but Vivianne always tells me to save it for the show. It's more dramatic that way. Clothing is optional here, but my body has always been treated as a sacred altar. For the pleasure of the *chosen*, not the masses. I cross my arms and tremble visibly, my teeth chattering a little.

Viv looks back, shakes her head in an 'I told you so' fashion and keeps walking. We reach the glass doors of the spa, a private entrance from our side of the compound. Viv hands me off to the staff, and they get to work. None of them speak to me except Lucy. She runs the whole place. A beautiful Russian woman with top-notch esthetician skills. Her injections are the best in the world. We certainly encourage the natural approach but facilitate all kinds of modifications. I encourage anyone to become the version of themselves they've always dreamed of being. Sometimes, that means bigger lips or fewer wrinkles. We also have a state-of-the-art plastic surgeon. I've never felt the need, but to each their own. Happy followers, happy compound and money is no object here. You would think we would have plastic Barbie and Ken dolls walking around, but when given free access, the obsession with extreme beauty doesn't have a chance to fester and form itself into a pustulant wound. Just like the drugs. No one is addicted to anything here because nothing is off-limits or restricted. There are rehab facilities available, but they mostly sit empty. People find purpose here and a reason, something to live for. We put them to work on the compound where they are best-suited skills *and* capacity-wise. Everyone has something they bring to the table, and we bring that something out of them through therapy and tests. They want for nothing and seek nothing except something to worship, and that's where I come into play. The inner circle worships me differently, but the rest of the compound worships me in their own right. I am the face of this highly coveted, award-winning, elite lifestyle facility. Those who come here tend to treat me like a celebrity, and we all know how the masses treat celebrities. It's two sides of the same coin.

Since the rumors and the following death threats started, I don't do many live public appearances anymore, not even on the public part of the island. Vivianne and her lackeys take care of that. My life is too valuable and my time is better spent elsewhere, according to Viv. Which is a far cry from when she used to leave me at the bar without saying anything to get laid without a care in the world about how I got home. Secretly, I think she likes being Cephalonia's second face and voice. None of us say anything to the public that she doesn't write first, and we never do it without her to field questions and reactions afterwards.

I received the full spa menu today. Blowout, mani & pedi, facials, massage, steams, baths, masks and waxes. I am fully prepped and pampered for the next few days of rituals. Tonight, is the opening ceremony. It's the big show and the first test. We determine if the prospects can stomach just a taste of what's behind the curtain. After tonight, they will have one chance to back out of their initiation. They are, however, vowed to secrecy. Not a whisper may pass their lips of tonight's activities if they return to being less involved in the nitty gritty. The penalty for what we call treason is death. You won't spill another secret because you won't have the chance. In the last three years, no one has ever decided against joining the inner circle. Everyone craves power and recognition. Everyone wants to be special. In a world of participation trophies and 'everyone wins,' I provide something remarkably different. I set them apart from the rest of the world, and in turn, they believe they are something exceptional.

The truth is no one here is special at all. They are all expendable to me except the twins of course, I could never replace them. All the followers are the same to me although I suppose I know most of the sinners' names. Come to think of it, maybe I don't know as many of them by name as I thought which makes my point all on its own. I don't care to know them. *As if* Zeus knew all of his worshipers by name. He only knew the ones he bedded. I guess he's got one up on me. I rarely sleep with anyone now, but there was a time before I became listless and disinterested that I participated in most of the group sex around here. It's not like we all sit around getting to know each other beforehand, asking awkward and useless first-date questions. So, I only know followers by their ability to be seen amongst the crowd and not much else.

Lucy is quiet today as she finishes up my wax and the pain distracts me from the passionate urges I've had all day. Usually, she's talking my ear off. For a split second I think about asking her why she is so silent, but I don't. If she wanted to tell me, she would, and I would pretend to listen because I like Lucy. She's not a part of the few; she's of the many, but she is as hardworking and brilliant as they come, and I enjoy our little chats.

"You're all finished, Cali." Her accent is nearly non-existent. She once told me that English was vital for her to be taken seriously, so she learned to speak it perfectly.

"Thank you, Lucy, and thank the rest of the staff for me, please..'

"Our pleasure as always." I am about to get up to leave when Lucy clears her throat. "Cali, before you go, I wanted to ask you for something." her voice is unusually timid.

"Lucy, you can ask me for anything."

"Please don't take this wrong, but there are whispers. I don't pay any mind to them usually. I just do my job…" Her voice trails before continuing. Whatever this is about, she's having a hard time articulating it. "I just want to know that I am safe if someone *was* to pay attention to those whispers."

"Lucy, you would never be implicated in rumors or whispers regardless of who is paying attention. You're safe, and you will always be safe."

"Thank you, Calliope. You know my loyalty is never a question."

"I know that Lucy or you simply wouldn't be here. Do you need anything else before I go?"

"No, that was all."

I put on my robe and leave without saying much else, but I give her the warmest smile I can muster. I meant what I said. I've long suspected that Lucy had an inkling of what we do in the shadows, and I would never throw her under the bus. Her only tie to this place is the spa that she runs for the compound. There is nothing that traces her or anyone innocent to our side business of punishing the guilty.

Viv and Zander are waiting for me outside the glass doors. I don't plan to tell them about Lucy because her loyalty is not a question in my eyes, but it will be for them.

"Is there something I can do for you two?"

"We're here to ensure you make it to the opening ceremony this time."

Zander's eyes darken at his sister's joke. He hates it when I get all melancholy and moody which has been my default mood lately.

"Don't worry, Zand, I won't lock myself in my chambers. I'm looking forward to the initiations."

Zanders' eyes darken even more as if it's equally as concerning that I have suddenly retaken an interest in things, but he doesn't speak a word. If I told him it was because of Aztyn he would lose his shit.

"That's refreshing," Viv says without looking up from her tablet.

Zander scoffs and runs his fingers through his hair, which he styles in a shaggy but effortless way that drives me wild. He's also in turmoil over my recent behavior creating even more heat between my legs. Viv follows without noticing that her brother is having a full-blown personal moment. I pick up the rear as if I'm making sure *they* make it to the initiation. By the time we sit down to eat dinner together in my chambers Zander is back to his charming self and Vivianne has turned off her tablet and actively listens as we converse and joke at each other's expense. It's like we are university students again and a part of me longs for a timeline where we had stayed that way. I can almost visualize it in my mind's eye and in turn I nearly ask them to reconsider. I nearly beg them to stop the madness here and now and go back to a time before. The harsh reality of knowing there is no going back and no escaping what we have done is what stops me. Zander squeezes my knee under the table sensing my growing discomfort. He is unbelievably perceptive, and I am grateful for it.

"We better get you dressed." Viv says picking up her tablet again.

Vivianne is always on a schedule. It's what keeps her sane in this insane asylum. It gives her a false sense of control as if we have ever had any control over this. Zander leaves while Vivianne dresses me. The gowns I wear on initiation night requires assistance. Every inch of the bodice of the black ball gown I have chosen for this evening is beaded. The tulle off-shoulder sleeves accent my decolletage sinfully. The dramatic tulle skirt gives me movement as I stroll around the room and lightens what would be a cumbersome dress otherwise. Viv fastens me in, and I take a deep breath. The room is suddenly boiling, and I feel a little faint. The hungry way Aztyn looks at me flashes through my mind and unbelievably the room stops spinning.

"Are you ready, Cali?"

I look at myself in the mirror. I want to hyperventilate. I'm not ready. I was never prepared for any of this but instead of blurting that out I say "On with the show, Viv."

I can hear the murmurs behind the curtain. Everyone is waiting for me. They have been waiting for what feels to them like eons to see my face. They all want a piece of me to take with them: A glance, a touch, an acknowledgment, my arousal, my interest, my body. They fear and worship me, but they will never *love* me. I once dreamed of falling in love, as any little girl would, it just never happened for me. Instead, I fell in love with something else, *power*. Now that I have all the power I could ever dream of, I am not sure I want it anymore. It doesn't thrill me like it used to and truth be told my soul longs for the one thing I can never have that I scarcely admit to myself I even desire. Aztyn thrilled me, poured life back into my bones and I could settle for a little lust before death if I can never have love. It's *only* moments like this where my heart beats so hard I swear I can hear it that the mask I wear cracks. These moments make a

66

sentimental fool out of me. I'll never find love here, not where the cursed and the damned come to play. With that thought I slip my mask back on, and I am ready for the show: *lights, camera, action.*

I become a different version of myself in this cathedral of sin. All three of us do. The red lights are usually dim but brighten upon me when I appear from behind the red velvet curtain. The crowd collectively gasps or perhaps I am just delusional enough to think they do. I don't usually pay much attention to them in these situations, but tonight I scan the room intently. I am looking for *him.*

The initiated are in the middle, ready to present their gifts and sins at my feet. The soon-to-be initiates stand around the perimeter of the room. They are only permitted to watch this evening's events. I sit on my throne, a little higher than the twins who flank me. It is everything Hecate and Persephone would be envious of. High-backed and upholstered in velvet and intricate carved skulls, spirits and symbols adorn the wood. They are stunning and a little frightening. Some of my best design work in our space of worship.

Actually, the entire ritual room is my magnum opus, including what happens within it. The sunken pit where the initiates stand is all leather for easy cleanup. Dark corners with smaller leather couches and more red velvet curtains line the walls for the more discreet during the evenings when we have fewer rules. Slick black flooring fills the rest of the room. The red lights bouncing off the dark black walls give the effect of the entire room being in a giant black hole. High windows made of deep red and darkly shaded stained glass tint the moonlight cascading in, adding to the ambiance of the entire evening. Behind us a red neon cross hangs on the wall just above my head, when the lights dim it looks as if it's floating above us. A lot of civilians think an upside-down cross is worship of the devil but they are wrong. It's a symbol of devotion and that is the currency here. Not just their adoration of me but to their belief in the cause and the justice we take into our own hands. I scan the room again, but I still do not see him. I don't even know why I am looking for him.

"I would like to begin tonight's ceremonies by apologizing for my absence and welcoming our new initiates into the inner circle. What you are about to witness is a taste of what happens here. If, when the ritual is over and you choose to stay, you will give your sacrifice. Suppose you choose to return to regular life at the compound. In that case, this is the last reminder that your silence about the events that take place here this evening is non-negotiable." I pause for dramatic effect and take the opportunity to look for Aztyn again. My mysterious stranger *would* know how to blend into the shadows of *my* room.

No one commands a room like I do. I can disarm you so underhandedly that before you know it, you're begging to confess your deepest, darkest secrets *or* I can make every person in the room stiffen and pucker with one glance.

I continue with a disinterested wave of my hand toward the pit. "You all know what to do."

Various members of the inner circle lay gifts of jewelry and different things they believe are to my liking at my feet. As much as I love power, material things were always just a bonus to dating men with money. These gifts are sold or sent somewhere. I don't know and I do not care. After the gifts the purest mix of molly I could have my chemists manufacture is passed from my fingers to their mouths like communion.

The lights dim even darker. The new initiates begin to get antsy, not knowing quite what to expect. The energy in the room is palpable, and I used to live for it. It's not long before bodies are bumping into bodies, and mouths are on mouths, amongst other body parts. As the orgy begins, I feel nothing and gaze off dissociated into the crowd. Having already given up finding his face I find it strange to suddenly feel the bile rise into my throat. The distinct feeling of being hunted fills my veins again and it electrifies me once more.

His eyes are on me I can feel them, and then his voice whispers in my ear.

"They think you're untouchable…"

I wonder how he has slipped past the twins and my own eyes to wind up in the shadows behind me, but the hairs on my neck are standing at attention, and I cannot find the words to ask him.

"Cat got your tongue, Little Muse? I wonder what they would think if they knew what I've done to you."

I compose myself enough to choke out some words, "You shouldn't be here speaking to me like this. It's against the rules." My voice is breathy, and I am visibly shaken. I can feel the sweat building beneath my dress. My hands grip the arms of my chair. He's so close I can feel his breath on my neck as he speaks.

"When I catch you again, you won't be telling *me* what to do, and I'll make you pay for every time you have. That's a few times now."

"Excuse me?" I hiss nearly whipping my head around to face him, but I do not want to alert the twins to his presence. They would most likely have him excommunicated on the spot, or worse.

"You heard me. Keep your eyes focused across the room. You'll find me this time."

I should look anywhere but the direction he told me. Instead, my eyes are glued straight ahead. My heart pounds in my chest, waiting for the dim light to illuminate his face. When it does, the room filled with the moans and whimpers of group sex suddenly quiets to nothing. It is just his eyes locked on mine and nothing else. His mouth a crooked grin, no doubt pleased with his trick of only being seen when he wishes to be seen. Admittedly, I am too. I see nothing but him now, and all I feel is the buzz that pulsates through every cell in my body like shock therapy. I want to float towards him as if he's caught me in a trance. My skin prickles at the thought of his breath having been on my skin again. I shift in my seat, and his grin grows wider. I am relieved from the intensity when Zander gently taps my knee. I can barely tear myself from Aztyn's gaze, but somehow, I make eye contact with Zand and nod my acknowledgment.

The pit has commenced their sex ritual, and the security will draw the curtains, giving the participants time to clean themselves up for the next part of this evening's festivities. More than the sex, the lavish gifts, the drugs, and the money, this final act of the evening always rekindles my love for what we do under the cover of darkness. The pledge always does something villainous to me. It's hotter than any smut I'll ever read. There's something about the sinners pledging their undying loyalty to me and the cause that makes me wet.

The pledge is as follows: *I pledge my undying loyalty to ensure stolen justice becomes justice served. We are Calliope's Reckoning, the right hand; under her wisdom and guidance, and I *insert name here* give myself to her and the cause. Body, mind and soul. And so, it is.*

Then my heathens swipe a ceremonial dagger with a ruby-encrusted hilt across their palms and let it drip into the center of the pit. To be more precise, the emblem on the floor. A gold plate with the scales of justice and the brand of our little cult. The initiates will receive something to match that brand tomorrow evening, but I get to deliver that adornment personally.

By the time Aztyn recites his pledge I'm practically squirming in my seat with my knees pinched together. It wasn't the usual stimulant of the evening's festivities that had me this way. It was the way his eyes never left mine throughout the entire lineup. I barely watched the other initiates. I couldn't tear my gaze away from him. The intensity of this revelation is coursing through my veins, and the adrenaline is the most intoxicating I have ever felt. I whimper out loud as Aztyn squeezes his hand and the blood drips down his impressive forearms dropping from his

72

elbow upon the seal. This earns me a devilish smirk from Aztyn and a scolding stare from both the twins. I collect myself and close my eyes briefly before closing the ceremonies. I stand from my seated position, careful not to let my knees visibly buckle and take a deep breath. Aztyn is no longer in my view, but that is perhaps for the best.

"Welcome to the gates. Ours are not to heaven, but you will be delivered all your wildest desires within them. Those of you with justice unserved will get your dues. Together, we will make sure of it. You have put your trust in me, and I will make sure all your sacrifices have not been in vain. You are now part of an elite and carefully chosen coalition within Cephalonia and there is great honor and privilege in that, but most of all there is protection. From this moment forward I absolve you from all the sins you may commit in my name and the name of my reckoning. If there is a god, may he have mercy on all our souls and considering I believe in one I extend *my* mercy and an invitation to believe in me instead."

The twins stand, and Zander takes my hand as I step down from my throne. I can feel Aztyn's eyes burning on me but I do not look for him this time. Instead, I gaze at Zander and take his arm as he escorts me from the ritual room. When we have begun to walk down the hallway towards Vivian's chambers, Zander drops my hand and walks off towards his own without saying a word.

"What the hell is that about Viv?"

"Oh, I don't know, perhaps your little stunt with that initiate during the ritual," she rolls her eyes for dramatic effect. "You usually keep your cool a lot more than that."

Both the twins know how the pledge makes me feel on a normal night, Zander especially has been a recipient of that stirred desire many times but Vivianne is right. "I just couldn't help myself tonight, I guess."

"Aztyn Diamandis is a fine specimen of man. He never struck me as your type, though. When I met with him, he was quite reserved. You usually like your men a lot more intense than that."

I hike my dress up as we enter her chambers. I am even more intrigued by the man who is hunting me. Reserved is not a word I would use to describe him and Vivianne is an excellent judge of character. If she didn't see the side of him I have seen he must be one hell of a smooth operator. Vivianne begins removing my dress, and I tremble as I leave it. Not from the brisk cold air that hits my fevered skin but from the pleasure I find in being *his* prey.

.

Aztyn

Your face haunts my dreams
So I become a nightmare haunting you in return
They think you're a savior
Except I've seen angels and you woman are no seraph
With horns for a halo
Always on your worst behavior
But I guess its true... the devil was an angel too.

Chapter Five

Calliope Veritas is an angelic and ethereal being only when she sleeps. The rest of the time, she is a force of nature and has the most commanding presence I have ever seen in a woman. It's fucking infuriating. Not because she is a woman. I *love* powerful women; truth be told, nothing makes my cock harder. Mostly because I know the majority of them want to surrender their control, and I am more than happy to take the helm of that control and give them what they desire. Calliope is no different but my intentions in coming here were far from getting the bratty little succubus in bed.

She enrages and maddens me because of who she is and what she has escaped punishment for up until now. I've been watching her for a good hour, her chest softly rising and falling as if she's some kind of princess in a storybook awaiting true love's kiss to break the spell. Her eyes flutter softly as she dreams, a sleepy smile on her lips. I wonder if she's dreaming about coming on my face in the greenhouse. Unfortunately for her, this isn't a fairytale, more like a true crime documentary.

My name is Aztyn Diamandis, and I will kill Calliope Veritas.

Calliope is a hauntingly exquisite woman, and I will enjoy edging her towards death and burying my cock inside her as many times as I like before slitting her throat and watching the blood pool beneath her. The black, silky sheets she is sleeping under only highlight the curves of her form, a form I have had in my hands before I was so rudely cock blocked. I shift in my seat as my erection becomes uncomfortable. I don't usually fuck my prey but she does something to me, and a large segment of me is disgusted by it.

What's even more twisted is my pursuit of her *exhilarates* her. I could see it all over her flustered face when she saw me in her private gardens, when she led me to the apiary and I could smell how aroused she was in the greenhouses. Calliope has been running her entire life and *wants* to be caught.

Her track record of fucking the wealthiest, most eligible bachelors, bleeding them dry, and moving on like a black widow is no secret. It's just an 'overlooked' part of her back story the media chooses not to disclose. I spoke to many of her previous suitors, and the hysterical thing is, even *now,* they would all walk straight off a cliff for her if she asked. That pussy must be out of this fucking world. I know it tastes like my undoing. I feel no shame in being the last man to fuck her.

Even more overlooked by the media are the events that take place in the dark around here. I don't give a fuck what happens to Cephalonia or the cult after I take Calliope's life. I only care about my revenge and the sweet justice of doing to her what she has done to so many, some may have deserved it but not all. It's not like she is some innocent woman off the street. Her crimes, if proven, would put her away for life: murder, abduction, conspiracy, production of illegal substances, racketeering. *My* hands are not the cleanest, mind you. I can now add stalking *her* to my list of felonies. Maybe you can teach an old dog new tricks. I know what I am doing is wrong. I could have killed her a thousand times and slipped away into the night, and no one would have been the wiser. I could kill her right now as I sit at her bedside, watching her sleep. I could knock her out with some chloroform, take her to the cliffs over my shoulder, slit her throat and toss her into the ocean, the sharks would have her devoured bones and all before daybreak. I can't bring myself to do it because there is something about Calliope that enraptures me. A part of me is jealous of all the men she has left in ruin. I want to taste her surrender and I want her to give it to me willingly before I take my revenge. I want to be the one to devastate her, ruin her in the sweetest ways. She's been my Little Muse since my vendetta began and I may be a psychopath, but admittedly, there's a bit of a romantic in me. I hadn't written poetry for years until I made it my life's mission to end hers and then like a light bulb in a dim room, divine inspiration took its hold of me.

Despite what it must look like, I did not come here to drool over her while she sleeps. I came here to leave another poem, wax-sealed and wrapped in ribbon. This time in a place that will give her that tremble of excitement she so desperately seeks. I want her to know I showed her mercy. She wants to be hunted and if anyone deserves that honor, it should be me.

The sun is coming up, and she is beginning to stir increasingly. I need to leave but can't bring myself to do so. All I want to do is crawl into her bed and inhale the breath from her lungs. I linger as I pin the letter to the bed curtain closest to her angelic face. I watch my hand reach out and tuck a few stray strands of hair behind her ear, and I am horrified by my actions. I cannot control myself around this woman and for a moment, I doubt my factual reasons for being here. I clench against the impulse to wake her up with my cock already in her. I can't think about much else besides the way she was grinding herself against it in the greenhouses. Twisted little slut. I shake my head so I can regain focus before I surrender to my own urges.

Calliope Veritas stole something from me I can never get back. That cunt killed my brother. He may have been a misogynistic asshole but to my knowledge, he never did anything so wrong as to be murdered in cold blood for it. They claim she is a twisted angel of mercy, granting justice to those whose justice has fallen short. Many have been denied their wishes due to lack of evidence to support their claims, but I can prove that the bitch doesn't follow her own rules. I knew my brother like the back of my hand and I have my research connections too. *My* justice will be poetic pun intended. I leave the same way I came and ensure my camera hacking skills went undetected. There is another ritual tonight, and my presence is expected.

Calliope

He watches me sleep; this should terrify me. He was in my bedroom, one of the most secure places on the compound. I am trembling but not from fear. Why have I never felt more alive?

Cali

Chapter Six

Aztyn Diamandis bypassed my security and cameras and broke into my bedroom to watch me sleep. His execution was flawless. I click my teeth while watching the footage in my office, his calling card safely in the vault in my panic room. There is not even a glitch on the screen in front of me. Aztyn is a fucking ghost. I am inordinately impressed. I *should* be terrified. I *should* tell the twins and let Zander deal with it. He's more than just a psych major turned cult leader. He's also incredibly possessive over me and loves the violence as much as I do. I don't want Zander to kill Aztyn though. I don't want anyone to touch one hair on his head. I want him to finish what he started in the greenhouse. I want to burrow my way into his brain. His obsession with me makes me obsessed with him, and my entire body tingles with that compulsion's electricity. I want him to hunt me; the chase is exhilarating. I sit back in my desk chair with a cheeky grin, inspecting his immaculate handiwork again, but it is short-lived because Zander bursts in the door without knocking, scaring me nearly half to death.

"What the fuck, Zand? You know I scare easily."

"Fuck you, Cali. What are you doing here? I've been looking for you all morning." Zander's gaze is murderous. He's furious with me, and it makes my clit tingle. I still haven't been satisfied and he is a force of nature when he lets his darkness take over. I kissed him in the middle of an argument once, and then we fucked for the first time and the sex was incredible. Zander fucks like he was made to be used for the pleasure of a woman.

"Don't speak to me like that, Zand. I'm working." My voice is calm and borderline playful. I know not to gode him in this mood.

"You don't fucking work around here..." His gaze softens slightly, but I can still feel his rage in the air. I must have stepped in it this time. My mind flashes to the previous evening, and suddenly, I feel a twinge of guilt.

"Well, maybe I want to start," I flip my hair, knowing my perfume will float in his direction. Zanders' favorite thing about me is how my scent lingers even after I am no longer in a room. "What's eating you anyway?" I offer, knowing full well what's wrong. That was lousy phrasing because his eyes return to their former harshness.

"As if you don't know. There was practically a fucking wet spot left behind after you watched that recruit's offering! First, you lock yourself in your room for weeks, and now you're moaning during the fucking ritual? What the hell is wrong with you, Calliope?" His voice nearly breaks at the end, but I feel every word in my chest. His posture is dominating, and I can't help but torment him a little.

"Those are some big feelings, Zand. Who the fuck cares? Are you jealous it wasn't you making me wet?"

Zander slams his fist down on the table. "I got over you a long time ago. That pussy isn't anything special. I bet you're fucking wet right now you dirty little *whore*."

Zander is baiting me, and it's working. I soften my gaze and look him up and down slowly, my eyelashes fluttering when they reach the apparent bulge in his jeans before continuing. "That's a shame. You fuck the best when you're in a murderous rage."

"I didn't come here to *fuck* you, Cali. I might be jealous, but I wouldn't fuck you again even if you begged me."

"Then get the fuck out of my office Zander. I've never begged you before. I am not about to start now."

I'm beginning to lose my patience with his little outburst.

Zander leans over the desk dominating me with his build and his voice hisses in my ear. "I know you better than

84

anyone here, even Vivianne. You might not beg, but it will be me you come to when you fucking lose it and need your head fucked straight, and this time, my door *won't* be open." He straightens himself before turning on a dime and slamming the door so hard I feel the reverberation in my chest.

Zander has never denied my desires before. He has always been the one I come to when I have come down from my bouts of rage and need to be put back together again. The thought of him rejecting me is sending me right over the edge. Maybe I'm so easily triggered because I've been slipping for a while. Aztyn is just a temporary distraction from the steep slope I am plummeting down but Zander is always the one who puts me back together and he's furious with me. I need to fix this, but all I want to do is crawl back into the black hole that is my bed and sleep until death claims me.

The subsequent intrusion is Vivianne, who is about as pleased with me as her brother. Her hair is wild and looks ruffled which is out of character for her. She is pacing my office occasionally looking at me and then sighing in frustration, her hands moving wildly at her sides as if she's arguing with me in her head. I know better than to speak because she *is* arguing with me in her head and because

Vivianne is a master wordsmith. If I'm not careful, Viv will desecrate my already fragile state.

"What were you thinking, Cali?" She finally says, tears brimming in her big eyes. I fucking hate it when Viv gets emotional.

"I don't know why everyone is so bent out of shape about my behavior last night as if it's never happened before." I know why this was different, but ignorance will be my best bet here.

"Don't play stupid with me, Calliope Veritas. We don't mingle with the fucking recruits. Don't you remember why we stopped?"

I do remember. Vividly. Before I was untouchable, I was free to participate in the free love around here. That freedom came with a cost. People can do wild and unthinkable things to receive divine favor when they believe they are entitled to it because they had a taste of it once. What I did that day was necessary to save my life, but it haunted me still. It was also the beginning of all this inner circle nonsense so sometimes I wish I had just let him spill my blood upon the grounds that day. Instead, I spilled his and sealed my fate.

From that moment forward, I didn't fuck anyone but the twins. It was safer that way. They were more understanding of my whims and moods but power was an intoxicating drug, and the withdrawal of divine favor can be excruciating. I should know, especially feeling the wrath of Zander only moments ago. Now when blood is shed here, it is not without reason and not without supreme order or else it gets fucking messy. Blurred lines and all.

"Ahh, so you do fucking remember," Vivianne says blankly, pointing at me. I realize I am absentmindedly fingering the scar on my waist from the knife he stabbed me with. "Zander is feral. He's talking about leaving."

"He wouldn't leave me?" My voice betrays me, and instead of being a statement, it comes out like a question.

"Don't be so sure. Watching your eyes light up like that when you've been dead-eyed for months was difficult even for me let alone Zander. You cannot pretend you don't know how he feels about you. I love you Cali but Zander would die for you."

"You wouldn't?" I offer her a chuckle, trying to ease the tension in the room. Viv is my best friend, and our sexual proclivities have never changed our friendship for each other.

"No, because who would clean up your mess?" She doesn't smile, but I can tell she is calmer. She paces in front of my desk a few times before continuing. "At the risk of setting you off there is something else I need to say to you."

She looks at me earnestly silently begging me for mercy. My blood is already boiling before she speaks.

"If you continue this foolish, selfish, and dangerous behavior, you'll lose more than just Zander. You'll end up risking everything we've built, and then none of us are getting out alive. You can want to die all you want but don't kill the rest of us for your flavor of the week."

I feel my jaw twitch and the drop in my gut.

"All of this would be nothing without me. I will fuck, moan over and do whatever and whoever the hell I want, and if you two don't like that, too *fucking* bad because you're in it for the long haul, just like me. *Get. The. Fuck. Out.*"

"Cali, I…"

I don't allow her to continue because I've already tipped over the edge. My laptop flies through the air and smashes against the wall like punctuation. Before I know it, the desk lamp is in my hand, and there's a bookcase toppled over. I don't even see Viv scamper out of the room because my vision is already black. When it returns, I am sobbing, my office is a mess and my hands are bleeding. I stumble down the hallways with tears fogging my vision until I reach my chambers. I slam the double doors behind me and slink to the floor leaning against the solid once holy wood. I scream at the top of my lungs until I have no breath, and the fury stirs within me again.

The next place I find myself is in my gardens. Broken pieces of my marble statues lay in ruin around me. I am spiraling which is a dangerous place for me. My mind flashes to the cliffs, and as if I was teleported there when my vision returns once more, I have my toes over the edge and I am screaming into the abyss. I have been here on the edges of my cliffs with a yearning I dare not name out loud but never have I had such an urge to step off the edge. I do not want any of this anymore. I have not desired it for longer than I care to admit. This epiphany was inevitable the moment I became more God than mortal. I am no longer shouting at the wind. Instead, I am watching myself lift one foot ever so gently as if my next step would be into a soft patch of grass instead of thin air. I am calmer than I have been in years.

There is something peaceful in the quiet that surrounds me now. Nothing but the sound of the ocean crashing upon my rocky grave. I close my eyes softly and the peace of my final decision beckons me forward. Vivianne will use my death as a publicity stunt and immortalize me post mortem. Zander will be devastated but ultimately will find freedom from the burden of loving someone so incapable of love. These are the things I tell myself in my last moments.

I lean forward, letting the wind flow around my body, keeping me suspended as if by magic. With my eyes still closed, it almost feels like flying. I feel an urge to laugh as a smile creeps into the corners of my mouth. Suddenly, something crashes into me. For a moment, I think I have jumped and hit the steep rocky side of the cliffs but I feel no pain and recognize the feeling of the soft wild grass beneath my limbs.

My eyes snap open to see Aztyn's face. His lips are moving, but I can only hear a ringing in my ears. I feel a wetness on my skull and bring my hand to it. When I look at my hand, it is hard to tell if any of the blood is even new or a result of my crash out. I close my eyes again in an attempt to get the ringing to subside and the sun's brightness to cease burning my retinas. Aztyn's voice floats faintly into my ears like TV static.

"Are you fucking insane?"

"I wasn't going to jump," I whisper unconvincingly.

"Bullshit. What the fuck else were you planning on doing?" I can feel him cradle me into his arms, and when he lifts me from the ground, I feel weightless.

"My head hurts," I squeak.

"Consider yourself lucky," He scoffs at me. "Keep talking to me in case you have a concussion."

"Why were you out here?" I try to open my eyes again, but the pain is blinding, so I quickly squeeze them shut. A strained moan escapes my lips.

"I was watching you and good fucking thing too."

"That depends on your perspective…" My voice trails off at the end of my sentence as a heaviness settles over me.

"If you suffer or die, Little Muse, it will be by my hand do you understand? I won't even let you take that satisfaction from me," his arms shift below my body to shelter me from the sun. "Stay with me now."

"Did you just threaten to kill me?" My body is in panic mode, and I begin to struggle. I was going to step off a cliff a moment ago but now for whatever reason fight or flight has kicked in. The struggle is pointless as Aztyn's hands clasp around my limbs holding me tighter and my vision begins to fade not unlike when I faint from the heat. I can feel my body going limp and his grasp loosening in response. I am utterly helpless and in the hands of someone who I think just threatened my life.

.

Calliope

Aztyn threatened to kill me... didn't he? Yet he saved me from death. What the fuck does that make this, and why do I still want it? There's entirely more wrong with me than I thought. I don't even know what's real anymore.

Cali

Chapter Seven

I don't dare open my eyes. Zander, Vivianne, and Aztyn are arguing and haven't noticed I am awake yet.

"Who the hell do you think you are?" I can hear the strained clench in Zanders' jaw.

"I didn't see anyone else there to save her. So, I guess a *hero*." Aztyn's voice has no trace of emotion, but I know there is an irritating smirk on his face. Zander's response solidifies that knowledge. "Give this guy a fucking medal." He claps his hands slow and deliberately.

"You still haven't explained what you were doing there in the first place." Vivianne sounds worried, but she's actually distraught that her flawless security system is in fact, not infallible.

"Got lost." He answers with a simple statement not open to dissection.

"I highly fucking doubt that." Zander is not convinced, and Viv won't be either.

"If I had *not* been there, she would have fucking jumped. *Maybe* we should focus on her mental health instead of why I was there. A thank you wouldn't hurt."

He is equally irritated and infuriating.

"He's right, Zand." Viv says with a sigh.

Zander says nothing but my door slams and that says it all. I know Zander and he's going to the library. To find an answer to the problem that is me. Fixing problems is what keeps Zander sane here. We all have our vices.

"You'll have to excuse my brother. Thank you for saving her from herself. I don't believe for a second that you were lost, by the way." I can hear the lilt in her voice, and I know how Viv's eyes sparkle when her voice floats like that. She's fucking flirting with him.

"I wasn't." Aztyn's voice is deep and assertive, but he is not flirting.

"I don't suppose you're going to tell me anything either?" She pauses and the disappointment of her advances being denied drips from her next words. "Well, I suppose we will have to deal with that later."

'I'll stay with her until she wakes up."

"That won't be necessary." Vivianne has collected herself and her usual curt nature has returned.

94

"I wasn't asking."

"Neither was I."

There she is. I know the smile I hear is threateningly sweet. I'd like to open my eyes and see this showdown firsthand, but that would ruin the vibe.

"I won't be far." Aztyn doesn't need permission to be in here and knows how to get back in. Vivianne will think she's won, and Aztyn will visit me at his leisure as if anyone could stop him. I hear the door close softly and wonder where he's going.

"Would you like to explain yourself?"

Busted. I open one eye very slowly to see Vivianne staring at me from the chair at my bedside. I open the other eye in defeat. "At this time, no, I would not."

"That won't fly with Zander so you better figure out how you'll charm and lie your way out of this one."

"Maybe I'll just tell him the truth." I fiddle with my blanket like a child.

"Wouldn't that be a nice change of pace? What is the truth exactly?" Viv leans forward in the chair, awaiting my answer.

"That I don't want this anymore."

"Well, then Aztyn should have let you jump." Viv rises from the chair and I watch as she walks to my bedroom door. She opens it to leave but hesitates. "None of us have a way out anymore, Cali. Try to enjoy the ride."

The door falls closed softly behind her and so do my tears. Viv's intention was not to be cruel, just truthful and my tears are not from sadness but from finally accepting that truth.

None of us will ever leave here alive.

After crying myself to sleep, I am awoken by a hand brushing against my cheek.

"Aztyn?" I croak, and the hand is abruptly removed. My eyes snap open to witness the brief shadow of sadness across Zander's face before it hardens.

"You are *unbelievable.*" Zander shakes his head. His jaw clenched. "Why...why would you try to kill yourself Cali and for the love of god why are you so hyper-focused on that asshole?"

"I'm not ready to talk about this with you." I sit up so we are eye to eye as he sits on the edge of my bed.

His hand reaches out to cradle my face again. His eyes are misty and I swear his bottom lip quivers. "I'm so sorry. I shouldn't have said what I did. I'd never turn you away. I couldn't. I love you Calliope. I'll always love you even if you can never love me."

I fight the urge to tease him for his outpouring of emotion. I rarely see the vulnerable side of Zander anymore and know I must tread carefully. "It wasn't what you said. Please don't blame yourself because of our little fight. I love you too Zander… just in my own way. I'll *never* love anyone the way you love me."

"You could have talked to me, Cali. Way before all of this."

"I don't even know if I would have jumped." Zander hangs his head, so I return the sentiment of my hand on his face. "I'll be okay, Viv set me straight. Doesn't matter how before you ask, just know she did."

I can't tell Zander what his sister said. He would be furious. She won't tell if he asks either because she knows it.

Zander lies down beside me. His head on my chest and his arms wrapped around my waist. Instinctively, I lean back and run my fingers through his hair like when he would collapse in my dorm after exams. I close my eyes, and I am there. The smell of books, student angst and microwave food wafting in the air of my reverie.

It was in those moments that I almost thought I loved Zander. I would search my entire heart and soul, looking for that knowing about love that everyone always talked about. I would feel sad for myself in those moments too, because if I could pick someone to love, it *would* be Zander, and if I had loved him maybe we wouldn't be in this mess. He would have finished his psych degree, and I would have settled down and done something meaningful with my life. I am lost in this daydream for a moment. Of what could have been if I wasn't such a demon of a woman. Incapable of love and obsessed with power.

"I wish I could love you, Zander," I whisper the phrase I always did.

One I haven't said since those days. My attempt at comforting him after the horror of my actions.

"The way you love me is enough." His way of accepting who I am and assuaging my guilt just like back then. He squeezes me gently. I almost begin to cry right here on the spot but I hold it back. This ordeal has left me uncharacteristically vulnerable and emotional. Maybe I don't want to die. Perhaps I just want a reason to live. Maybe I just want to feel something, *anything* to live for.

After some time, Zander kisses my forehead and leaves my bedside. I am unable to leave the spot I am rotting in. I watch the sun go down from the big windows. Someone at some point must have drawn the curtains open. I have avoided this view because I don't deserve it after all I have done. I finally allow the tears to fall again and this time they are droplets of relief. I am relieved to watch the sun sink below the horizon as if the ocean swallowed it. I watch Nyx paint the night sky with expert brush strokes and my heart yearns for something I cannot name. The sea reflects the endless universe and my boundless yearning right back at me. I close my eyes and drift in and out of consciousness. The scrape of the chair on the opposite bedside jerks me wholly and violently awake. My entire body snaps towards the chair and Aztyn's stoic and ruggedly handsome face greets me. I blink several times in response.

"I'm not some kind of dream if that's what you're wondering."

"That's exactly what a nightmare would say." I stare at him blankly.

"What makes me a nightmare, Little Muse?"

"The fact that you threatened to kill me for one."

"What else?"

I shift myself into a seated position, never taking my eyes off him, "That you get into places you shouldn't without anyone knowing how."

Aztyn's grin reveals that he takes pride in his work if you could even call it that. "That's not what's bothering you. Try again." He is devilishly handsome, overdressed for attending my bedside in a crisp black-on-black suit. His blue eyes sparkle even in the dark.

"That I love the way it feels when you *hunt* me." My voice is barely above a whisper.

"Good girl." He growls. His grin turns feral, the sparkles in his eyes feeling more like a predator's glean but his stiff posture relaxes.

He is sinking into the chair and cocking his head to the side, and I've never felt more vulnerable.

Instinctively, I pull my blanket up to cover myself, shifting uncomfortably, and his grin grows wider.

"So, are you here to make good on your threat then?" I ask, and my voice shakes against my will.

He doesn't move a muscle. Something I don't recognize flashes in his eyes.

"Not tonight, Little Muse."

I lower my blanket cautiously. Fortunately, I had Zander bring me my sad girl clothes. I am dressed in my biggest and softest black oversized tee and boy shorts but I still feel naked in Aztyn's gaze all the same.

"What are you here for then?"

"To make sure you don't do anything stupid to ruin my fun like you attempted today."

I chew on my words for some time before speaking again.

"I wouldn't dare," I say with a whisper of fire.

"That's all good and well, but I prefer to keep a watchful eye on my… obsessions. Especially when they act erratically."

I say nothing but pat the empty spot beside me in my bed. The look of shock on his face makes me burst out laughing. The annoyance that follows makes me laugh harder.

"Suit yourself," I say seriously once I've collected myself and returned to my view.

After a few minutes, I feel his weight beside me, which comforts me strangely. I feel so safe in his presence and I damn well know I shouldn't. That seems like a concerning red flag but I rest the thought and clear my mind. Even his silence is comforting. I feel him relax beside me and I turn to face him.

"There, you can keep a very watchful eye on me from right there *and* take in the view."

"The view is unrivaled and unparalleled." He says this quietly without taking his eyes off me. I feel my cheeks flush and before I can turn away his hand brushes my hair behind my ear stopping me dead in my tracks. His face comes so close that I close my eyes in anticipation of his lips meeting mine, my heart fluttering wildly in my chest. His lips linger on my forehead and I melt with every passing second.

"You need sleep, Calliope." It is not a question. It is an order. The way he says my name sends electric shocks into my brain. I open my eyes to ask him a question I've never asked anyone.

"Will you stay?"

"Until dawn, they'll be back to check on you in the morning. They won't be too happy to find me here."

I take a risk and lay my head down on his chest. He has removed his suit jacket and loosened the buttons on his shirt, exposing some of his rippled build. He stiffens at first in response but I feel his muscles relax against my skin and his breathing slow. Eventually his arms move to cradle me. The gesture of intimacy causes all the emotions I had tried so hard to bury from the day to bubble up into my throat and I sob silently. I have never wept in front of *anyone*. Aztyn's hands run over my body but he says nothing, allowing me to dig up the grief that has consumed me and occasionally wiping my tears only for more to come pouring out. One hand moves to my hair and he runs his fingers through it, calming me enough that the sobs stop racking through my body.

"Sleep now, Little Muse." He whispers so quietly I'm convinced I imagined it until his hand squeezes mine a second after. I press back in reply.

When the sun peeks over the horizon and kisses my face awake, I find myself alone and feel his absence in my soul. The familiar ice queen chill returns to my veins and I shiver. This man will be my unravelling, and there is nothing at all I want to do about it.

Calliope

Viv is right, I might as well enjoy the ride. Besides, Aztyn seems set on being the vehicle for my demise so that must be where this peace comes from. It's out of my hands now and I've never felt more free.

Cali

Chapter Eight

I haven't heard from or seen Aztyn in days. I haven't left my room either but I have started returning to life. Zander brings me food from the kitchens, all my favorites: Rich soups, warm bread, Snickerdoodles, fancy French pastries, extravagant charcuterie boards, and midnight toast with jam. Sometimes he lies with me and other times I know Viv is outside that door coaxing him from my bedside.

When I am not with Zander I am lounging around my chambers, journaling through my emotions and reading all my favorite books. I don't want to leave my sanctuary but my soul yearns for my gardens and the sound of the ocean crashing into my cliffs. I don't understand why Aztyn didn't kill me the night he held me in his arms. He could have made it look like I succeeded that evening where I had failed earlier in the day. I'm sure that's something that he is capable of. I'm even more sure I wouldn't be the first blood he's spilled. In the darkest hours I quietly ask myself why he hasn't visited me. He can move in between shadows as he pleases and he hasn't even at the very least left a poem at my bedside. I don't dare ask Zander about him but I do ask him about Vivianne.

"She's still angry with me?"

"You know Viv. She still hasn't gotten over mother."

The twins biological mother committed suicide shortly after they turned 16. No one loved Viv the way her sweet mother did. Viv never forgave her for her final act and didn't even go to the funeral. I don't know if she's ever been to her mother's grave site but I do know she wouldn't tell us if she had. Vivianne looks exactly like her mother and isn't the only one who had a tough time forgiving the late Mrs. Belmont. Mr. Belmont was obsessed with his grief and took that obsession out on his wife's mirror image. Viv showed me the scars once. He was a vengeful and vicious man. When he died, I swear that girl smiled the biggest smile I have ever seen. All the family money was left to Zander, his *perfect son* who instantly gave control of the estate to his sister. Mr. Belmont must have rolled over in his grave when he realized he forgot to put a clause preventing that action. After that Viv *tripled* the family money and we used a combo of theirs and mine to fund and develop Cephalonia after we all dropped out of university and lost project funding from the school.

I must go to her if I want to fix things and be allowed out to my cliffs again. I better come correct too. She may need me as the face around this place but she can punish me as long as she wants under the guise of protecting me from myself. As for the official ceremonies that were to take place, they are on hold indefinitely. She will have told everyone that I am experiencing health issues or was called away on official business. Whatever she tells them it won't be the truth. The truth would break the hold I have on people. It would make me too human to them. They would see me just as flawed and broken as they are. Soon they would lose their devotion and then they would turn on us and each other.

If I can't give them what they came for I'm just another bitch on a power trip. Power is a delicate dance. To maintain it you must be an unattainable standard of your success. To maintain a god-like status, you must keep your humanity to a minimum. They have to want something they believe only *you* can give them. That's just business babe. I've dated enough finance bros and CEOs to know it's true.

I dress myself in black leggings and another oversized T-shirt. I brush my hair and pull the separating strands into a messy bun on top of my head. I grab a bottle of Viv's favorite wine from a Bala Ontario winery in Canada. Viv insists they make the best blueberry cranberry wine in the world and I tend to agree with her. It never fails to butter her up.

When I knock on her chamber doors no one answers so I walk down the corridor to her office. Viv spent more time designing her office than she did her chambers. She once told me a bedroom is just a place you sleep but an office is where you spend your time. *Disgusting.* That statement rings true for her at least. It's where part of her annoyance towards me comes from. I'd rather spend time in my black hole or gardens than toil away in my office like her. She thinks I lack discipline and I think she lacks the ability to let loose and have any kind of fun but that's what the wine is for. Maybe I can recreate our study nights in her dorm and turn her favor nostalgic and in my direction again.

When I reach her office, the door is slightly ajar, and I can hear the ending of a phone call.

"...make sure you dig deep. He passed our initial security check but there's more to him than meets the eye. Thanks Ivan."

Ivan is head of security, former CIA, and as crooked and dirty as they come. I love Ivan but we rarely call him directly. Whatever has Viv on the phone with him must be severe. I knock quietly and after a moment she calls out to me.

"The door is open Calliope."

I enter the room with a bow presenting the wine before me. "Truce?"

Vivianne clicks her teeth in response but goes into a drawer in her desk to fetch two wine glasses. She places them on the desk and motions for me to pour. After the glasses are filled, she breaks the silence.

"Should you be drinking in your condition?"

"Condition? You make it sound like I'm pregnant."

"No, thank god for that just suicidal… alcohol increases suicide idealation."

"So do pushy overprotective friends…I heard."

Viv takes a sip from her glass and I follow suit. She is warming up to me, well she's at least talking to me which bodes well for my reconciliation, time to dazzle her.

"I'm sorry Vivianne. I know I broke open an already festering wound and I should have talked to you or Zander about what was happening. Instead, I pushed you both away and isolated myself until I was helpless to the emotions drowning me."

Viv shifts in her seat and swallows another sip of wine. "This has nothing to do with Mamma," she pauses here for another swig. "You know you didn't even write a note. You didn't even think your act through enough to think about how we would feel. Zander especially would have blamed himself forever."

"I know, I wasn't thinking clearly…"

"No, you weren't thinking *at all*." Vivianne takes a long drink from her wine and sighs heavily after she swallows. "No point in dwelling on it now. I am eager to return to the matter at hand which is finishing the initiation rites."

"Do we have to talk about work tonight? Can't we just have some fun? Like we used to?"

"That would require a time machine and some fancy CIA brain manipulation."

I lean forward and point to the bottle. "Or just the rest of this delicious cranberry blueberry wine." I wink in her direction but she still seems less than impressed with me.

"Come on killjoy, let's put some music on in your bedroom and dance around in our underwear, scream-crying the lyrics at the top of our lungs."

Viv shakes her head and lets out an exasperated sigh. "Seeing as I am the only one who works around this fucking place, no. I have things I need to do to keep this place running. If you want to play, go ask Zander…leave the bottle though."

"Can I go to my garden tomorrow?"

Viv looks at me, the wheels turning in her head. "You don't need my permission to go to the gardens Cali. You don't need anyone's permission to do anything."

"Without being chaperoned?"

Viv rolls her eyes. "That I can't allow. Not because I'm afraid you'll jump. If you want to kill yourself there is nothing we can do to stop you. I cannot allow you to go unchaperoned since I still have no idea how Aztyn got in there in the first place."

Aztyn won't come to me if I am still being escorted and I am desperate to see him. I am also terribly curious about where he has been the last few days so I take a risk and ask Viv.

"What happened to Aztyn anyway?" I try to appear nonchalant, though I know she doesn't buy my facade.

"Nothing. From my observations he's been the perfect cult member."

Everything makes sense now. That's why he hasn't been to visit me. He is also under surveillance and intelligent enough to assume he would be. I leave Viv and she hugs me tightly which is unusual for her. She's not really the touchy-feely type. As much as she says she is not worried about me, I can see she's shaken about my suicide attempt and her keeping an eye on me is her way of assuring I don't get into any more trouble that she can't fix. She's right to be nervous about Aztyn. He did threaten to kill me, although she and Zander don't know that, actually they don't know a lot of things.

Something about him puts everyone including me on edge. Except I enjoy the state of panic he puts me in. A little too much as I feel the withdrawal from his intoxicating essence. I'm practically chomping at the bit to see him again even knowing that the next time I see him could be the last time I see *anything*. The thrill rises in my chest until it warms me from the inside out.

I know I will die; I just don't know when which is no different than anyone else but I just happen to be in proximity of my death clock and can hear the ticking. When I die at least the handsome psychopath will be a decent view before my final breath. I already know he's going to fuck his prey before he kills it and my nipples harden at the thought. Something tells me Aztyn knows how to handle a woman and then some and before I return to the earth, I think my dying wish will be to let him handle *me*. I also suspect from

112

his threats of punishment that Aztyn likes to take control and although I have *never* surrendered to a man for some strange reason, I believe I'd surrender to him of my own free will and that thought scares me way more than the certainty of him wanting to murder me.

●

I saunter down the halls to my chambers. My left arm stretched out with my fingertips grazing the edges of the walls like a child and a fence on their walk home from school. The carpet is soft, and I am barefooted as usual. I stop to squelch my toes in it. When I arrive at my room there is a new stack of books on my pillow and a letter this time, not a poem, from Aztyn.

Little Muse,

Here are some of my favorite books of poetry. I took the liberty of borrowing some of your well-loved books. My obsession with you consumes me. I thought it was a fair trade.

The fact that you will see the knowing that I also took the one you were reading at your bedside is just a bonus. I plan to read that one last.

Az.

What an infuriating, pigheaded, son of a bitch. I almost rip the letter to shreds and throw the stack of books across the room but my senses catch up with me and I just stomp my feet a little in a spoiled princess way. When I am done, I thumb through the books he left me, five in total. I assume he took the same number of books from me since he called it a fair trade although nothing about this seems fair.

His books are in excellent condition even though they have been read many times. Franz Kafka, Edgar Allan Poe, Tyler Knott Gregson, r.h.Sin, Atticus. My curiosity takes over. He has taken my book hostage but I justify with my neuroticism that poetry is a collection in a book format so I wasn't exactly starting a new *book*. I can smell the scent of him mixing with the scent of the books. Mahogany, tobacco, buttery scotch and old paper envelop my senses and it is like he materializes before me. I am moved by the words on the paper and the thought of him so twisted and yet so intellectually stimulating.

They do say that serial killers tend to be incredibly educated and charming. I'm not sure Aztyn is a serial killer but he's certainly no stranger to being Death's right hand. I read the entire evening away, devouring the different prose and poets like a five-course meal. Love is not something I am wired for but this psychopathic stranger has me bewitched. I suppose this is how those prison pen pal romances get started, except their dangerous criminal is locked safely behind bars and mine is stalking me on my compound and not the least bit shy about his intentions to end my life.

Aztyn and I are a match made in hell. I have never been so interested in another person in my life. I don't usually invest too much time learning about *my* prey, just the basics to manipulate them and all men are virtually the same. I honestly didn't think a man could be so complex, besides Zander, but even his complexities are simple enough for me to navigate.

Aztyn almost makes me forget he's stalking me. It feels more like courting. My penchant for dark and tragic romance has come to haunt me and my attraction to the villain will prove fatal. I always did like the stories where one of the main characters dies the best. I bet this was far from Viv's intention when she told me to try to enjoy the ride. Well, *this is me trying..*

Aztyn

You run through my veins like the sweetest poison
A wicked drug I can not come down from
I think the darkness in me recognizes the darkness in you
I want you to feel the suffering I feel
I want to break you
Mold you into something made just for me
Little Muse,
I'm going to make you feel alive
Make you crave me like I crave you
A high only death himself could survive

Chapter Nine

I have made a grave mistake. I should have let that sorrowful broken little bird jump from her nest. She was willing to do the dirty work for me and some incredibly idiotic notion came over me. I just had to have it my way I suppose. Watching her standing on the edge of the bluff crying into the wind, her foot dangling over the edge like some kind of twisted ballet made something within me I thought I had lost long ago come alive again.

At one point in my life, I had set out to do virtuous and honorable acts. I thought I would be making the world a better place. I soon learned that pursuing justice is too heavy a cross to bear on your own. Corruption pays and it poisons. They draw you in, weave you a narrative that plays to your objectives, and manipulate you to do their bidding, all the while you are delusional enough to believe you are performing justifiable actions for ethical reasons. I am no one's scapegoat. So, I took a path of my own choosing and got swept up in my delusions of gray areas and rationale for my actions.

Calliope Veritas' attempted suicide awakened my humanity again and that was a plot twist I wasn't expecting. My initial impression of Calliope was not that she was some damsel who needed saving. Quite the opposite. Her kind of corruption is *precisely* the kind I take pleasure in eliminating. My quest to understand her lore and my obsession with observing her have made her slightly less despicable than the filth I usually find myself punishing. In my pursuit of others this has never happened before. Usually, I just find *more* reasons to spill blood, *more* grounds for my motives. The further I dig into Cali and the more I get to know her, the more my compulsion with her heightens in a way I never expected.

The last few days, I have been under surveillance as expected and I have had to act like a model cult member. I can't even hack into the system to watch her, and not knowing what she is doing is driving me mad. Vivianne is a shark and she is excellent at what she does. I do not want to cause any more suspicion than I already have. I don't need her looking into me anymore than she did for me to get this close. It has been excruciating to be away from my Little Muse and I physically ache to be near her. Her exotic scent lingered on my skin the next day after laying with her through the night and every so often, I catch a phantom whiff of amber and jasmine and it causes my stomach to plummet, and my breath to immediately catch in my lungs.

There is another part of me however, that made the vendetta in the first place. That version of me is hungry and feral for its revenge. That *she-devil* who has somehow bewitched me still *murdered* my brother and although *I* may deserve that kind of end, I am *certain* he did not. I still want her to suffer endlessly and I meant it when I said I wouldn't let her take that satisfaction from me. I can still feel her tears on my chest, and it induces the desire to carve the skin beneath her trail of tears away so I can keep it forever. I couldn't help but soften for her when she began to sob in my arms that night but it was a temporary lapse in judgment. I forgot about the wraith she still is as I watched the wind caress her body and whip through her hair on the edge of those sharp and jagged cliffs.

It will not happen again. Try as she might to tempt me otherwise with her sadness and inability to accept her actions. Why the fuck should I feel bad if she clearly cannot live with what she's done? Consider me the Grim Reaper who will deliver her to her fate. She will beg for mercy just like the ones before her when she feels the life draining from her limbs. *They all do.* Confronted with the true possibility of death, *everyone* wishes for more time.

Cali doesn't want to die; she just wants to feel alive. She's afraid of how I make her feel as I stalk her like a fox stalks a rabbit, and nothing makes you feel more alive than terror clawing at your insides. I will be Calliope Veritas' living nightmare and when I have had my revenge I will finally rest in my crusade against the wicked until Death deems it is time to call me home to pay for my own mortal sins. I hope wiping the wicked from the earth has redeemed my soul enough for some eternal peace but I doubt it.

She does have *excellent* taste in literature. My Little Muse has a penchant for tragedy and devastation. Why is the girl who has everything so *broken*? That's the next question I have a fascination to answer. It can't just be what she's done. I saw her eyes flash with desire as we all devoted our blood to her. She does still take some pleasure from her position so what is it that plagues her soul so fervently that she feels her only escape is death?

I'll choke the truth out of her pretty little mouth if I have to.

.

Calliope

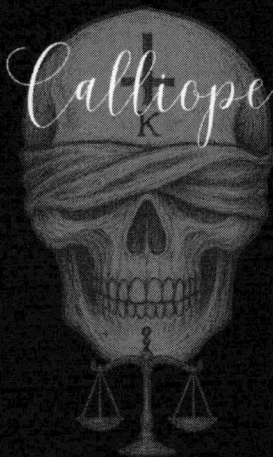

I don't know why but his absence makes me feel
hollow again. I desperately need to be brought back
to life, and I have never felt more alive than in his
relentless pursuit of me. When he held me as I sobbed,
I realized something dangerous. Aztyn can kill me in
the end. I've made peace with death, but I want him to
be haunted by my absence when I'm gone. I want to
seep into his bones until my voice summons him to the
afterlife. Aztyn Diamandis will hunt for me long after
he has taken my life.

Cali

Chapter Ten

I have a desperate and gnawing need to see Aztyn so when Viv suggests we get back to business with initiations, I agree maybe a little too eagerly. I play it off as a chance to return to my life and forget about my little episode. This lie earned me a quizzical look from Zander but at least Vivianne was satisfied.

Tonight, I will brand my new initiates with the symbol of Cephalonia's inner sanctum. A skull with a ribbon across its eyes and an upside-down cross on its forehead with the kappa symbol right below the scales of justice capping out the bottom under the skull's jaw.

Cephalonia shares the name of the greenest and most fruitful Greek island, rumored to be a paradise for the Gods. Originally spelled with the Greek symbol kappa, which is why it is present in the brand. I have always been fascinated by Greek lore, namely due to my own name's origins.

Calliope was the eldest sister of the Nine Muses and she presided over poetry and eloquence. It's some cruel twist of irony that Aztyn happens to have affectionately named me Little Muse and leaves me poetry as his calling card. I wonder if he is aware of this irony? Something tells me that there is not much about this orchestration that is not calculated or intentional as everything he seems to do is and it makes my body rush with a heat that emanates from my core. No one has desired to know me as much as Aztyn does even if it is to serve his own purposes and it makes my insides curl. He is more intentional in his pursuit of me than any man I have ever met. All the men before him bowed to whatever version of myself I created for them, never even bothered to ask themselves if it was real.

Aztyn will never bow to me but he will know me better than anyone else ever has because his *need* to know his prey governs him and because I am relieved to confess all my sins to something other than my journals without fear. He already despises me so nothing I confess will matter. If anything, it will fuel his desire to take my life and the sweet release of death at his hands will be my abolishment.

I also have a desperate need for him to return my books. I shouldn't care about the opinion of my stalker on my choice of literature but after devouring his favorite poets as if they were my last meal and feeling so close to understanding his psychopathic yet hopelessly romantic nature through them, I find myself curious about his interpretation of his selection. Is Aztyn Diamandis possibly just as disastrously fragmented as I am? We are fire and fuel—never meant to last, only meant to burn in each other's inferno until we eventually snuff each other out, one way or another. I have gladly accepted *my* fate. I need him to unmake me and destroy what little grip I have left on reality. I need him to give me the one thing I desire above all else: escape.

I have done these rituals enough times that I should not be this full of nervous electricity. It is Aztyn that I am nervous about branding. I know exactly what it will do to me to mark him in a way that will outlive me. I hope it burns his flesh into the next life, so deeply that even when the proverbial slate has been wiped clean, I will remain, pulling his soul towards mine inexplicably. How's that for poetic justice?

I need to find a way to stifle my desire tonight. I cannot risk a public showing of it again. Not just for the sake of my image but for Zander's sake. Tonight, I must be as frigid and unyielding as a winter storm. I need to be stoic and unmoving. There is a delicate balance that only I can restore here and I must do so while I still have the opportunity. To steady my nerves, I find myself in the gardens.

Zander has been through here and cleaned up my wreckage. He is always cleaning up my mess. Vivianne would have the staff do it but Zander saves me the embarrassment of their gossip. Besides, he knows how I like things. It's as if that day never even happened. Any flowers or greenery I had wounded beneath my feet have been pulled and replanted and the remains of the marble statues I desecrated have been swept up and replaced. Zander worships and honors me through his meticulous care of me. He likes to act tough sometimes but behind closed doors he is soft and sometimes trembles at my touch. It's sweet how nervous he gets before he fucks my brains out.

I run my fingers through the flowers in my garden. I imagine myself like a honeybee pollinating as I go, my hands sticky with the sweet orange powder. I stop walking and close my eyes to inhale the fragrant air deeply through my nose until I feel like my lungs might burst. With my eyes still closed I exhale slowly until I can't possibly blow any more air out. Then I dance through the garden to my fountains to rinse my hands. Doing so I glance at the statues of fairies and mermaids frolicking in the middle. I spot what appears to be a letter fasted to the hand of a pointing mermaid. I immediately wade into the fountain pool with little thought and clamor anxiously to the note.

The middle of the fountain is quite deep, and I have to jump to snatch the message, careful not to get it wet. Once it is in my grasp I carefully move towards the edge of the fountain and immediately upon reaching dry land I rip open my newest correspondence. It's blank and my disappointment must show heavily on my face.

He made me get in the water just to see if I would. How *fucking embarrassing*. I can't picture Aztyn wading through my fountain pool but I would have loved to have seen it. I bet he had that all-consuming and aggravating sneer on his face. Two can play at that game. I wonder what Aztyn looks like when there's *jealousy* on his face. Part of me wants to crumple the blank paper or rip it into a thousand pieces. Instead, I bring it to my nose and inhale the heady scent of him. I tuck it into my pocket to put it safely with the others in my safe room. I've had enough humiliation for one day and retreat back to my chambers. Fool me once; hell hath no fury like a woman scorned. Tonight, my frigid demeanor towards Aztyn will have two purposes.

My ritual attire for the evening is a two-piece ensemble. Black, of course. My midriff is exposed. The skirt is mostly sheer with two slits up the sides. The spaghetti-strapped top dips low between my cleavage reaching just under my sternum. I admire my curves in the mirror the way the dress cuts my body in sharp but flattering angles, my hips creating a perfect hourglass. I am sin dipped in lust which is exactly the vibe I set out to achieve. I call for Zander to escort me to this evening's events and his knock on the door steals me from my mirror.

"It's open, Zand," when I see his reflection behind me in the mirror, I turn to face him with my most enigmatic smile on my face. "How do I look?"

Zander's jaw is slightly ajar, and color blooms across his cheeks. I wink and stick my tongue out, breaking the spell I have over him momentarily as he chuckles at me.

"You're always the best view on this island Cali, but *this* is something else entirely."

I grin genuinely, this time as he drinks me in. I know he can smell my perfume wafting towards him. I wore *his* favorite, the one he can't help but inhale off my skin with a growl behind his teeth if I let him get close enough. I can see the restraint in his muscles. He's unsure of my intentions and I enjoy watching him squirm. I bite my lip and look him up and down. He's dressed impeccably as always, his tailored black suit echoing the empty void I am wearing. His curly hair is pushed back and messy like he used to wear it in university. It gives him a boyish charm and it's my favorite.

He clears his throat, the timber of his voice reverberating up my spine.

"Does our resident goddess approve?"

I cock my head to the side and nod before strolling towards him. Zander is a head taller than me so when I press myself against him, I look up at him through fluttering lashes and I know it drives him wild.

The art of seduction, of playing to a man's fantasies, always came far too naturally to me. Zander places a finger below my chin and tips my lips to meet his. He is always right on cue. For a split second I have remorse for what I am about to use him to do. He is no stranger to me using his cock to quiet the voices in my head but using him to make another man jealous feels wrong. The moment is fleeting however, because the thought of Aztyn being jealous makes me wet and I lean into Zander's kiss even more. His tongue meets mine and explores my mouth and his teeth nip at my bottom lip as he breaks our kiss.

"Come on, Cali, we better go."

Walking into the ritual room, I keep Zander on my arm and forcefully push him down onto my chair before I sit on his lap and face my congregation. Viv looks back and rolls her eyes at my antics. I do not break character. I stare out at my audience with a bored expression. I focus my eyes above the crowd's heads so as not to accidentally meet Aztyn's eyes although I would love to see the expression on his face right now. I will still have to brand him but I'll cross that bridge when I am in front of it. I shift so that I am sprawled across Zander's lap absentmindedly running my finger along his jawline. He unknowingly plays his role perfectly. He sits straight with an arrogant confidence, his fingers mimicking my own across my thighs, my skirts draped daintily down my throne. A cockier than thou smirk on his face. He no doubt *has* found Aztyn's gaze. Their rivalry already embers long before my little game which will ultimately set fire to them both. Casualties of war and all that jazz. Vivianne clears her throat and Zander takes this as an invitation to dip his head down to nip at my neck eliciting a hiss from my teeth before I stand to speak. It takes everything in me not to look for Aztyn.

"Welcome back, my initiates. I offer my humble apologies for my absence," I pause here and nod to the crowd. Now my arms spread in front of me in a grand gesture, "Tonight, I brand those of you who chose to stay with our seal. Like the others who have come before you, including all of us on this platform."

Each of us now reveals our brands. Mine is already peeking out of my ensemble on my hip. I've had an artist tattoo a butterfly over the teeth of my skull, and outline my cross in red. Vivian's is in the middle of her outer thigh and Zanders is on his chest right over his heart. It started as a way to prove our loyalty to each other. As we stepped into the roles we play now, we thought it appropriate to include the heathens.

I step forward to address them further, "You may be asking yourselves why we would brand you. You can remove a tattoo or piercing, but a brand is *permanent*. We are all a part of this circle permanently bonded in sin. You may leave here one day but you will always carry Cephalonia and what happened here during your time with us, with you."

I find Aztyn's eyes now. I immediately wish I hadn't, but I hold his gaze firmly. The chill within them hits me hard and my bones are suddenly like frost-covered branches. There is a different kind of darkness that clouds his face now. It is ominous and I am shaken by doubt for a short time. Then the heat of his humiliation returns to my cheeks. My face is undoubtedly a reflection of the fury I feel

130

deep in my chest. I grin devilishly and it almost seems I got under his skin in a way he wasn't aware I could.

Zander places his hand on my shoulder while he stands behind me, his other hand finding my hip as his fingers graze my brand. Again, he is inadvertently right on cue. Aztyn's eyes darken, but he is no longer looking at me. He's staring at Zander, his eyes flickering back and forth between Zander's face and the many contact points he has with my body. Instinctively my hand reaches back to caress Zander's face and Aztyn's eyes snap back to mine. He is furious and I can feel his fury deep into my hollow bones. It does not deter me whatsoever. If anything, it ignites me more.

Vivianne hands me the brand and I stick it into the lit pit of embers in front of me. Viv calls the initiates by name and they come to receive their mark one by one bearing their various chosen flesh. When she calls Aztyn's name I nearly freeze. Facing him in such proximity is entirely different than putting on a show up here out of his reach. He wouldn't dare try to kill me now, there are too many witnesses but his threatening aura will speak volumes.

I involuntarily tense up when he begins his ascent up the stairs. As he walks, he slowly undoes each button of his shirt, never taking his eyes off mine. I long for him in a way that betrays my anger. When he reaches the step before me, he silently taps his chest. Zander tenses behind me, his hands gripping me tighter in response to the subtle challenge. The branding rod I hold suddenly feels like it weighs 100 pounds and my hands tremble. As I press the red-hot brand into Aztyn's chest he doesn't even flinch. He just stares darkly and into my soul. If he didn't hate me before he hates me now and I have practically sealed my fate. I might as well start digging my own grave for what I am about to do next.

When I am finished, Aztyn moves to the side with the others I have branded. Zander then relaxes as I continue my work on the last few. When I have finished, I step forward out of Zander's hold.

"You belong to something bigger than yourselves now. You belong to Cephalonia," for the last part of my speech, I look directly at Aztyn, "You belong to me."

He shakes his head slowly back and forth just enough for me to catch. The scowl on his face looks as if it were etched in stone. I dismiss the crowd to their rooms and thank them for offering their flesh then I find Zander and place my hand on his arm as he escorts me out of the ritual room and back to my chambers.

I am nothing but a dead woman walking to my execution.

Aztyn

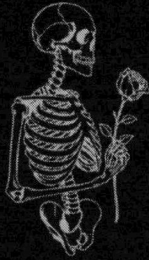

I will burrow into your soul until it's only my hands
you crave wrapped around your throat
Until I consume your thoughts
And your body responds only to me
My face will be the last you see when the devil calls
you home
It will be my name you call out until then when you
need to be released
I may not be your first but
Mark my words I'll be your last.
Fino alla morte piccola musa

Until Death Little Muse

Chapter Eleven

I will make that little bitch pay for what she did tonight. What a disgusting display of power she doesn't yet have a right to yield. All this childish game playing because I stole her books and then forced her to get a little wet to retrieve a blank letter? I didn't expect her to jump into the fountain nevertheless, it was amusing...actually it was downright comical. The look on her face when she realized it was unmarked was priceless.

Okay, maybe I pushed her buttons intentionally but that's no excuse for her immoral mating display. She practically performed live porn for an audience. Except it wasn't for the crowd it was specifically for me. I'd like to cut off every appendage Zander laid on her, gift wrap them, and hang them from her four-poster bed but I can't maim Zander *or* kill him. That would be incredibly stupid and a slight overreaction. He's her pawn in our chess game and needs to stay put.

I burst through the door of my room and hit a button on my phone which supplies *my* version of the video feed to Vivian's tech team. I need to access my personal feed in Calliope's room and I don't want to take the chance of them zooming in on what I am doing. I place my earpiece and press my feed link. She's not in the room. *Fine.*

I urgently flip through my camera angles of the live feed until I find her in the hallways. She's with Zander *of course*, and they're acting like teenagers. If she fucks him, I don't know if I will be able to stop myself from killing him. It's not like I haven't watched a girlfriend or two get fucked by a buddy or three, and I have had my fair share of group sex, but for some reason when he touches my Little Muse, I feel a rage inside me like I have never felt before. At this point if I wanted to cut off every piece of skin that he touched her with, he'd end up sliced like Thanksgiving turkey. Nothing but a gaping carcass would be left behind.

I am confident she will leave him at the door and wait for me to arrive. That's what this is: *Aztyn bait.* Unfortunately for her it worked like a charm. She's going to beg for my god like forgiveness tonight. She's already tried to tell me what to do several times, plus she tried to kill herself intending to rob me of my poetic justice, and now this dog and pony show.

I'm going to spank her ass so hard my handprint will be there for a week and shove my cock so far down her throat she won't be able to swallow right for just as long. They're taking their sweet ass time getting to Cali's room so I switch through my cameras until I find Viv. She's in her office as usual. I can guarantee that her annoyance with her brother and Calliope is perpetual. I feel Viv would gladly take over when Calliope ceases to exist. It's not that she doesn't care for Cali. It's that she doesn't care for the way Cali operates. Vivian's organizational and public relations skills are bar none and her intelligence is sky-high. She would be quite dangerous in power not that Calliope isn't. That one is as dangerous as they come but Vivianne is calculated and has more control over her emotions than Calliope who's currently acting like I ditched her on prom night. I quickly flip back to the feed I am eager to see but I do not like what greets my eyes at all.

Zander has Calliope pressed against her door and I'm waiting for her to send him away so her worst nightmare can take its shape. When she pushes his chest back from hers and opens her door, she pulls him in with her and my rage paints the world in a single violent hue. I switch to her bedroom feed, not my most gentlemanly camera placement sure and yes, a complete invasion of her privacy, but she's not shy about her nudity, and it's not like I put one in her

136

shower. Although I never imagined using it to spy on her sexual activities I cannot stop watching, it's no wonder I have to keep an eye on her.

Just fucking look at her behavior

The sick attraction I have to my current complex infatuation is distorting my logic. I do not like Zander touching what is mine let alone *fucking* it. They've made out enough now I speculate because Calliope removes her clothing slowly until she's completely naked then backs up as she pulls Zander forward towards her and sits down on the edge of her bed. She pushes him down to his knees with a devastatingly seductive smile and he does as he's told. Her head kicks back as he settles between her thighs. Her hand reaches into his hair and pushes his face further as she begins to whimper and moan.

Now I've decided to cut out his tongue and each finger that smells like her sweet cunt before I slice off the rest of him piece by piece. When she cries out in ecstasy, I feel physically ill and don't know how much more I can take. Something flickers across her face and I think she almost loses her nerve but as quickly as it appears it is replaced by that devilish grin and I want nothing more than for her to look at me like that.

What is wrong with me? If I didn't know I was sick in the head before this, I do not doubt it now. I shouldn't want her for more reasons than I can count but finding out how broken she is makes me want to break her beyond repair and rearrange her as I please. I want to ruin her even more than she is already ruined. Stain her soul even blacker than the pitch black it is already.

When she pulls Zander's face to hers and rips his pants off, I can't help but get a little hard, watching her taste herself on his lips makes me want to spit her cum into her mouth and see how much she likes it, and I bet she fucking *loves* it. Regrettably for her it also reminds me of the unfinished business we have. Which provokes me further because I was the one who primed that pussy and now, he gets to reap the benefits?

He climbs on top of her and I want to march down the corridors, rip open her door and drag him clear across the room but I smother the murderous impulses. She flips on him so it's her on top and seats herself down on his cock. I wish she had closed the curtains that surround her bed but then she wouldn't be able to watch herself in all her fucking mirrors like she is now. I shift my erection in my jeans.

The only reason she gets off is because she's watching herself. Zander is nothing but a good-looking toy beneath her. Her head kicks back and she cries out again but this time she throws her middle finger up behind her back as she cums. Zander doesn't notice because he can barely contain himself and I swear to God if she lets him cum inside her, I will fuck her so hard I'll rearrange her insides and from that moment forth only I will fit inside that pretty little pussy.

That little bitch knows I'm watching her. I've seen enough. Too much if I'm being honest. I rip the earpiece out, chuck it onto the desk, and slam my phone screen beside it. I can't kill Zander no matter how much I want to, and boy do I fucking want to with every fiber of my being. I also can't keep this bloodthirsty rage inside me. It will leave me vulnerable. I need some catharsis. I pick my phone back up and look for my files on a few of the cult members.

Calliope and her inner circle have made many powerful enemies and many of the members are spies of some sort or another. I know one of them is a sleazy reporter who just happens to have a penchant for underage girls. Calliope and Vivianne are unaware of this man's private proclivities although they know his employment choice. I too would be ignorant of his fetishes if it wasn't for a young girl who made a now redacted complaint six years ago and was paid off by his magazine. My contacts run deeper than Vivian's. I've planted roots in places where she's barely scratched the surface.

I quickly find his dwelling number and rush out of my room slamming the door behind me and clicking on my personally curated feeds. Once I slip into the shadows, I can sneak around undetected. The compound is under video surveillance but the public part for the Normies has plenty of blind spots unlike the private inner sanctum. I don't need to hack anything except the camera outside that sick pedos room and that will be like a walk in the park compared to everything else I have hacked so far. Don't get me wrong, the compound's security is impressive and highly sophisticated. *I'm just better.*

I haven't killed anyone since I started hunting Calliope, which is different from my usual targets because killing those who stand in my way doesn't usually come with such grave consequences. She's my final mark. I've secured enough funds and land and property worldwide to live peacefully for the rest of my days after this. I'll still carry my sins and misdeeds but at least I can lay down the cause.

Strangely enough, the closest I have ever come to peace in this lifetime was holding that enchantress while she sobbed. I wish I could erase that from my system's memory. I have never been described as soft or comforting and being that unguarded with her was a mistake. When I arrive at the reporter's dwelling, I have a momentary change of heart. I didn't come here with this as a part of my mission. I gathered information on various cult members to know who else was trying to get to her. Going in blind and naive could get me killed. Although plenty have tried in the past, no one has succeeded because I do not rush in without taking a look at the whole picture. Then I remember why I am even standing outside this man's door in the first place. Flashes of flesh, a mouth on a mouth that is not fucking mine. Calliope must be punished and this dude is a piece of shit. I'm doing the entire cult a favor.

I usually prefer a cleaner kill and usually I spill only what must be spilled but I know for a fact this incident will be handled internally with no official investigation to take place, and as far as I know Vivianne doesn't have anyone with criminal lab access on the payroll, nor does she give a fuck about the peons enough to investigate further. Her main concern will be whether or not this is a threat to their trio. In any case I'm no amateur and left no damning evidence behind. Not the kind to condemn me anyway.

I want Calliope to know what I am capable of, and I've left her a calling card. This is not a warning, it's a fucking threat. If Zander touches her again stupidity be damned, I'll most likely kill them both on the spot. No one will lay a finger on Calliope Veritas from this breath and into the dark. My hands will be the last to touch her skin and my name will be the last name she cries out in ecstasy until I decide I am ready to end her life. She wants that too or she wouldn't have pulled this little stunt.

She just wanted to make me jealous but she needs to learn her place and who she's dealing with. I'm not some overgrown trust fund kid with Mommy issues; I am a different breed. I was stitched together by darker hands. It's time she found out exactly how dangerous a game she is playing. I do not belong to her, but she will wear my name, in blood and in bliss.

I stand back to admire my work. I've made a bloody mess, literally. There's blood sprayed all over the room. I somehow managed to keep most of it off myself but I still have to burn and dispose of everything I wear.

It's a shame, I usually wouldn't murder someone in my good jeans but Calliope got the best of me. There was no time to think through my wardrobe choice. Luckily for me, during the initial struggle the prick got a good shot in and nearly broke my nose, so if anyone does catch me leaving,

I'll just say I have a nosebleed. By the time anyone wonders where this garbage human is no one will remember seeing me.

I don't see anyone returning to my room, which is just as well. I wipe all the cameras of the evidence of my existence just in case, and I immediately change. There are plenty of places to burn my soiled clothes on the island and when I am done, I'll throw what's left over the cliffs. I check on Cali, she's sleeping soundly and so is Zander beside her. She thought she'd be safer that way. My Little Muse is as intelligent as she is cunning. She knows I won't risk blowing my cover but what she doesn't know yet is that I have already made my presence and displeasure known in a way she will not be able to ignore. My creative side outdid itself this time.

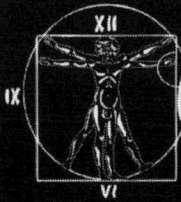

Calliope

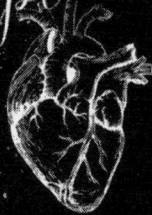

When I set out to make Aztyn jealous a part of me knew something like this could happen. He is after all an unhinged psychopath who has made his intentions with me crystal clear. This little 'art installation' of his muddies the waters. If I weren't mistaken, I'd think Aztyn's heart was bleeding for me.

Too soon?

Cali

Chapter Twelve

I startle awake from the obnoxious phone vibrating beside my ear on the bedside table. Groggily, I smash the screen with my eyes closed until my finger finds the right button. Make that the wrong button. The click of the speaker echoes in my room.

"Calliope? Get dressed and wake Zander. It's important." Viv comes in loud and clear on the speaker.

"Fuuuuuck Viv. What could be so important at this hour?"

The clock on my phone says 6:45 AM.

"You need to…you need to see this for yourself. In the dwellings. 812."

I can hear the panic in Viv's voice. Whatever it is, it's serious. I smack Zander in the chest, and he groans.

"We're coming, Viv, just relax." I hang up and strike Zander again, harder this time. "Your sister is freaked. We need to go."

It takes us only a little while to meet up with Viv and it takes even less time for me to figure out what's got her so spooked. I can smell the familiar metallic scent before I even reach her. I have no doubt whatever this is, it was meant for me to see it.

"I can't…will not… go back in there," her hands shake as she points to room 812. "The boys are on their way to clean this up and I have relocated all the other members in this wing temporarily until this matter is resolved."

Vivianne is leaning against the wall smoking a cigarette, her back to the room's door which only means one thing. That what lies past that door is a horror beyond her capability to spin into gold. Zander stays with her and I go in on my own.

Opening the door, it takes a moment for my brain to comprehend what it's looking at. The smell of blood fills my nostrils and my eyes struggle to focus on what's before me. A nude man, suspended by red wire midair arms outstretched as if hanging from a cross. Sort of a twisted version of the Vitruvian Man. His heart was removed and articulated outside the gaping chest wound suspended

146

midair by the same red wires. A blood trail trickles like an oil slick down the victim's body, pooled like spilled wine on the dark hardwood floor. In front of this altar to madness is a shiny black folder untouched by the blood stain. I pick it up and leaf through the few papers inside. It seems our heartless friend here was a reporter with an appetite for drama but worse than that it appears his appetite also applied to underage girls. I tuck the folder under my arm and shift my perspective of the horror before me.

Something I instantly recognize catches my eye suspended just off to the side and perfectly placed so that it is nearly invisible or camouflaged from most viewpoints in the room. I know this one will not be blank. I snatch the letter from its wire and rip it open. No poem inside but written in blood is four words I recognize.

"They may all belong to you, but you belong to ME."

I stuff the letter in my pocket hoping no one else has laid eyes on it and won't notice its absence. I know no one on the camera footage will be seen going in or out of this room. I know that Vivianne will bury this so far into the ground that she won't even allow us three to speak of it again. It's mesmerizing and hauntingly poetic.

There is a rot in me I can't carve out, after all what kind of person understands the villain. Though I am no stranger to blood and murder this should horrify me. It should leave me a shaking mess like Viv. This is the work of a psychopathic madman, a warning for letting Zander fuck me. It would be kind of romantic if it weren't so disturbing. I am fucked up beyond all help. Was I always this broken or did I become it slowly?

Fear reverberates through my bones but another sensation is here too. Aztyn has reignited something that had been slipping from my fingers. He has made me untouchable again in a way that is not dependent on anything within my control. I was his the moment he started hunting me whether we knew it or not. He is consumed by me as I have been by him which complicates things at the very least. I could go out there and expose him right now and this could all be over but I don't move a muscle or say a fucking word. I just stand there gawking at what Aztyn has done like it's behind a red rope framed in gold. When Zander finally comes in, he is horrified and appalled. I'm unsure if it's because of my calm demeanor, the appalling scene, or both but he leaves me there in my silent and obsessive observation after taking the folder from my grasp. It's not until the boys come in to clean up the mess that I remove myself from the room and walk back towards my own.

It's a little inebriating to find a man who not only shares my penchant for *extracurricular* activities but also wants to own me in a way that sets feminism back a few decades. I *must* be rotting inside to even think this way but I can't help myself. His little display protected me from someone else trying to get to me and revealed an advantage of mine in this game that Aztyn had successfully hidden... until now that is.

I get to him as easily as he gets to me. Despite the warning bells in our heads, we are inexplicably drawn to one another. The two of us are broken, fucked up, rabid creatures. Neither one of us is capable of love in the traditional sense of the word, but both are capable of overwhelming obsession for one another.

The two of us will burn the world in our destruction of one another and the mere thought makes me want to melt into a puddle on the floor. If his end goal *wasn't* to murder me, I think he would make a perfect addition to the ruling faction. He's already proved he would never let anyone get close enough to breathe on me, let alone harm me. I don't need to wonder if he'll keep me safe. He already made it clear I am very much off limits. He made it so clear that I know I have to end things with Zander like yesterday. He's no stranger to my hot and cold moods, so it shouldn't be too difficult. I still love Zand in my serpentine way and I don't want to see 'Art by Aztyn' featuring my former lover anytime soon.

I need a shower to wash off the stench of death that has permeated into my skin. I do not need to look for Aztyn. He will find me when he decides and I will surely pay for my breaking of the rules. I hop in my shower and the frigid black marble meets my feet. The icy water seizes my skin, stealing the heat in an instant. I let it crash over me, ruthless and immediate. I hadn't realized how warm I was. I close my eyes and put my face under the water, its thunderous current drowning out the voice in my head.

A voice that tells me that there is no escape. Not from Aztyn, not from here, not from my sins. I am in perpetual limbo and at the mercy of those who know none. My cleansing is interrupted by someone's hand fisting my hair, dragging me out of the shower and throwing me to the floor, a sopping wet mess. I look up at my assailant with tears already brimming my eyes from the pain. Aztyn peers down at me, his eyes dripping with venom.

"Well, that was fucking rude." Gods alive. I just can't help myself.

Aztyn looks momentarily shocked by my words but quickly regains himself.

"The only thing you should be doing right now is begging for my forgiveness."

"Here's something you should know about me," I say in defiance. "I. Don't. Fucking. Beg."

Faster than I can comprehend Aztyn has bent down to my level, his fingers grasping my jaw hard

"You will."

Just as quickly he rises back to his mountainous height dragging me again by my hair into my bedroom. My limbs scramble for purchase but I'm still soaking wet so I look like Bambi trying to walk for the first time. He tosses me onto the floor again. I land forcefully and every muscle aches with the impact.

I scoff at Aztyn, "You're going to bruise me if you keep throwing me around." I squeak out between the vibrations shooting through my body.

"Oh, I'm going to do more than bruise you, Little Muse," Aztyn smirks down at me, "Get on your knees."

"Why don't you *make me*?"

Fury and something else cloud Aztyn's face.

"Careful what you wish for."

Aztyn's teeth are gritted and his hand is quickly around my throat. He effortlessly lifts me just enough that my legs scramble once again beneath my body and my lungs gasp for air. He swiftly places me directly on my knees in front of him before releasing his grip.

I cough hard but stay where he put me.

"Holy *fuck*. You're psychotic."

"Watch how you speak to me Calliope. My patience is wearing thin."

My knees are already starting to burn.

"As is mine, Aztyn Diamandis. What if I tell everyone what you've been doing in your spare…"

Aztyn has once again come down to my level and pinched my jaw between his fingers.

"Why don't you stop running this pretty little mouth of yours and use it for something more useful."

Aztyn releases my face and calmly walks to the edge of my bed. Then he simply sits and I cannot help but watch him, my jaw smarting from the corrections. His fingers snap and he points to the place on the floor before him.

I laugh sarcastically. "You want me to beg for your forgiveness on my knees? I'm not even sorry. So, what if I fucked Zander. I *don't* belong to you."

Aztyn doesn't even flinch. His voice is as calm as ever.

152

"I warned you once already, but maybe I didn't make myself clear. If I have to get up and drag you over here I will but the harder you make this on yourself the worse off you'll be in the end."

He sounds like someone's father. I am still infuriated when a different sensation threads its way through me. My clit pulses with every word he speaks and a wetness builds between my thighs that is foreign to me in every way. My pussy is betraying me. I don't precisely desire to be dragged across the floor a third time so I rise to my feet and yet again he stops me in my tracks.

"Ah Ah Ah, you *vicious* little thing you've been quite difficult this evening. You can crawl to me, ass up, princess."

"Are you fucking serious?" My voice also betrays me. I sound like a teenage girl whose father denied her request to attend a party.

"As death…would you rather I *make* you again?"

I can't believe I am going to crawl for this man. The indignation must show in my face because he seems pretty pleased. With a heavy breath I drag myself forward as per his instructions.

"Eyes on me. I want to see the hate in them when you look at me."

My eyes flash to his against my will. His voice is gritty and commanding. My core is slick with heat and every

153

thought vanishes. I am ruled by the ache that is pulsing low and hungry. I crawl, my eyes glued to his until I reach his indicated destination. I shift to my knees, my hands still flat on the floor before me, my eyes never moving from his. Aztyn shifts his jeans and a little groan escapes his lips.

What a fucking perv.

As though I am not equally as aroused. I lick my lips seductively and play into the moment. My hands reach up to his knees.

"So, you want me to apologize, do you?"

I wink, and then my expression falls flat

"I don't apologize either so go fuck yourself."

For added measure, I give him the finger and remove my hands from his knees although I don't dare get off mine.

Aztyn smiles wickedly. Those predatory eyes gleaming at me.

"Such a wicked tongue. It's too late for apologies anyways," Aztyn unzips his jeans pulling them down and kicking them off behind me. He's not wearing underwear and a cock more than I bargained for and exactly what I wanted springs out in front of me. He's not just going to fuck me he's going to invade claim, and sanctify my insides.

"You'll mind your perfect teeth or you will be picking them up off the floor."

He cannot be fucking serious right now. He thinks I'm about to blow him as a substitute for an apology.

Wait, that works for me and isn't much of a punishment.

"That's all?" I question him suspiciously.

He gestures to his raging hard-on but says nothing. Aztyn is sharp featured and sinful but also a complete psychopath which is evidently not a big enough factor to deter me. Before I can overthink it, I rise off my knees and take the tip of him into my mouth, my hand grasping the shaft. He moans as my tongue glides up and down in time with my hand.

My head game is superb. It's not the first time I've used it to get something I want. In this case I'm trying to avoid Aztyn's wrath so I do all my best tricks. My other hand cups his balls as one of my fingers reaches for that sweet spot. When I hit it, his eyes roll back and he lets out a deeper needier moan. My teeth graze his shaft and he tenses for a moment. Fucking serves him right. I quickly release them using my mouth to ease any discomfort.

Like the flick of a switch Aztyn's demeanor changes. His hand fists my hair and he shoves his cock so far in the back of my throat I gag. My head is tilted slightly back and his hips are angled so he's face fucking me. The sting of fresh tears presses behind my eyes and he chuckles.

"That's it, Little Muse now open your fucking throat before I force it open."

I breathe deeply and attempt to relax the muscles and drool spills from my mouth. The back of my throat already feels bruised. Why did I think he would let this be enjoyable for me? His other hand grasps my throat and I gag again. I fucking despise him with every fiber of my being right now and yet I am the wettest I have ever been. I want nothing more than for him to fuck my pussy like he's currently fucking my face. Aztyn's head kicks back when he catches the venom in my eyes, and I can feel his cock twitch. Abruptly he removes himself from my mouth without releasing my throat. He stands and scoops me from the floor. I can feel every muscle in his body tense with arousal.

"Are you going to fuck me now?"

I am disgusted with myself. Writhing with the desire for his cock to rearrange my insides and borderline begging. I'm fucking pathetic.

"Only good girls get rewards. I said you would beg for my forgiveness, and that's exactly what you will do next."

He sits on the bed, throwing me over his knee, my ass in the air. I can feel his cock pulsing under my stomach as I lay balanced across his knees.

I am trembling, but I don't know whether it's from fear, anticipation, or both. I attempt to wiggle my way out of his grasp, but he pins me there firmly. He's stronger than I predicted. His naturally muscular physique easily overpowers me.

"You're not actually going to spank me, are you? Who the fuck…"

I am interrupted by his response, a hard smack on my left ass cheek eliciting a yelp that makes Aztyn chuckle.

"You're a sick fucking bastard!"

Aztyn slips two fingers inside me, feeling my slickness and laughs again.

"If I'm sick, you're terminal Calliope."

"I fucking hate you." I spit with as much poison as I can muster and try to escape again but this time, he holds me down so tight I almost can't breathe and I sputter for air.

Aztyn shoves the fingers he used to check me inside my mouth.

"You might hate me but that cunt is *dripping* for me."

He follows this up by removing his now even wetter fingers and three violently hard spanks come across the same cheek as before. He whistles sharply and I can already feel the bruises forming as my skin pulses and I whimper pitifully.

"You know what to do if you want this to stop, baby." He whispers into my ear as if it's the sweetest words anyone will ever utter.

The fact that he called me baby is maddening and reignites the fire in me. I dig my long stiletto-shaped nails into his thigh as I fight to get free with all my strength. He lashes me again twice, this time on the other cheek. I involuntarily curl up against him from the sting and pant heavily, weighing my options as his hand rests against my ass, squeezing just firmly enough that I begin to cry silent tears. My entire body aches from the abuse this evening, and he's getting off on the thrill. The more I struggle, the more I will regret it. He's made that abundantly clear. Submission does not come easy to me. I have never submitted to a man in the bedroom or otherwise. I cannot believe what I am about to do. I don't do it quickly enough for Aztyn's liking and he spanks me again. The pain is blinding, and I choke out words I thought I would never say as quickly as possible.

"Gods alive, please just stop. I'm fucking sorry, alright?"

"That's not what I asked for Little Muse."

I can feel Aztyn's hand rise from its resting place, and before he can swing it back down, I scream the words he's looking for.

"I'm sorry, I swear. I'm begging you Aztyn, *please!*"

"Do not let another fucking hand touch you again besides mine. Calliope, do you understand?"

"Yes, I understand."

I squeak out barely above a whisper. Aztyn throws me back down to the floor, and I can't bring myself to watch him but I hear him collecting his jeans and putting them back on. I listen to him leave. I'm unsure how because my door never opened or closed but I know he's gone. Leaving me wet and wanting someone I have no business wanting. Aztyn has taken a part of me I have never given to anyone and I loathe him for it just as equally as I yearn and ache for him. I crawl into bed and sob myself to sleep.

Calliope

Aztyn has bruised and practically beaten me. I despise
him, yet something inside me screams for him to
return to my side. Is this my proper punishment? To
crave him now more than ever? Maybe I don't hate
him. Maybe I hate myself. God, how I loathe how
pathetic this makes me feel. Longing for something I'd
never have was one thing. Thinking I could have it
with this brute is another. If there's a god, he must
fucking hate me too.

Cali

Chapter Thirteen

I can't even sit down. When I inspected Aztyn's damage this morning I was black and blue from the multiple impacts on the floor and the violent spankings I received. I've never been spanked so hard that there were little pinpricks of blood from the vessel's bursting. I could have made things easier on myself if I hadn't resisted with every ounce of stubbornness I have in me but something tells me that if I had just given in that I would've disappointed my Nightmare. He expected me to fight him. It is what fascinates him about me. I am not afraid of him and he gets high off it. I have already made my peace with death. I was already busy destroying myself before he came to set his destruction upon me. There is nothing to stop me from burning this place to the ground and taking everyone with me. Those with nothing to lose are the most dangerous, and I have already lost everything in this place including my soul. I am just as broken and damaged as he is, if not more and he loves it. He loves how dangerous and unhinged I am. It feeds something inside of him. I want him to consume me and take whatever remains of my innocence. I want him to feast on the last flicker of light within me and leave only shadow behind. He could eat me alive, and I would call it mercy.

"Calliope, are you even listening?" Viv practically stomps her foot.

She hates having to repeat herself. Except that's precisely what we have all been doing for the last hour so it's not exactly hard to guess what I just missed.

"Also, can you sit? You're making me nervous."

That's a hard pass on the invitation to sit.

"*No*, I won't sit because I stand by what I said regardless of whatever I just tuned out."

This earns me a stifled giggle from Zander.

"The guy was a lowlife pedophile as well as being a reporter. Whoever killed him did us a favor."

Vivianne looks at Zander for help but he simply shrugs his shoulders and says, "Sorry Sis, I can't argue with Cali's logic."

Viv throws her hands up in the air exasperated with us both.

"This is going to come back to bite us in the ass. I don't know how our team missed both a pedophile and a killer but if you two want to ignore the problem then fine."

"Are we done here then?" I ask impatiently.

Viv waves her hand in dismissal and I amble to the door. Zander catches up with me in the halls and I wish he wouldn't because I know that Aztyn watches my every move. I can't bring myself to be cruel to Zand but I can ice him out until he gets tired of my shit.

"Hey, I was thinking we could go splash around in the ocean like we used to when we first bought the island."

I can see Zander in my peripherals. So hopeful and bouncing with nervous energy like a golden retriever puppy.

"I'm not feeling well…maybe another time." I lie *badly*.

"I could come to hang out with you then. We can read together."

He's stopped bouncing. He knows exactly what's coming.

"Zander, listen…"

'No, you listen to me Calliope. One day, I'm not going to be here. Do you understand that? You'll go to reach for me and I will not *be here*."

163

I can see the hurt in his eyes, which kills me, but this is for his own good.

I know Zander. It's okay."

I stop walking and hug him as tight as I can without wincing. He does not hug me back, which is just as well. I kiss his cheek softly and linger momentarily and he melts into my frame. When I let go, he simply turns and leaves me to walk the rest of the way alone.

When I open the door to my chambers, Aztyn is waiting for me. Something about his demeanor has changed from last night. The air in the room lacks its usual edge when he is around. He simply watches me walk to the edge of my bed and sit down very slowly. I try not to suck any air through my teeth from the pain but I am unsuccessful. Aztyn looks like a child who just had to shoot his dog. I look at him curiously a little taken aback by his reaction.

Aztyn slides his fingers through his unusually messy hair, and when he looks at me again, I can see the red rims and dark circles.

"I shouldn't have been so rough with you, Little Muse. That's not exactly how I wanted our first encounter after the greenhouse to go."

164

I chuckle.

"Are you telling me my Nightmare has a conscience?"

"A rare occurrence."

He looks disappointed, likely in himself, before the softness returns to his face.

"I'm sorry."

"Too late for apologies," I tease him only a little. "Besides, I liked it, remember?"

His turn to chuckle.

"You're in no shape to receive the kind of apology you deserve."

His temporary smile falls.

"Can I spend the day with you? I can help you stay comfortable."

He now points to my bedside table and I can see he has returned my books with sticky notes sticking out of the pages.

"I was going to write in the margins, but I thought you would hate that."

I reach for a book and flip through. He annotated each one with his thoughts and emotions. I'm speechless. So, I look up at him and smile softly which he takes as an invitation to sit at the foot of my bed, his eyes watching my entire body tense as I try to get comfortable. I feel his eyes roaming as I take off my hoodie and he inspects the bruises just beginning to form themselves. Who knew seeing me in the pain he caused me would turn him into a proper human being? Aztyn is more complicated and complex than I could have ever imagined. I look at him curiously as if seeing him for the first time again. He seems genuinely remorseful, if you could believe such a thing. I pat the bed beside me and he scurries up before I change my mind like a small boy who's just been forgiven for drawing on the walls. I forgive him but I shouldn't. He is evil incarnate but are we not cut from the same cloth?

I know what they call me behind my back. They think I'm some kind of succubus demon in league with the devil and it is their fear above all else that makes them worship me like a fucking goddess. Aztyn is not afraid of me but something tells me he would worship me all the same in a way that I would never grow tired of. I have long grown tired of the weight of my crown and the coldness of my throne of bones—Queen of the Condemned. I catch Aztyn looking at me just in time to see a single tear fall from my eye.

"Little Muse, tell me why you're crying."

His voice is so sweet and calm it coaxes more tears to fall.

"Can I tell you something?"

I sniff back my tears but they do not stop falling softly upon my cheeks.

"You can tell me anything. Your secrets are safe with me."

I laugh at the irony of it all. Of course, my secrets are safe with my Nightmare. At least I won't die with them on my conscience. I take a deep breath but all that comes out is a whisper.

"I never wanted any of this and it was all a terrible accident."

Aztyn says nothing, but his features are soft and comforting, so I continue a little louder.

"I killed a man who wouldn't keep his hands off me who had assaulted me once at a frat party before I started this place. It's why we have such an extensive vetting process."

I'm rambling now, but I can't stop I desperately need someone, fucking anyone to understand the things I've never said out loud.

"I stabbed him to death before there was a ritual room before the gold seal was placed at the scene of my crime."

I am frantic and Aztyn reaches for my hand silently reminding me to take a breath and I do.

"They immortalized me for it. They *bowed* at my feet, Aztyn. They covered up my sin and pledged their undying loyalty to me."

I squeeze his hand while looking at him through blurry eyes.

"Before you take my life, you need to understand that I never meant for all this. I only wanted to create a place where people could heal from the injustices that are sometimes thrust upon us. I never intended for us to take justice into our own hands. I had no choice but to give them what they had given me so freely without ever being asked. I had no choice."

I collapse into his arms, and I sob once again. What is it about this man that makes me so fucking soft? How is it so easy to unburden myself to him when I have never been able to be this vulnerable with anyone who dares get close to me? Yet this mountain of a man who smells like cigars and whiskey and times long since passed can bring me to my knees with any small ounce of kindness he shows me. Perhaps because I know his compassion is genuine and that he has no obligation to do so. His only obligation is to himself and his mission to end my life. He is close enough to kill me now and yet his arms feel like a home I have never had, solid and safe. He could snap my neck and instead his hands are running through my hair and he is shushing me softly as the emotions I've held onto for so long break free against his shores once again.

He is the lighthouse in my storm, and when he turns the light out, I will crash upon the rocks and become dust on the wind. The sweetest escape. I turn from him, embarrassed that I am so easily turned into a puddle by his presence and he holds me tighter until the tears stop and my breathing returns to normal. Aztyn places his hands gently on either side of my face and brings it to meet his. He kisses the dimples of my cheeks where the tears had been falling, the tip of my nose, my forehead, and finally my lips, so tender I could start to cry all over again.

"I am sorry someone ever touched you without your permission."

His voice is uneven and he is physically distressed as if he is fighting every instinct inside himself.

"Do you remember his name, Calliope?"

"I'll never forget it… Alexander Samaras."

Recognition flashes in Aztyn's eyes, his face falling and his grip on me tightening slightly.

"You're certain, Cali?"

I nod, unsure of what his reaction means. Aztyn rises from my bed a million emotions playing on his handsome features.

"I need to take care of something. I don't want to leave you now but this is important. Please forgive me."

"Will you come back?" I whisper, my eyes brimming with tears again.

"I will and I'll stay as long as you need me."

I want to say I want him to stay for the rest of whatever is to be the length of my forever but this thought shocks me and so I say nothing. He leaves through my stolen doors and another irony comes to light.

The girl who has never fallen in love, fell in love with a man who could never love her back.

Aztyn

A fallen angel weeps upon my shoulders
Let me kiss the pain of descent from your lips
I can not take away the past but I can give you
something you are owed
I'll storm the gates of heaven just to demand your
wings
I'll become a monster whenever you ask, just to see
you fly again.

Chapter Fourteen

I was wrong about Calliope. I'm never wrong. The devil was an angel first but they painted him a demon. She's not a monster, she is a fallen angel with clipped wings and she doesn't deserve to have her life snuffed out by me. I will however do everything I can to see that she comes *back* to life. I was wrong about something else too and it almost cost me my honor. Like Calliope, my killings are also always justified.

Alexander Samaras is my brother. Half-brother to be precise and I usually wouldn't make that distinction but the occasion calls for it. He was the evil right under my nose my entire life. Nothing makes sense now and my head is reeling.

My Little Muse has no reason to lie to me and I can spot a tell like a World Series poker player. She unburdened a truth she had never uttered out loud. I could see it in how she looked at me with the desperation of a dying soldier and felt it in her collapse after she confessed her sins. I pace the floor of my room as I try to process the breakdown of my purpose here. I could leave now and sail away to the islands on my map and live the rest of my days on the fortune I've stashed but I still have an itch that needs to be scratched.

Calliope was supposed to be my final act and if I'm being honest with myself, I don't think I can leave her. Leaving her chambers just now felt like the most excruciating torture. I will not leave her in this place to die, not at someone else's hands or her own. A thought dawns on me the reality of which brings me to my knees. What if she does not want to leave with me? I have not been very kind to her and that's saying the least. Instead, would she rather take her own life rather than escape from this hell with me?

A fury rises threatening to boil me from the inside out. Another thought extinguishes it almost immediately, humbling me to my core. The *obsession* that I could not understand the *reason* for saving her life I could not find, my *hesitation* to end her life at every opportunity I have been gifted, and the intense *jealousy* I felt when she let Zander fuck her has all boiled down to one thing.

That deeply wounded sadness in her eyes that first day I saw her pulled at me to search for an answer to its presence. You can always tell a monster by the sparkle in their eyes. They always run around with that 'cat ate the canary' grin. Calliope is cunning and puts on a good performance but she is only masquerading as a demon. She is what this place has made her and she is broken because of it.

I need a new plan, one to get us both out of here, but before I start calculating that pipedream, I need to find out if my Little Muse even desires to run away with me and I need to apologize for more than just getting the story wrong. I need to tell her everything. Well not everything, we all have secrets to take to our graves and I have more than my fair share. I will however, offer up what I think is pertinent information and give her the vulnerability and transparency of that information that she deserves. Once we both escape, she can go wherever she chooses and be whomever she chooses to be. I'll be able to leave her knowing she's been delivered from a fate far worse than the death I would have given her. To wither in a place that cannot hold you is not living, it's slow erasure. When you exist somewhere that breaks you, it's not living, it's waiting to die. My Little Muse deserves more than that. An overwhelming urge to be by her side while I still can blisters up inside me. I change my clothes into something more comfortable for spending the day with her.

When I reach Calliope's chamber doors, I walk right in and lock them behind me. My entrance does not phase her and she smiles at me sweetly when she looks up from one of the books I annotated. She looks me up and down lingering on the gray sweats long enough that I notice her cheeks blush when she realizes I have caught her leering. I can't help but smile back at her.

"I've never seen you dressed so *casually*."

Her voice is coy and teasing.

"Can't very well lay in bed with you all day in a suit or my jeans."

She laughs and I see a flash of another life for a second. One in which we met long before the world turned us into creatures of a darker variety. I'm starting to not recognize myself when I am with her.

"Come. Sit."

She pats the bed and it takes everything in me not to run to her like a golden retriever.

I crawl into her bed beside her and she immediately moves her body to fit against mine. I pick her up and place her in my lap, and a slightly pained squeak escapes her. She settles quickly into my lap, her head leaning against my chest and her legs sprawled across mine. She thumbs my musings as she silently flips through the books, she's read a thousand times and I just watch her for a while. Every so often she scoffs at a comment she disagrees with or taps her finger on something she does agree with. She sighs a little if she really likes what I wrote as she fingers it softly. I inhale the intoxicating scent of her, breathing deeply. I don't want to disturb this moment but I must. I close my eyes and will myself to break this lavender haze we have found ourselves in but she breaks the silence first.

"Your heart rate and breathing pattern changed. What's wrong?"

She doesn't look up at me and her muscles don't stiffen in flight or fight. She's simply that observant.

"I'm impressed Little Muse. Not many people are that perceptive."

"I didn't get where I am today without being able to read people's body language like a book. Spill it so I can continue reading your absurd comments on my literature."

"You like some of them. I can tell when you sigh and touch them softly with your fingertips,"

I whisper into her ear. *Her* heart rate picks up now but she says nothing waiting for me to oblige her request. I shift underneath her and she wiggles right back into place. I take a deep breath to keep myself steady. What comes out is a question and even before it leaves my lips, I know she will be displeased by it.

"Why have you never asked me why I came here to kill you?"

"I don't care why. I have made peace with my sins and with death."

I can hear the annoyance at my question and the honesty in her voice.

"Now stop pussy footing around."

I groan audibly. "Vulnerability is hard for me Calliope," I sigh and run my fingers through my hair. "Alexander Samaras is my half-brother."

Her body stiffens and her heart races but she waits.

"I came here to kill you because I was under the impression that I would be killing a hypocrite and setting the scales of justice right again."

Calliope hops off her bed and immediately regrets it due to the pain she forgot she was in. I rush to her side and she lets me hold her. She is visibly shaken.

"I don't understand what this means."

Her voice is barely above a whisper.

"It means I'm not going to kill you, Little Muse." I whisper back, nestling my mouth against her ear. I pick her up and place her back into her bed.

"What are you going to do?" She asks meekly.

177

I cup her face gently in my hands. "I'm going to save you and help you escape from here…if you want me to."

I stand at her bedside because she has not invited me back into her bed.

"What happens after?"

"You can be whomever you choose and do whatever you choose. That will be none of my business."

Her face sours.

"You don't care what happens to me after we escape?"

I shuffle my weight back and forth nervously. I don't even know why I am anxious but I didn't expect this reaction from her. Why is she so hung up on what I care about?

"I said it wasn't any of my business. I didn't say I didn't care."

"Do you want it to be your business?" She's elevated, her voice wavering with an emotion I cannot place.

"What is with the inquisition to my feelings? Does it matter what I want? I'm offering you a way out. That's what *you* want, isn't it?"

"Being vulnerable certainly *isn't* your fucking strong suit."

"As if it's yours?"

Now I am elevated. How did we end up in an argument? The fire in her eyes is intense. There is something

178

she wants to say but she is waiting for me to say the right thing first except I don't know what it is that this infuriating woman fucking wants from me.

"This was not my intention, Calliope."

"What was your intention Aztyn? To let me know you care enough about me to help me escape but not enough to stay with me after?"

The confusion must show on my face because she mirrors it.

"Why would you want that Calli?"

She doesn't answer. She just stares at me burning a hole right into my soul. I rack my brain for a hint of what the fuck is going on here and it dawns on me.

"Are you asking if I have feelings for you of a romantic nature?"

"Would you have done any of the things you've done if you didn't?"

Calliope has caught me off guard. I thought I would have to convince her to escape with the man who stalked her to kill her. I did not know I would be confronted by a petite blonde firecracker about my feelings for her.

"People like us don't get happy endings Calliope. This could never be anything but a catastrophe," I shrug my shoulders. "I do however, think I could fuck you without being disgusted with myself now."

179

"Are you fucking kidding me? What about me disgusted you that suddenly doesn't any longer?"

If she could get up easily, I'm sure she would hit me right now.

"I just meant fucking and being attracted to the woman who murdered my brother without reason would disgust me, there's nothing about you that physically repulses me."

"Oh! Well, thank Lucifer the serial killer stalker can fuck me without being repulsed by the fact that I murdered his brother now that he knows he was a piece of shit rapist!"

She's so angry I can feel the heat radiating off her and she's vibrating. She's pretty cute when she's riled up. Reminds me of Tinkerbell, small but deadly. I smile at this thought and she immediately gets more enraged assuming I am laughing at her. Watching her get so worked up is almost as funny as watching her jump into that fountain so she's justified.

"I'm not a serial killer. I'm more of a vigilante, I guess."

"A vigilante?"

She laughs ironically.

"At least I'm doing something important. Who are you? Spiderman? Do you wear a fucking cape too?"

I deeply regret using the word vigilante. She's never going to let this go. Now she has me vibrating.

"Spiderman didn't wear a cape and I think you know that Calliope."

Why was *THAT* my retort? My calm and collected demeanor is visibly ruffled. She knows it too judging by her smirk and the way her eyebrows are raised.

"Why don't you tell me what you want instead of being so god damned impossible?"

"Fuck. *No.*"

There is so much defiance in my Little Muse. I will enjoy breaking her. I say nothing but there is a smirk on my face. I just stand there letting the weight of her own words sink into her skin. The longer I stand there staring at her the less confident she is in her insubordination. I take my eyes off her and sit in the chair at her bedside. My posture is relaxed as I lean back in the chair watching her again.

"I won't ask again."

She squirms, battling with her inner brat. I've unnerved her enough that she decides to try a different route.

She finally whispers, "You don't understand. I want you to *want* to stay with me."

"I already told you I would stay as long as you wanted me to. Why are you fretting so much?"

"I don't want that to be the only reason you stay."

I think about my response very carefully. I've wound her tighter than a screw and she's barely hanging on by a thread as it is.

"I've never done anything I didn't want to do, Little Muse. You are not an obligation. You are an *obsession*. I won't leave your side if you do not ask me to."

I stand again and walk towards her until our noses are practically touching, "But don't think for one second you can play me like a fool. Mark my words Little Muse, if you let anyone touch you to make me jealous again or ask me to leave even once you will never see my face again. Do you understand me?"

Calliope swallows hard before nodding her agreement. So, she does know when to shut her fucking perfect mouth.

"That's my good girl."

Calliope

I'd like to hear what kind of plan this man has for escaping from this island and our lives as we know them. He doesn't love me but he is obsessed with me. I don't know what an obsession is without love. Every man who's ever been obsessed with me has claimed love as their reasoning. I've never experienced the kind of obsession Aztyn has for me. So either the men before him didn't love me, or they loved me and were not obsessed with me at all. I think I like Aztyn's obsession better than love.

Cali

Chapter Fifteen

I swallow hard and nod my agreement. His face is so close to mine I can feel his breath but then he moves to give me some room to breathe.

"That's my good girl."

My breath wavers and I am feral for his praise, something I have never craved. Aztyn's eyes flash with acknowledgement and then fire. He licks his lips like he's about to eat me alive and I whimper out loud like a cornered rabbit. I am so vulnerable. Practically bedridden from my punishment means I'm easily subdued. He could be lying to me luring me away from here where it's easier for me to go missing and then turn up dead but even if that were true would it matter? I look him up and down analyzing him. His warning echoes in my head. I don't understand him one bit and I want to be angry with him but I can't when he looks at me that way. I sigh and look down at my hands which are clenched in my bed sheets.

Aztyn places his pointer finger under my chin tipping it upwards so my baby blues fall upon his impossibly blue ones.

"There is no reason for you to ever lower your gaze Little Muse. When you feel the need to do so, let your eyes find mine instead."

My lashes flutter, and he leans down again, his nose brushing mine gently before his lips meet my own. This kiss is needy and romantic, building in intensity and then softening against me. One of his hands is fisted in my hair while the other trails down my jawline and then delicately grips my throat. I moan into his mouth as our lips part and our tongues explore each other. No one has ever kissed me the way Aztyn is kissing me right now. I feel like I'm floating and if I wasn't in so much pain from my punishment, I might actually let him make love to me. I imagine even his tender side is a little rough around the edges, the thought of which makes my hips rise involuntarily.

Aztyn chuckles and breaks our kiss but leaves his hand at the back of my neck.

"If you invite me back into your bed, I'll take care of that for you."

"You don't need an invitation to be in my bed."

My voice is breathy and wanting. Aztyn grins cheekily, walks to the foot of my bed and crawls up beside me.

Immediately his hand is back in my hair and his lips have returned to mine. His other hand however is moving my blankets and removing my sweats. I lift my hips again to assist him and kick them off. This leaves me in a simple black thong and my university tee shirt. Aztyn doesn't miss a beat. The hand in my hair moves to my throat, while the other explores what's underneath the waistband of my panties. He stops kissing me but doesn't pull away.

"So wet already."

Aztyn clicks his teeth as his fingertip slowly swipes along my opening. I whimper as he teases me and my hips rise again.

"Don't be greedy now Little Muse, I want to enjoy devouring you."

Aztyn slips a finger inside me and tightens his grip around my neck as he watches me rock my clit against his hand. I can't help but be greedy. My punishment was like being run hard and then put away wet. There was no release. He squeezes harder and slips another finger inside me allowing me to continue rocking myself against the palm of his hand. Kissing and biting my neck he elicits sharp intakes of breath and soft moans from my unoccupied lips as his fingers move in time with the rocking of my hips. The hand partly responsible for the shallowness of my breathing now pins my hips down instead of restricting my throat. His mouth moves from my neck straight to my clit and the moan that slips from my mouth is guttural, my hands move to his hair, my hips buck against his skilled tongue that feels as though he's currently swirling a language he very clearly wrote against my clit. I'm coming undone.

"Oh my God Az, don't stop."

His fingers and mouth move in tandem, hungrier than anyone has ever been to make me come. I can't stop myself from tipping over the edge.

"Oh fuck, I'm coming…I'm fucking coming."

The heat and electricity are something I've never felt, rolling over my body repeatedly. Not only did I not look at myself in the mirror once but from the wet sounds of Aztyn cleaning up my mess he coaxed me to a peak I have never reached with a partner. When the aftershocks roll across me Aztyn pinches my jaw forcing my mouth to open and aggressively spits my own cum inside before kissing me. No one has ever attempted that either but it makes my pussy pulse faster and I moan into his mouth once again as I swallow. He pulls away placing the fingers he used to bring me to climax where his tongue had been and I lick them clean swirling my tongue the way I did before he started face fucking me during my punishment and he groans remembering. Aztyn takes his fingers out of my mouth

"I've wanted to do that since I watched you ride Zander's face and realized he was nothing more than a toy you used to get off. I wanted to make you come."

I feel my cheeks blush.

"I've never had a partner who could make me come without my...help. Let alone soak the bed."

The grin on Aztyn's face makes me giggle. He looks so pleased with himself that I can't contain my own pleasure from trickling out. What is it about this man that makes me different? It's as if I could just close my eyes and slip into some kind of domestic bliss induced coma. That will never happen for us. Aztyn was right when he said people like us don't get a fairytale but maybe this doesn't have to end in catastrophe either. Perhaps we could create our own twisted version of love and happy endings. Sitting here laughing and holding my gut with him makes me feel like that could be possible. For once I see potential where at one point, I only saw death. My Nightmare has already given me something that I never thought possible, a chance at having a life outside of this place. I begin to cry soft tears and Aztyn wipes them away softly, his hands lingering on either side of my face.

"Little Muse, you feel everything so deeply, one second you're laughing hysterically and the next you're falling apart. What can I do to stop these tears?"

"Let's just run until we're dead Aztyn, please do not leave me behind."

Az cradles my head into his chest and kisses the top of my head.

"Oh, Little Muse, I'll run with you. Even if you begged me to, I'm not sure I could leave you. Not in this lifetime and in the next I think I'll find you before the world twists us wrong."

He kisses the top of my head again, then brings his finger under my chin lifting it so he can kiss my lips so tenderly I feel the urge to cry. Before I can he places his lips on the tip of my nose and the giggles pick up instead. The kind where you cling to one another and laugh against each other's skin. I've never been this intimate with anyone and suddenly I'm frozen with fear and insecurity sits heavy in my chest. My giggles stop and I shake Aztyn off of me.

"Well, I suppose we're done here for today then?"

Aztyn is confused and takes a moment to recover before speaking.

"What exactly are you on about?"

I roll over to exit the bed trying to pretend I am not as sore as I look. I glance back over my shoulder at him coldly.

"What, did you think we were going to do, cuddle?"

Even as I say this, my heart is crumbling.

Aztyn scoffs but doesn't move.

189

"You're like a fucking stray."

"Excuse me?" My head whips back around.

"You heard me."

Aztyn sits up but doesn't make any moves indicating that he will be exiting my chambers.

"When I was a little boy, I loved bringing home strays and wild animals, but you know what, sooner or later they all bit me. Usually after a heartwarming moment, do you want to know why Calliope?"

He doesn't wait for me to answer, instead he quickly reaches over to pull me back into my bed and to pull me back into his arms. He holds me firmly and my struggle is absolutely useless.

"When you're not fed love on a silver spoon, you learn to lick it off knives."

"You don't fucking love me Aztyn you said so yourself."

I struggle to say as I squirm against him, trying to wiggle myself free, when all I really want is for him to hold me tighter.

"Is that what I said Calliope?"

Aztyns hold breaks on me but I'm no longer squirming to break free. I'm lost in contemplation.

"I don't believe you ever even said those words yourself."

190

Damn it, he's got me there.

"Fine then… We can cuddle."

Aztyn laughs and kisses my neck as he speaks.

"My Little Muse you are such a stubborn and vicious little thing. Still so much fire even after such a thorough punishment."

He pinches my butt cheek just enough to produce a surprised shriek from myself and more feverish giggles from both of us.

I still don't know where I stand with Aztyn. I'm not even sure how I feel but I know I've never felt this way in all my life and I want to see how this story ends even if it ends in flames and tragedy. Which it most certainly will. Nothing good lasts long here.

Aztyn and I spend the rest of the day in bed. I order food from the kitchens and we have lengthy discussions about his annotations in my literature while we stuff our faces. We do not speak anymore of escapes and there is no power struggle happening here, just simple bliss. At some point he takes it upon himself to open the glass doors and windows letting the ocean air in. I watch him curiously. I can't remember the last time someone opened those. If I

191

had to compare Az coming into my life to anything I would compare it to this moment. Like the windows inside my soul were thrown open and I rack my brain trying to remember if that had ever happened before. I smile softly to myself observing as he walks around my room fingering various objects and listening intently as I answer his probing questions. He is relaxed, I can tell by the way he saunters around. How rare a sight this must be to witness this man soften. I feel privileged to be a spectator and a content sigh escapes my lips prompting him to look up at me, with a boyish grin spread across his face. How can I simply be this delightfully effervescent? This cannot be sustainable. I must have fallen into a coma that day I tried to kill myself. None of this can be real because I do not deserve to be this euphoric.

I do not deserve any of this.

Calliope

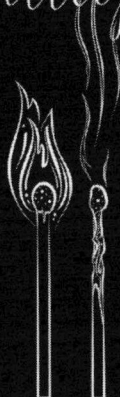

My suspicions that I have never truly loved another
soul have been confirmed by my absolutely
unfathomable feelings for Az. The suspicion that I
lack the capability or capacity to love another human,
has been debunked. I don't know which revelation
surprises me more, but this can not end in anything
other than me burning my entire life to the ground.
Not if I want a chance at freedom.

Cali

Chapter Sixteen

I'm not sure any lover I have ever had would describe anything but my skin as soft. I have been an ice queen my entire existence but I am a softer version of myself in Aztyns hands.

You see when a girl grows up without either of her parents something glacial festers where she should feel their love. When that girl grows up living in survival mode learning to manipulate people for her own gain it spreads until there is no hope of warmth. Until now that is.

I hadn't factored in meeting a man who not only takes care of me emotionally but can quite literally put me in my place. Like the gods that only answer at night made him just for me. Last night before we discussed our escape plan Aztyn told me things that should have made me run for the hills secrets he's been holding onto. Watching him unburden himself at my feet and beg my forgiveness for keeping his past from me made me love him even more. I should have thrown him out of my bedroom and my life. The information he divulged to me is dangerous not just for me but for everyone here.

Instead, I held that formidable man's face in my hands and whispered that he never needed my forgiveness and that I could forgive him for anything as long as he could do the same for me. Last night was a test of my ability to stomach all that he is and still look him in the eyes. Tonight, will be an exploration of his capacity to accept the darkness that lives within my bones. All my nightmares have learned my name and it's about time he joined the rest.

Tonight, members of the inner circle will get their own justice, and I will continue to solidify my throne in hell. Even the devil himself won't deny me that privilege when I arrive, I've sold my goddamn soul for it. Vivianne's team has already secured the assets. Our members are being prepared for their part in tonight's soiree, and I too have been prepared by way of the spa. As I make my leave through the frosted glass doors a familiar face greets me.

"I'm glad I caught you."

Vivianne smiles sweetly as if she doesn't know exactly where I will be at any given second. My eyebrows raise prompting her to drop the facade but I say nothing and just begin walking.

"Was your treatment satisfactory today?" She prods me, keeping pace.

"Meep… Morp… Very satisfactory. Thank you, robot Vivianne. You may return to your charging dock."

Vivianne ignores my behavior.

"I was wondering if I might speak with you about the sacrifice this evening."

"Cut the crap Viv. What is going on with you?"

"Just thought that since we're keeping secrets from each other, that we must not be friends anymore, just colleagues."

My heart beats like a drum in my chest and I can feel my face getting a degree or two hotter but my expression remains stone cold. There's no telling what secret Viv has stumbled upon. I need her to tell me.

"Ever the dramatic one. What are you talking about exactly?"

"When were you planning on telling me about Aztyn?"

"What about him?"

I stare blankly at her. At least we're getting more specific.

"Well to begin with, you're sleeping with him."

"How do you know that?"

"We have security cameras everywhere Calliope, please."

Aztyn could have told me he stopped scrubbing the cameras or whatever the fuck he does.

"That doesn't mean we're sleeping together."

Vivianne scoffs, "Why else would he be in your room?"

"Maybe we're friends," I laugh.

"You sleep with your friends."

"Do you have some kind of point you would like to get to?" I ask impatiently.

"I just thought we still told each other those things, not to mention the fact that you should have told me from a trinity standpoint."

Vivianne's face falls. She's more hurt that I didn't tell her personally than angry about the potential security breach. I need to play to that note.

"I'm sorry Viv, I just wanted to…"

"Keep something for yourself?"

"Something like that."

If I was a normal human being this might be true. Truth is, I could care less who I flaunt my sexual conquests in front of. I have never been shy about it before. I just need Viv to back off.

"When you're ready, Zander should hear it from you."

Shit. Zander.

I nod but choose to say nothing. Zander will not take this news well and in normal circumstances I would just let Zander happen upon this information himself and watch it all blow up in an infernal blaze of testosterone and pissing contests. For Zanders safety and wellbeing, I need to be the one to break it to him, but not right now there's too much to prepare for both in keeping up appearances and my escape. Vivianne and I walk in silence for a while before a thought dawns on me.

"Tomorrow night I think we should all have dinner in my room, I'll tell Zander then."

Vivianne is hesitant to agree as if she already senses my intentions but she lets it go.

"I think I can schedule that for you."

"You will. Move anything for any of us that conflicts with my request and tell Zander his presence is mandatory."

I chew on my own words for a moment before continuing, "It really should be done tonight but I don't want anyone to spoil the reaping, and Zander's mopey face will certainly do just that."

"Speaking of the Reaping," she expertly segues the conversation, "We have the sacrifices in custody. They're being cleaned up and prepared. Apparently, one put up quite a fight for the boys. Someone must have warned him we were coming."

"Make sure they are compensated heavily for their troubles. Let them have their pick of the offerings before they are disposed of or whatever you do with them."

I wave my hand nonchalantly ignoring the security breach as if she asked me a question about my shoe choice for the evening.

"And for the widows?" Viv inquires. There is often a rotating staff when it comes to 'the boys' and if the sacrifice gave them trouble this means Ivan is currently hiring the replacements.

"The usual should do."

"The usual won't do this time, some of the bodies are pretty mangled."

Viv's face falls in mournfulness. One of them must have been one of her current beaus. She loves her men dangerous and stoic.

"Then double it, triple it if you have to. God, silence really is getting more expensive."

I toss a soft smile her direction to let her know that I acknowledge her melancholy even though I know she won't discuss it. Vivianne is married to her career, no piece of ass will ever change that. Sex is 'a biological base need' as she so eloquently explained it to me once. God, I bet she even schedules her orgasms.

$$\spadesuit$$

Aztyns face greets me when I arrive through the doors of my chamber. He is such a striking specimen of man. All rippled muscles and olive skin his impossibly almost azure-colored eyes bear straight into my soul. I have never been a lover girl but his mere presence makes me want to melt. The scent of him in the air that lingers after he is gone makes me crave him again. With him I can drop the facade, the curtain can close and I can be exactly the woman I am without restraints. No stage, no adoring followers, no other man, has ever been able to give me that feeling.

The last time I felt soft was the day I buried my mother. It is not a feeling I am comfortable with if I think about it for too long. Vulnerability is not exactly a strong suit of mine, a quality that my Nightmare and I share. I often sense his own trepidations ripple through his body as mine are right now. He too can sense when I am unsure of us and I can see it on his face as if he can taste my fear permeating the air between us. His head tilts slightly sideways in my direction, the predator in him so strong I can see that glean in his eyes as if he might eat me up, until only my hollow bones are left.

"You look ravishing, as always."

He practically growls when he says it, and it makes my insides quiver.

"Wait till you see me in my dress. Tonight, is a very important event. It calls for very special attire."

"I am very much looking forward to the sight of you." His jaw twitches and my legs tremble.

I am so easily brought to my knees by this man. I wonder if he will see me differently after tonight. If seeing the wretched divinity in me will resurrect the god unmade and feral in him. What I am about to do, would turn the stomach of most but then again, his choice of artistic expression should have turned mine. It is possible we're just a match made in the deepest bowels of hell.

As he moves towards me, I can feel the carnality between us lust dripping heavily in the air and I drop my robe as if he had commanded me to do so. In an instant his hand is at my throat and his lips are inches from mine.

He doesn't kiss me, instead he tilts my head, his lips trailing along my neck until they reach my ear, his breath hot against my skin as he says, "Under normal circumstances I would paint your insides with my cum so I drip down your legs during your sacrificial ritual this evening."

My knees buckle but he holds me firmly in place.

"What's stopping you?" I ask with bated breath.

His grip tightens on my throat as I watch his internal battle take place. His restraint wants to crumble in my presence. He may soften me, but I awaken something in him. He has searched for me long before his misinformed vendetta formed. Where he has only found boredom and discontent in the women before me, he has now met his match in intellect and substance. I challenge everything he knows to be true.

"I want you high off the power you wield when I bury myself inside you tonight Little Muse and I am not a man who spoils his appetite."

His mouth crashes into mine, the kiss violently wanting and needy and I revel in it. This man reveres not a holy relic in this world but he worships me as if I am the only thing on this planet that gives him the life in his bones. It fills me in ways the devoutness and piety of my followers never could. Every beast no matter how cursed aches for a soul who won't run.

I gasp for breath when his lips finally leave mine and his hand returns to his side.

"If you're not going to make yourself useful then you may take your leave and I will commence getting ready for tonight's ritual."

Aztyn chuckles dangerously and I know I'll regret saying that later.

"Consider this your one pass to order me around Your Highness," he says with a deep bow that makes me ache for the evening to end before it's even begun.

Although I have lost most of my gratification when it comes to the rituals and responsibilities I have here, this particular ritual always puts a little pep in my step. Revenge is a business just like anything else, I don't do any of the dirty work. I won't even be the one exacting revenge; I am just the facilitator. The one they look to assuage their shame and guilt. I take the blame they cannot reconcile within themselves. I take pleasure in their revenge and I play the part of the villain so delectably wicked. I have to put on the show, set the stage, make them believe that what they did was nothing more than a normality with the depraved nature of what I will do with the spoils of our war on injustice. What they will witness sets them at ease. There's something a little Elizabeth Bathory about it all but I always did love the drama of the Renaissance era.

The dress I am slipping into needs no assistance tonight and I need no escort. Both Viv and Zander know that if I am the moth then the reaping is the flame. It is the only part of cult life I will miss when I escape and I don't know what that says about me as a person but it is much too late to dwell on that now. My dress is snow white and two pieces. There are two slits up the sides of the skirt and the top is structured like a Grecian corset showing off my waist as if it was molded to me. I look like a fallen angel, the dress clinging to my figure, my long blonde hair cascading down my back. I take in my appearance one more time from every angle possible and a familiar feeling creeps over me. The cat ate the canary grin affixes itself to my face and I have shifted from almost innocent to walking temptation. Usually at this point in the evening I would make myself come while I watch in the mirror but I want Aztyn to be the source of my orgasm tonight so I refrain. My body's muscle memory has kicked in despite my decision to abstain and I'm already soaked with want. I take a deep breath focusing back on the task at hand shutting my chamber doors behind me.

.

Aztyn

Oh sweet enchanting siren
Sing your mournful song
I am not another man you will drag down to the
depths to make chum of
I am more than mortal flesh and sinew
You can not pull deaths shadow into the sea
Your song still calls to what's left of my soul
So instead I'll take all of you
Every tainted and fouled piece
Instead I'll make you <u>mine</u>.

Chapter Seventeen

I do not know what awaits me tonight at the Reaping. Actually, I have had little idea what to expect since I joined the inner sanctum. If there's one thing Calliope has garnered from her followers it is their silence, which means they either fear her greatly or respect her immensely. That's the only way to receive that kind of loyalty and looking around the ritual room I gather it's the fear that stokes the fire of their respect.

Zander and Vivianne take their seats but I barely glance in their direction. My gaze is fixed on the curtains where I know my Little Muse will emerge. I can taste her excitement in the air and the room smells like her skin, exotic and intoxicating. It takes everything inside me not to barrel through the curtain to the small room on the other side so that I can keep her all to myself.

Part of me wants no one but me so much as to make eye contact with her ever again and the other part of me wants them to see every inch of her as if she was theirs for inspection. Both counter parts threaten to rip me apart.

The hum in the room is palpable. When she finally emerges, my eyes roam the incredible form of her and for a moment she is frozen in time. The portrait of a deity in all her glory. My Little Muse is a superior specimen of female. She commands attention effortlessly and without words. Her mere essence stops time. If only they knew how soft and vulnerable she can be when she surrenders to me. How she melts in my hands and allows me to mold her into whatever I choose, whenever I ask.

I swallow hard as her sapphire blue eyes meet mine. I have never been enchanted by a woman but Calliope is enrapturing and I am spellbound as she begins to speak. Her voice is seductive and it makes you want to give her anything she would ask of you no matter how depraved and mad. Like heroin calls to the soul of an addict, she is a walking siren call to whatever is left of my soul. I feel it calling to me now and every muscle screams in protest as I resist the summons.

Her request to remain one of the crowd instead of asserting my dominance as one of the favored leaves me in a very interesting position. I could care less about sparing Zander's surface level feelings. In fact, if it were up to me I would make him watch as waves of ecstasy crash upon her body like poetry until he crumbled in the realization that he will never again touch what is mine, while rubbing his nose in the naked truth that he could never make her come the way I do. My girl has never asked me for anything and I am inclined to oblige her every whim from now until the end of time itself. I have mostly taken what I wanted from women in my past and there was never a thing in my life I wasn't willing to turn my back on but I would rip the entire earth in two and release the bowels of hell upon what remained if she asked me to. She does not realize it yet but I am the only villain in our story and I will kneel only to her.

Calliope is speaking but I cannot hear her. The blood rushing in my ears is deafening. She is like watching an angel descend from the heavens well maybe not an *angel*. Her silhouette is unbelievably stark against the contrast of the dark hole this room is modeled after. She glows like something otherworldly and I'd go blind just to keep watching. Her gaze finds mine and she flusters for a moment but she doesn't break character. Such a willful creature my Little Muse. A walking sin. She doesn't want anyone to know about us and I want the opposite. I want to rub *everyone's* noses in it. I want to come and go from her presence as I so choose. It's partly why I sometimes 'forget' to replace the feeds. I don't care who knows. No matter which way Zander finds out he's going to throw a punch or two in my direction so trying to spare his feelings is a pointless endeavor.

Zander hates the idea of her choosing me over him. His romanticism of her led him to believe in the end they would wind up together, because who could ever love her, accept the things she's done and that she is incapable of the normal definition of love…but him. He never fathomed a man like me would come along. One that matched her unhinged and sinful nature, one who can rationalize the evil she's done and still put her up on the pedestal with a crown and a throne. One who sees his own darkness in her ready to be brought out. Not one who hides his sins stacked up behind the gravity of hers hoping no one will ever notice the pile that belongs to him.

The truth is as much as the 'trinity' values trust and loyalty, they would sell Calliope out in a heartbeat. The twins would save themselves or at least try to, Vivianne has intertwined the three of them into the very little paper trail this place has besides from what they have established as a legitimate business which kudos to Vivianne. It's a shame to see it all crash down around them but Calliope has a plan. What remains of this place when we leave will give the twins everything they need to start over. Everyone will get off scot free. She really is brilliant My Little Muse. I will admit when I first started working on escape plans, I never gave a thought to what might happen to this place once we were gone, but Calliope has thought of every little detail I could never have prepared for. Her attention to them is remarkable and it goes to show that she has indeed calculated almost every move and is a force to be reckoned with. I once thought of her as a rabbit or a mouse. Small and easy prey. Calliope is a predator right down to her very bones, just like me, she only looks easily dominated, but she could give any man a run for his money.

She fine tunes what was already an art for me. Nothing catches that woman by surprise and all the while she plays spoiled and bored princess because if she played the game by who she really was there would be much surprise and quite a lot of hard feelings when the twins realize the only reason she is close to them is so she can play the role she likes best. Queen of the Underworld…but not the devil. Vivianne and Zander underestimate her, the entire island does. They see her as the face of this establishment like she's the bait that draws them here. They don't see what I see and it's because they never bothered to look. Even Zander is smart enough to know that peeking behind the curtain only reveals more darkness. Her being more calculated and cunning than them does not suit their narrative of her. There is a very sinister and evil edge to that little demon and it is by that edge that I am charmed and smitten. She has orchestrated more than she takes credit for and still she cares for them, her little peons. Enough to rewrite their time spent here and erase all she has done in the process.

I think I love Calliope Veritas. I am not a religious man but maybe some dark force made her just for me. My piece of heaven on earth. My reward for being Death's right hand. If something awful awaits me in the afterlife my life with Calliope will make it worth all I have done and my knees buckle at the thought.

Our escape cannot come soon enough. Every day here is a wasted one. She will never be all she can be here and as long as she's here she can never be free. Like a songbird in a cage, her melancholy melody permeates even the grounds of this land and all who walk here feel it. I felt it the moment I stepped onto this island and the moment I looked into her eyes for the first time I recognized it as hers. I will free my sweet sorrowful little songbird and she will sing a song made just for me and her. The melody of her freedom will be the music we dance to for the rest of our lives. It's all worth it if I can hear what her laugh sounds like when she is unshackled. When she cries in the middle of the night because she cannot reconcile what she has done. It will be I that holds her and reconciles for her. She will never know suffering or pain again as long as I have anything to say about it. She will be my Queen of Darkness; my Persephone and she will never again have to worry herself about the plight of mortals for I will be the one to bear that weight. I'll shoulder the weight of her sins alongside my own. She is worth every cross, every scar, and every burden fate can conjure.

She looks at me now as if she can hear my thoughts threading through the space between us. I see her falter for a split second, but one deliberate nod from me seems to renew her strength and onward she carries. Calliope is clearly finished with the ceremonial part of the evening. Several large men bring in a hooded figure who is still trying to put up a fight despite being what I assume from the muffled sounds is gagged and from what I can see is hogtied. The crowd parts as they walk the figure to the pit which now has a copper tub placed over the drain and a rope with a hook on the end of it. Calliope claps her hands gleefully and draws my attention back to her.

"Oh, I do love it when they have some fight left in them."

She scoffs looking directly at me before the room snickers with her and her gaze roams the crowd once more. She motions for the hood to be removed and a large man with a handsome but brute face whom I know to be named Ivan, nods and does as he is commanded. The group of men that do Calliopes bidding leave without looking back once. The now unhooded man looks fucking pissed but terrified and the drum of energy in the room thrums to his fear. This is about to become a grim unravelling indeed. Calliope brings out a black folder and pretends to thumb through it.

"Henry Theodore Mason. Age 45. Balding. Mild case of erectile dysfunction"

Calliope laughs a little and leans forward

"Nothing a little Viagra can't fix right Henry? You don't mind if I call you Henry, do you?" .

My little muse, once a mouse in our cat and mouse game, was a cat all along, and she likes to play with her food. Henry still gagged spews what I'm sure are a very colorful river of words no one can hear. Calliope clicks her teeth in response.

"Now, now Henry. Is that any way to treat your hostess? You've not been harmed aside from what was necessary to obtain you, you've been fed excellent food prepared by my chefs, your favorite dishes if I recall, and no one has mistreated you. In fact, you killed several of my men in obtaining you and just in case you were worried, your little informant, you know the one who told you we were coming? He has been disposed of accordingly."

Henry's face falls. His little mole within Calliope's organization must have been someone close to him. Henry is slowly starting to realize he is not going to win whatever game is being played.

"Although my boys, now they would be warranted in exacting some revenge, wouldn't they? They haven't and won't because that's not quite why you're here…is it? Do you want to know why you're here…? Henry?"

Henry nods and swallows hard. The melancholy on his face growing by the second.

"Then for the sake of putting on a show, indulge me a little while I introduce you to the crowd." Calliope clears her throat and begins again.

"Henry Theodore Mason. Age 45. Balding. Erectile Dysfunction. We got all that. Let's get to the real juicy parts. See it says here that you buy girls off the black market and what you do to them is let's be honest with each other. distasteful."

You can hear the disdain and loathing dripping off Calliope's teeth. Henry begins to struggle against his gag and Calliope motions to Zander who rises from his chair and removes it gruffly then takes one step back from the vile man coughing and gasping for air to return to his lungs.

"You have no proof, you fucking crazy bitch."

Calliope pretends to pout.

"Now you're just trying to hurt my feelings. Crazy bitch I may be, but I did not apprehend you and go to all this trouble to look this nice to have no proof. I'm crazy, not negligent."

Her face returns to its 'I have a secret' grin.

Calliope throws the folder to Zander who holds it out for the cretin to examine and once he has seen enough his expression is less indignant and more resolved to his fate. Zander returns to his seat folder in hand.

"Now I read and maybe you can confirm, but you were black listed from a particular trafficking ring? Bummer...and here's the kicker, it was because you lost one, a girl that is. Isn't that right Henry?" Calliope asks curiously.

Henry's face flashes in horror. As he begins to understand and the fight he had in him is all but extinguished.

"That's right and I bet you remember her name don't you. I bet her face haunts your nightmares. The one that got away. So, let's bring her out...Jane...come on down to the pit."

Calliope is like a twisted talk show host and it is magnificent to watch. The crowd parts for a young woman petite in stature wearing a white ceremonial robe who looks at Calliope like she is a savior and doesn't even glance at the man who is at her feet. Henry however is looking up at Jane as if he has seen a ghost and is too shocked to speak.

"Now her name is not really Jane. That's the name her traffickers gave her. We know her as Sister Creedence. Now Sister Creedence came to us broken, beaten, and bruised. You must have really liked the way she screamed because you kept her longer than the others, didn't you?"

Henry is now silently sobbing as Calliope reads him to filth. She's better than me at this too. The thought makes my cock twitch and I am grateful for the dimly lit room. I am not one for theatrics like this. I save the drama for my poetry and art. This ceremony is her art and I am in jaw dropping awe of her as I watch her perform.

"She came to us that way but she is not that way now. We gave her a home here at Cephalonia, healed her body, mind, and soul. We washed her clean of any stain you or anyone else left upon her and now we will give her the revenge she so rightly deserves and has worked for. Sister Creedence, your final words to our guest Henry here?"

Sister Creedence finally looks at the man at her feet. I watch as she crouches down and whispers something that causes Henry to sit straight as a rod before she raises her voice loud enough for all to hear.

"May the swiftness of your death be the only mercy bestowed upon you."

The petite woman looks stronger and even more sure of herself as she looks up at her Queen and nods. Calliope rises from her throne and walks slowly down the stairs, the slits in her dress allowing her long and elegant legs to peek through and I am like an early Victorian man seeing ankles for the first time. In her hands is an obsidian hilted dagger, different from the one we use to give our blood offerings, which she presents to Sister Credence who bows deeply as she takes it into her steady hands with not even a sliver of hesitation.

Creedence secures the hook onto the rope that Henry is hogtied with and raises him just above the tub his head tilted down. Whatever the Sister said to Henry, it has broken him. He has resigned to his fate and is sniveling his last pitiful moments on this earth away as they all do. He fights no longer because he knows exactly what he is. Calliope has shown him the truth of it, and confronted him with a ghost of his past in the process. It is breathtaking to watch her. Her eyes sparkle even in this dimly lit room and I can tell this is the part she actually enjoys. Sister Creedence, staring directly into Calliope's eyes, holds the dagger in her hand at the ready.

"The justice you seek is in your hands Sister. Take it."

The Sister bows and swiftly slits the snotting and sobbing Henry's throat and his crimson blood spills into the shallow tub as she raises him higher still. The blood rushed like a waterfall.

Creedence turns to leave just as Ivan and the boys bring in the next cloaked figure and in turn Calliope grabs the next folder.

"We have a very special guest tonight my friends," she says gesturing for the figure's hood to be removed. "Let me introduce to you Father Templeton."

The Father looks confused as he blinks in the red light of the room. He turns behind him to see the first body still draining into the tub. He nearly throws up but fixates instead on the upside down cross behind Calliope and I am sure this feels like some sort of twisted dream to him. He is old in his 70's I would imagine.

"Father Templeton has quite the reputation around his little town of being the model Catholic citizen, but we know something they don't."

The crowd murmurs in agreement.

"You know nothing, you succubus of demons. God will save me."

"There is no God here Father, but you can feel free to worship me if you like, everyone else does," she hisses in response.

The father bows his head and begins to mutter nearly silent prayers.

"Do you remember why you became a youth pastor and began your career in doing the lord's work?"

The Father stops praying and looks up into Calliope's eyes slowly.

"You were 13 remember, and the neighbor boy Caleb he was 9 if my records are correct."

Recognition flashes upon the Fathers face and the wheels begin to turn. Calliope circles him like a vulture as she reads his file.

"You were charged with sexual assault as a minor after assaulting him every day for 3 years and to keep it off your record and to keep you out of juvenile detention and being tried again as an adult the courts and your lawyer petitioned for you to enroll in the priesthood as repentance and reform."

Beads of sweat pool on the holy man's forehead.

"I am an old man now; I have given my life to God."

"Revenge is a dish best served cold Father. Eye for an eye you know."

Calliope looks up as the crowd parts, "Ahh here he is now, Caleb, thank you for joining us this evening."

Caleb is a large man. He towers over Calliope and the Father.

Calliope addresses the crowd, "Do we believe in absolution through the institute of religion?"

The crowd answers in unison, "No."

"That's right because no institute can provide absolution and that includes me. Does my absolution grant you salvation in what may or may not be to come?"

"No."

"That's right," she turns to Caleb now. "Do you forgive this man after hearing he has hidden from justice behind a fake god and a fake belief that his sins can be absolved through anything other than what you deem is worth the transgression on your life?"

Caleb takes a step towards the Father, the shadow this man casts cloaks Calliope and the Father almost entirely.

"No."

"Well, you heard him folks, a life devoted to god is not enough for Caleb and you know what, it's not enough for me either."

Calliope dances around in front of them excitedly, "I almost forgot to ask you a question, Father. There were other sins, right? Here's your chance to get right with your God."

"We all give into temptation from time to time."

Calliope pretends to let this thought marinate.

"You know what? I suppose you're right Father except that's not supposed to include continuing to sexually assault little boys. Not even *your* God condones *that*."

"You have no proof. You are nothing but an incarnate of the Devil sent here to tempt me. In the name of God, I rebuke you. May all of you burn in hell for whatever has transpired in this evil place."

"Oh, I could have sworn these official complaints to every channel up from you right into the Vatican would have proved otherwise."

She hands him the folder and he refuses to look at it, the stack of papers scattering to the floor.

"That's just hearsay, you vile godless creature."

"I am my own God and religion is not an excuse to do deplorable and unforgivable things in the name of one."

Calliope practically sneers into the air as she hands the dagger to Caleb.

"Justice for you and every person he's ever led astray, or touched with his repugnant body against their will."

Caleb wastes no time hoisting this scum of the earth into the air. One large hand pulls the rope with a solid yank while the other slits the Fathers throat on his ascent. Calliope leans over the metal tub filled with the blood of the sacrifice dipping her hands in. The viscous liquid drips from her finger tips, as she cups it in her hands and raises them above her head. Stepping into the metal tub she descends into the scarlet pool, each movement slow, deliberate, divine. The silence in the room is deafening and the electricity in the air is palpitating. When she emerges, she is baptized and soaking. Her now scarlet dress clinging to her curves with her slender arms raised above her head. She looks like she has been carved into something between water and crimson stone, shifting but unyielding.

She is magnificent and I realize in this moment that I have most certainly fallen in love with this creature of death, with this Lilith incarnate, this poet's muse. She is a vision and I am moving towards her before I can think twice. My hand reaches and although she looks momentarily stunned a sickeningly sweet smile falls across her lips as she places her hand in mine stepping out of the tub. The urge to take her in front of everyone races through my body. I want them to watch while she climaxes over and over. While she calls me God and whimpers my name. I have never seen her more desirable. I think I'm a fan of female rage, at the very least I am a fan of hers. The look on her face is pure satisfaction but I can see the horror in her eyes. I can see the part of her that cannot fathom what she has just done. The part of her not yet lost to the madness. Her humanity is showing. The part of her that longs for an escape lives within those walls. It is there for but a flash of moment. Ivan and the boys come in and remove both bodies and the tub. I bow when she drops my hand and back my way into the crowd as she ends her sermon.

"The Reaping is not about suffrage. We are not entitled to the suffering of another no matter how much they have made us bleed. It is our role and privilege to rid the world of its blight. The Reaping is about taking justice into our own hands and offering a sacrifice in return. I am the vessel in which the sin is alchemized where the pain is transformed into something we can be proud of. We did good work today. As always you are absolved of your guilt, your sins and the dirt you think stains you. You are washed clean here in the present."

The roof above Calliope opens slightly to reveal what appears to be a storm made particularly for her as if she conjured it out of thin air. I know this must be some kind of parlor trick but it is magical to experience nonetheless. Thunder rolls and lightning strikes across what was the roof and I feel it reverberate in my chest. Calliope winks in my direction before throwing her head back and stripping out of her blood-stained gown. Some of the crowd follow suit while others just sway in the storm with their eyes closed. I keep my eyes on my Little Muse as the frenzied energy in the room picks up threatening to swallow us all whole. I let myself be consumed by it for a moment and for that moment I am outside of myself experiencing the pure ecstasy of the night with everyone else. As if I am anyone but who I actually am. As if I am not a devil in disguise. It is fleeting because the moment I realize I have lost sight of my muse the predator in me takes back over. The lightning creates a strobe effect and I grow weary of the hindrance immediately. It takes me longer than it should to find her.

She is sitting in her robe on her throne staring straight at me with a coy smile on her lips and I know instantly she watched me look for her and that it satisfied her. I do not move; I just watch her. Bodies are moving all around us, crashing into one another. The crescendo of their moans of pleasure drowning out the sound of the storm and yet her and I are the only ones in the room. Everything pales next to her; she is the brightest spot in an otherwise pretty dingy and dark world. Zander leans in to speak to her but her eyes never leave mine not even when she scowls and ignores him. He gestures in my direction and because she refuses to acknowledge him, he turns around and marches my way.

Aztyn

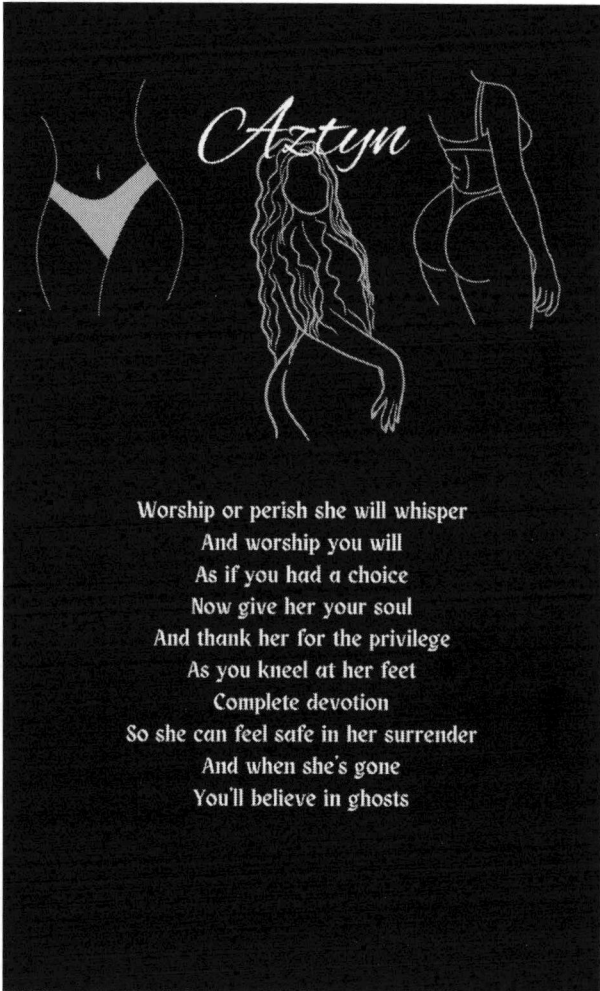

Worship or perish she will whisper
And worship you will
As if you had a choice
Now give her your soul
And thank her for the privilege
As you kneel at her feet
Complete devotion
So she can feel safe in her surrender
And when she's gone
You'll believe in ghosts

Chapter Eighteen

Zander bobs and weaves through the crowd but I do not move to meet him. I have nothing to prove here, but I know exactly what's about to happen. Zander swings and I let him land his punch. He needs this more than I do and if she wasn't mine before this will certainly seal the deal. He's no slouch and his next punch rattles my teeth. A familiar taste of copper floods my taste buds and I instinctively smile. The crowd doesn't stop, it seems to feed on the chaos our little fight has created. Zander rears back to hit me again but this time I dodge his attack.

"Now, now…it's my turn." I say clicking my teeth. "You haven't even told me what the first two were for."

This irritates Zander and knocks him off kilter making it easy for me to sneak in a light jab or two. He knows I'm playing with him now and he knows it's too late, he's done exactly what I want him to do. He's already lost so he doesn't hesitate to get his licks in. My nose is definitely broken and my left eyebrow has split making it nearly impossible to see a small redheaded girl in my way. Her voice jars me from the haze of vengeance and fury.

"Zander you idiot! What has gotten into you!"

Vivianne pulls on her brother pleading with him to stop.

"Awe, you're not going to let your sister stop you now are yah little buddy?"

I spit the blood out of my mouth onto his shoes and purposefully weave back and forth as if I am dizzy.

"Looks like he already won. I'm doing this for your benefit."

She huffs, not knowing the game Zander only just realized he was playing.

"Trust me, I'm the one who won here, and your brother knows it."

I smile, a horror show of blood between my pearly whites. This infuriates Zander and he almost rushes me again but Calliope has arrived and her presence alone could end a war.

"Are you boys about finished with your high school antics and ready to talk things out like adults?"

"This was us talking."

Zander shakes Viv off of him and pushes his way through the crowd and out through the curtains. He's probably going to his room to pout. Viv shakes her head. She looks tired now that I am watching her up close. The dark circles suggesting late evenings and the makeup covering them suggest that she plans to keep those late nights a secret. No doubt still trying to put together the pieces of my art project, the multiple security breaches by me in the last few months and an increased scrutiny by the Feds and the media. Someone's been leaking information and she doesn't want her comrades in arms to know. Can't keep anything from me though. I haven't told Calliope because she doesn't need to worry about those kinds of things before we make our escape. Besides, it's my job to worry about those things now. I'd rather she shut her brain off and let me handle the big bad wolves circling outside her castle gates. It's of no consequence to our escape anyways.

"I've got work to do. I'll have Ivan shut down the festivities… take him to medical."

She gestures in my direction barely a whisper over the sound of Calliopes devotees. Dionysus would be proud of her little collection of maenads and sacrifices. All around us people are giving into their most carnal desires all while eating and drinking decadent food and sampling the equally decadent delights from each other. I feel no shame in stealing her away from her followers because the only delights I want to sample are the ones beneath her robe and I want them *now*. As Viv walks away, I lean in to whisper in my goddess's ear.

"Fuck going to medical, I want you to take me some place I can worship you."

She shudders against me and grabs my hand to lead me through the swarm of bodies. When we make it through the curtain and the door on the other side of it, she finally speaks. The timbre of her voice instantly soothing my wounds.

"You could have killed him but you didn't, why?"

Her question is less a question and more a demand.

"Even a monster can restrain from being so my Little Muse. Whatever his reasons, he felt justified. Why take that away from him."

I shrug indifferently as we stumble over each other into the hallways like lovers do. She stares at me inquisitively with her piercing blue doll eyes and I can't help myself. I sweep her into a violent kiss and she moans into my mouth. Her body is electrified and responds to every palpitating touch of my fingertips. Her hips arch into mine and we stumble until her back is against the wall and my hand is at her throat. I don't care that we're both still covered in the remnants of blood and neither does she. As I kiss her, I can taste the blood in my mouth and I know she does too. I can see the stains of crimson on her skin and seeped into her blonde hair. She is the most disheveled and unhinged I have ever seen her, and yet I have never been more attracted to her, never needed her so deeply in my veins.

Calliope is no monster, she is just a deity, a lost goddess of all this world has forgotten, and someone needs to keep her safe from all the mortals that would hunt her down and burn her at the stake. I won't let that happen. They would mistake her judgments of justice for some kind of sickness, but she's truly a visionary and like the visionary minds before her she will be vilified for it.

I keep her pinned against the wall as I slide my other hand under her robe to the wet slit between her legs inciting a sharp inhale from her soft pillowy lips. Her pupils dilate with excitement. She's already dripping and I growl into her ear as I sweep my fingers along her opening and bring them to my mouth sucking her arousal off of them before crashing my mouth down upon hers so she can taste herself once again on my lips. We moan in unison and I shift my fingers back inside her as she rocks to find friction against the palm of my hand. She's so close to cumming all the foreplay of murder and ceremony bubbling inside her. I can feel her inner muscles contracting with every flick of my fingers but I want to savor this encounter so I remove myself abruptly and she pouts her lips ever so slightly, prompting me to turn her so that she is facing the wall my chest pressed against her back one hand ripping her robe from her body while the other lands a perfect smack on her ass cheek. She lets out a yelp and a melodic and intoxicating giggle follows. My cock twitches, the predator in me awakening.

Anyone could catch us here, and I know it fucking thrills her. Turning her to face me again, her body needy and naked, I sink down to my knees reentering her sweet pussy with my fingers while my tongue circles her clit. Calliope wraps a leg around my shoulder to give me more access and I sink my fingers even deeper inside her and her moans get louder and more frantic as she rides my face, her back arching against the wall as one of her hands grasps my hair and the other steadies herself.

I won't let her cum here but I can already feel her losing control and I bring her just to the edge of her bliss before stopping and she grips my hair harder in frustration.

Calliope Veritas may not be used to begging but tonight she's going to beg me for release. In one sweeping movement she is over my shoulder and I carry her down the hallway to her chambers. She fights and wiggles and protests against me trying to regain some sense of control, and I love the way she fights her surrender as my own arousal fights against the fabric of my jeans. Her whimpers of injustice fuel the chaos and lust within me. I just want to bury myself inside her but my patience is key. It will be sweeter for the both of us the longer I can resist my urges to take her on the floor of this corridor.

When we reach the door, I fling it open with one hand not bothering to close it behind me. I throw her down on the bed and the way she looks at me, her eyes wide and innocent, her mouth curled into the most devious of smiles, I almost give in to her right there. Instead, I undo my jeans and let them slide to the floor. She crawls across the bed towards me stopping at the edge sitting so pretty for me on her knees and I groan at the sight. I'm going to enjoy fucking her mouth until she chokes on it. I gently place my pointer finger under her chin before reaching into her hair and grasping it tight, pulling her mouth towards my cock. She inhales to speak but I don't give her a chance, the second she opens her mouth to do so I slide my cock in.

"Fuck... you look so good with your mouth wrapped around my cock Calliope."

Her tongue begins to swirl around the head as she tries to take all of me into her throat and my body shudders. It has never been this hard to resist my primal urges with another woman before, I've been patiently waiting to paint her insides with my cum but I focus on letting her think she's in control. I'm starting to lose myself in the movement of her mouth and she nearly wins this power struggle but I want to breed my little muse and I won't finish until I can feel her dripping down my balls as she screams my name.

I watch the tears roll down her cheeks smudging her mascara as she takes me and she's never looked more beautiful to me than when I've made a mess of her. I pull her head back and catch her off guard, I watch a little drool pool in the corners of her mouth and instinctively reach between her legs. She's even wetter than she was when I had her wrapped around my face and the longing to be inside her triples.

"God you're so wet for me you little succubus slut. You're going to cum so hard for me, like a good girl, but not until I tell you to."

"Who says I come on command?"

She snarls, all heat and fury—and fuck, if that doesn't make me harder than I already am.

"Oh, you will, and right before you do, you're going to beg me to let you. Now get on all fours and turn around."

"I've never begged anyone for anything."

233

She doesn't move and neither do I. God, I live for this tension between us.

"You can either do it of your own free will or I can make you Little Muse, but something tells me you might enjoy that more."

I smirk. I think I'd rather enjoy making her as well. My Little Muse crosses her arms in rebellion and the deviant in me steps up to the plate. She tries to escape but it's too late, I already have her in my grasp and she struggles but is no match for the fire she lit inside me. Before she can counter, I pull her legs out from under her hauling her off the edge and flip her around. I pull her hips back towards me and settle inside her right down to the hilt and she sighs so sweetly. She's given up the fight now and I fuck her hard from behind occasionally reaching around between her thighs to circle her clit with my finger tip giving her just enough friction to feel a flood of her wetness but not enough to make her cum. She's barely holding on, but she's not begging yet, she won't give up the struggle that easily. I use her arousal to coat my finger and slip it into her ass as I rut into her at the same time. The moan she lets out of her mouth nearly sinks me to my knees.

"I think I'm going to…"

"Not until you beg me princess."

I remove myself from her completely and flip her onto her back as she pouts breathlessly. I can see it all over her face. She wants to cum so badly and I'm going to bring her to the point of no return. I kneel my face between her legs two fingers in her dripping wet pussy and one in her ass as my tongue writes poetry on her clit. Her body writhes and shakes and I bring her to the edge and back expertly. Her body speaks to me in gushes and clenches and I know exactly when to pull back. Her moans are frantic and loud and I hope that Zander walks by that open door and hears our girl screaming the way only I can make her scream. The thought makes me precum a little and I finger fuck her holes a little harder in response.

"Aztyn...please, I just want to cum for you."

Her voice is pleading and breathy. Those are the magic words and I stand now taking in the dripping messy and wanting masterpiece I've created into my mind so I can remember the moment I broke her forever.

"That's it sweetheart, say it again…"

"Please Aztyn, I need you to make me cum."

I slowly put the length of me inside her. I want to feel her cunt grasp every inch as I slide my way down. She gasps as she takes me and her eyes roll back and I know I've got her exactly where I want her. I thrust in and out of her grinding my pelvis against hers in circles until she's chanting my name between moans over and over again. I can feel her tightening around me and I step up the pace.

"Now you can cum Little Muse."

That's all she needs to open the floodgates.

"Oh God Aztyn, I'm cumming...I'm fucking cumming."

"That's my good girl, just like that, cum for me."

I growl as I release inside her and I watch my cum spill out of her as I pull out and it nearly makes me release all over her again. It's like she was made to take my cock like she was made just for me.

Calliope

I never expected to watch a God fall to his knees for me. He is crule but the only kindness he posesses is mine. I am in love with a shadow, a beast in the night, a scourge to the wicked, and yet he is so easily undone by me. He may not be hell bent on killing me anymore, but this will destoy me all the same. It's why the Gods will always end up with each other. Mere mortals could never compare.

Cali

Chapter Nineteen

I sigh as I wipe the blood from Aztyns brow.

"You need stitches…and maybe your nose reset."

The need to care for him claws through me and I surrender to it without shame. I softly touch the scars on his face as I inspect my cleaning job. There's danger threaded through his beauty, subtle but unmistakable if you dare to look long enough. Fine lines left behind of different dark days. I take in his muscular form as he sits on the edge of my tub. He acknowledges my assessment of Zander's damage with an eye roll.

"Do what you want but you will be in attendance at tonight's dinner."

I press a little on the bruise starting to form and he winces. I shake my head and roll my eyes this time. Aztyn reaches up and grabs my face firmly pulling me down into a soft kiss.

"I wouldn't miss the opportunity to hang with my new buddy," he says sarcastically as he releases me.

"We need to clear the air when it comes to the twins. If we want this plan to work, we don't want them looking in our direction," I say, turning to start the shower.

It must be nearly 3 AM but I can't sleep like this, covered in filth and someone else's blood. The storm I 'conjure' out of thin air is little more than a rinse and a rinse is for the surface. I need something that touches the rot beneath, I need to be stripped bare and scrubbed to the bone. I hop in leaving the glass door open behind me.

The black slate tiles are still cold on my feet but the water is already hot. I need to cleanse myself of the Reaping and I close my eyes letting the warm water wash over me. The urge to curl up on the shower floor sobbing while I scrub my body raw that comes with the realization of what I have done hits me but I hit back and shake the thought from my mind. I feel Aztyn move in behind me, his arms pulling me into him the water cascading over us both. As he kisses my neck I almost forget as the night fades into itself. I turn to face him and open my eyes, swaying a little from the heat. His thumbs rub my temples and my head falls back, eyes closing again.

"I'm going to wash your hair now, Little Muse."

I just nod sheepishly. I've never had someone wash my hair before. Actually, I never much cared for showering with anyone previously but this feels different and I let myself sink into the intimacy. His hands are in my hair and he scrubs the remains of the evening out while massaging my scalp and rinses the remainder of the evening down the drain.

The multiple shower heads around us and the rain head in the middle above us keep us both warm from numerous angles but my nipples peak and a shiver runs through my body despite the humid heat. Aztyn stands closer to me as he washes my body and the scent of jasmine and vanilla fills the air. I watch him as he runs his hands over the curves of my silhouette. My breath hitches, sharp and shallow, the sob curling just beneath the surface.

The softness this brute of a man has within him shocks me every time I see it. Not all nightmares are bad, My Nightmare is as equally nourishing as he is punishing but only I see this facet of him. Like an offering he lays at my feet for accepting all of his darkness. His worship and protection of me is the only light he possesses and he gives it all to me.

He kisses me with his hand grasping the nape on my neck as the water rinses us both and I melt into him. Even knowing he will ruin me; I lean into his embrace. Aztyn steps out of the shower and grabs a towel to wrap me in as I shut off the water. I shiver even wrapped in the towel and he picks me up and carries me to my bed.

"I called down to housekeeping and had them change the bedding while we were in the shower."

The curtains are drawn and the room is dark and cool.

"Thank you." I whisper as he tucks me into clean sheets and crawls in beside me.

He wraps his arms around me and I bury my face in his chest. Our legs entwine together as naturally as a breath. Before I know it, I am dreaming of blood and sacrifice of a different kind.

It is the smell of breakfast that rouses me from my slumber. In place of Aztyn is a note in his signature style.

Little Muse.
Eat. I will see you tonight for dinner.

A.

There is the smallest of chances he went to medical after all, but the more realistic option is that he left to go handle that problem himself. Aztyn doesn't seem the type to need to rely on the skills of others.

The smell of maple syrup and cinnamon invades my nostrils once again and my stomach growls. I can already tell Aztyn had the kitchen make me my favorite cinnamon bun brioche French toast with real maple syrup that I import from Canada, and vanilla bean that I grow here on the island in my own personal garden.

Normally I would rot for three days, seeing and speaking to no one before emerging from my black hole but Aztyn has a way of encouraging me out of that state. Things are so different when I surrender a little and allow him to take care of me. As I'm chewing on a piece of mango from the assorted fruit accompaniment, I decide that I will spend the day in the garden reading under the gazebo in the hammock. I need to relax before this shit show of a dinner and I may even go for a swim after. There's a grotto on the beach side of the island that only I know of and I think I'm ready to share it with Aztyn. I think I'm also ready to share the rest of the escape plan with him. When he asked how we would be getting off the island discretely I told him I knew exactly how, and I think tonight is the perfect night to make good on my promise to show him before we make our final move. Before I can pick a book to read by the hammock, there is a buzz at my intercom followed by an eerily calm Vivianne.

"Cali? It's Viv. I need to see you in your office asap."

I hear her click off before I can respond so I groan dramatically for nothing but the pure satisfaction of being able to do so. I walk, no saunter really down the halls to my office and I find Viv exactly where she said she would be, she's sweating profusely and I find it kind of amusing but I keep this thought to myself. She shuts the door behind us.

"Give me your phone."

"Absolutely not," I say, snatching it close to me.

"There's an FBI agent here to see you give me your phone. You can get a new phone for fucks sake."

I probably shouldn't have sauntered through those halls.

"If he's here to see us, they've probably seen what's on our phones."

"That's not how it works, Calliope. Give. Me. Your. Phone." She says through gritted teeth.

I can sense she's too tense for my antics so instead I try reassuring her as I pass her my master gallery of nudie photos.

"Relax, we have our own private network here on the island, and what could they possibly know?"

Vivianne says nothing and instead shoves me out the door to the main lobby of the offices. For an agent to arrive on the island to speak to me directly is odd enough although not as shocking as Vivianne wanting me to handle everything solo without so much as a briefing. This whole endeavor has Viv spooked clearly, but she also knows I don't *need* a briefing. I allow her to give me one for her sake in these situations but I notoriously run off script without supervision. Enchanting someone is what I do best and that's exactly the task at hand.

I put on my public celebrity persona and walk through the main office doors into the lobby ready to put on the show. A different kind than the one my followers are used to. The biggest role of them all. I observe but one lone agent, tall but not quite as tall as Aztyn, late 40's I'm guessing by the grey in his espresso dark hair. He is handsome but rugged like a lumberjack. Like someone's dad showed up to collect them. If he was rich which I know he's not he would be exactly my type. Certainly not from around here.

"Why hello there sir, Calliope Veritas, and you are?"

The sickeningly sweet but soft southern drawl I can turn on and off always does the trick at disarming the suspicious, especially when dealing with a man. My accent is barely there but I kept enough of it to use to my advantage when needed. A furrowed brow and a scowl meets my fake introduction

"Agent Blake. FBI."

"Agent Blake, welcome to Cephalonia. Will we be having the tour? The facilities are really quite spectacular…"

The agent cuts me off.

"Spare me the niceties Miss Veritas, I want to talk about the reporter who is missing from your 'spectacular facilities' if you don't mind."

He barks gruffly.

"My office then."

I smile cheerily, not dropping my act for a second. He's playing hard to get but I play in a much different league than he's used to so I'm not rattled in the slightest.

When we arrive in my office Vivianne is gone but I know she's watching, she won't be able to help herself. I gesture to the chair in front of my desk as I settle into my chair behind it. Folding my hands in front of me on the desk my face stretched into a barbie-esq smile. I begin the dance.

"So, what can I do for you Agent Blake."

I sound sweet and easy to speak to.

He does not sit, but stands stiffly with his back to the wall studying me with his slate grey eyes.

"A reporter named Victor Kremchuck is missing, he hasn't checked in with his employer and when I asked your intake reception, they said he 'checked out' a few weeks ago…except no one has seen him."

He is doing his best to intimidate me.

"The name doesn't ring a bell, I don't know every patron of the facilities by name but they keep pretty good records down at intake so if they say he checked out, he must have checked out. Reporters, even agents such as yourselves sometimes find themselves in need of rejuvenation and relaxation. A break from the world's busy pace, or hilariously as common they think they will be the one to discover the secret."

I pause and laugh my best fake laugh before deepening my tone only a smidge, but it is enough to catch the man's attention.

"Except there is no secret Agent Blake, and like Victor there they all end up…checking out."

I lean back and look the Agent up and down like I might eat him alive.

"Well, most of them end up back home Miss Veritas, I'm curious, why didn't this one?"

He leans back on the wall, a smug expression crossing his features. Check and mate, or so he thinks.

"Last I checked, grown men are free to disappear if they so choose. Fathers do it every day. That doesn't mean I am responsible or that there is anything nefarious going on regarding his alleged disappearance."

I smile again as I rise from my chair.

"We both know the FBI has no jurisdiction here, least of all you."

The shock of what I have just said registers briefly on his stone-cold face.

"I'm far from an idiot Mr. Blake, we both know there is no active investigation here, but if you need any paperwork, I assure you my reception would be happy to cooperate and send it along, just leave your card at the front desk."

I begin walking towards him gesturing to the door.

"Shame you didn't want that tour Mr. Blake, you came all this way for what could have been a five-minute phone conversation, or even an email."

I chuckle my expression saying what my mouth isn't.

"Please do reconsider on your way out, any of our services completely complimentary for a highly esteemed member of the task force dedicated to finding this reporter, or whatever you overgrown boy scouts are up to."

The Agent smiles and scoffs, nodding his head.

"I'm a thorough guy. Thank you for your time, Miss Veritas. I can find my way out."

"See to it that you do."

I stand firmly at the door to my office and watch him walk down the hall and out the doors to the lobby. I hear the buzz and click of them locking behind him. So, I was correct in my assumption that Viv would be watching. I immediately burst open the door to Vivianne's office. She looks pleased with me; this will help me at dinner.

"Well done Miss Veritas."

I can hear in her voice that she's impressed. I laugh my real laugh and curtsey in front of her.

"He's not going to let this go."

"No, he's not." I volley.

"I'll have it taken care of. That's all. I'll see you at dinner."

Her coldness returns towards me. She's a diehard for her fucking brother.

I collect a book from my room, slip into a black sundress, and spend the afternoon in the hammock as the staff bring me various foods and drinks at my whim. After

248

all, I earned it. It's nearly time for dinner when a thought strikes me. Although Aztyn has given his blood to me in the initiation ritual out of loyalty to the cult and symbolism of the cause, I've offered him nothing tangible, nothing he can touch when doubt creeps in, and I think tonight in the grotto he and I will seal our fates once and for all.

My Nightmare deserves to be worshiped in devotion but unlike a pledge of loyalty, this pledge will be to one another, made with our bare souls and we can seal it by devouring each other in the inferno of our madness in the grotto that is our only salvation, crashing into each other upon the shores of our new beginning.

Calliope

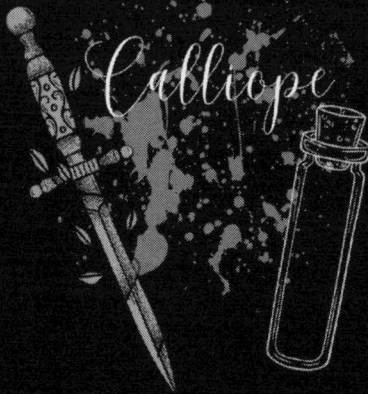

I want to give something to Aztyn that shows my devotion for him as he has shown me his. I have never found anything to live for, but I could live for him. Until Death himself comes to claim us both.

Cali

Chapter Twenty

This is going exactly as I expected it would. Zander inarguably still in a brutish mood sits across from Aztyn who is overtly still smug about it all. Vivianne and I sit across from each other both poised and polite but fiercely invested in the outcome of this negotiation. There is an untouched charcuterie board on the table, a well touched bottle of wine and a near empty scotch bottle. So far this evening has consisted of me trying to butter up Zander in between Aztyn quipping back and forth with him like some kind of ego contest the other two of us in attendance are not privy to, and poor Viv is refereeing it all. I am tired of negotiating, and exhausted by their pissing match and I am about to do what I should have done from the very beginning.

"Oh my good *GOD*. It's like the Sahara Desert between my legs right now."

The shock that registers on both those men's faces when I interrupt them and the almost spit-take from my friend across the table is worth any kind of punishment that might warrant me from Aztyn.

"I beg your kindest pardon?" Aztyn stares daggers at me now.

I tilt my head and flutter my lashes, softening my features.

"You heard me," my voice is breathy and they both hang off every syllable. "I think all three of us know what I would rather be right now."

I bite my bottom lip just a little.

The look on Aztyns face tells me to watch my step but I know exactly what I'm doing. Snapping back to my usual entitled persona I point in Zander's direction.

"You being even mildly civil," I turn pointing at the other culprit, "and you being minimally smug about whatever THIS is going on between the two of you, would make me gush like a fucking fountain right now."

Vivianne snorts from across the table before Zander pipes up.

"This man is going to be the death of you Calliope. Mark my words."

"If a tall, dark and dangerous man with a good dick game is the thing that takes me out, so be it."

"This is serious Calliope."

Zander slams his hand down on the table and leans across it towards me and Aztyn tenses but doesn't move, ready to protect me at a moment's notice.

"You have no idea what he's hiding."

I lean across the table until our faces are nearly touching, lowering my voice just above a sharp whisper.

"And neither do you, not finding anything on someone isn't evidence of anything."

Zander sits back in his seat exasperated with me and I can feel Aztyn relax his muscles back into a more casual state.

"She's right Zand. You know she's right. We all need to be on the same team, especially with this FBI agent sniffing around."

Vivianne can't argue with me because we both know neither party will surrender but perhaps they can yield to one another for both our benefits. Viv cannot risk losing Zander in all of this, and there's no way in hell that I am backing down about Aztyn. Besides once Aztyn and I escape, Zander and Viv will only have each other, so for the time being all I really need is a truce.

"He is the beginning of the end of all of us but if you are unwilling to see that, then I give up Cali." Zander stands and excuses himself for the rest of the evening. Vivianne does the same and leaves Aztyn and I to each other's company. I look at Aztyn and sigh.

"Sometimes you boys can be cavemen, you know that? Doesn't matter how brilliant you clean up, you're still animals underneath it all."

Aztyn grabs my jaw pulling me towards him and our noses almost touch.

"It's what you women like about us men. That underneath it all, were still just beasts, driven by an insatiable hunger."

"And what do you hunger for Aztyn Diamandis?" I stammer.

Aztyn pushes me away slightly and looks at me as if he might take me right there on the table.

"Would it make me the villain if I said that what I hunger for is to break you until you beg me to put you back together to my preference? To own you completely until you remember nothing else but me."

"Would it make me one if I said that's all I've ever wanted?" I whimper through shallow breaths.

His response is to kiss me deeply, lifting the soul from my body before standing and leaving me at the table. My body trembles as I catch my breath.

"I want to take you somewhere," I blurt out and Aztyn looks at me curiously. "Lock the door and follow me."

I lead Aztyn to the back of my closet and touch the trigger point on the shelf opening up the safe room. He looks less than impressed. I'm sure he's seen safe rooms before; he's probably even seen this one. When I press a second trigger point under the desk, he clicks his teeth.

"How do you think I kept finding my way into your room Little Muse?"

He stands there smugly and I can't wait to wipe that smug look right off his face. I smile like a Cheshire cat and climb down into the now exposed tunnel below the entire compound. Aztyn follows me down and begins walking down the tunnel's only visible corridor. I do not follow and press a third trigger point opening the wall in front of us. Aztyn turns around in bewilderment and I am pleased with myself.

"I told you I had an escape route for us." I chuckle.

Aztyn whistles. "Color me impressed, Little Muse."

"That's not even the most impressive part."

●

The second tunnel is only wide enough for one person to pass through at a time. I lead Aztyn down the sloping spiral. I open the door and we walk out into the grotto. Stone and salt make up the jagged natural walls of the cavern, in the middle of the space the bluest water I had ever seen almost entirely still aside from the waterfall stirring things up at the far end of the small secret paradise. Aztyns eyes widened in disbelief as he took in the cave.

"Out past that waterfall, is a small cove where a small rescue boat could be docked. The grotto behind the waterfall and the tunnel are all a secret as far as I know. The only people who know about the tunnel or the grotto are either dead or paid off extremely well."

"I have no doubt you can cover your tracks when you want to, but I was not expecting this."

Aztyn turns around to see me knelt down into the sand with an obsidian hilted dagger that I had slipped into my pocket contents while reaching for the closet switch in my right hand and my left palm outstretched. He lunges forward but my outstretched palm flips towards him and he halts.

"What are you doing now?" his voice growing impatient.

I think he has had enough of my antics today. From the moment I told him of my encounter with Agent Blake, he has been perturbed at my general nonchalance about it all even going as far as to call me 'flippant and brazen' when I told him to 'fucking relax'. I'm hoping my next stunt will change his brooding mood.

"I Calliope Veritas, pledge my undying love and loyalty to you Aztyn Diamandis. I give myself to you body, mind and soul. A vessel for you to yield as you deem fit. I will be the muse and you will be the sculptor of our life together, a life worth living in, one we don't ever have to escape from. I will live for you until Death himself calls his right-hand home, and time crumbles to dust around our graves. Where you go, I will forever follow."

I swipe the dagger across my palm without breaking eye contact. Ruby droplets quickly fill the cut and the warm liquid begins its descent down my wrist and arm. I pull a small glass vial from the pockets of my dress, the same dress I first saw him in. I hold the vial to the cut I have made. It quickly fills and I cork it tightly, handing it to him.   Aztyn looks astonished and hesitates at first before kneeling in the sand in front of me. After slipping the bottle into the breast pocket of his shirt he grasps my still bleeding palm in his and brings it to his lips as he sucks the blood from my wrist and hand and it is my turn to be astonished. After handing me back the dagger that I dropped into my lap Aztyn removes his shirt.

"Carve your name into my chest above the brand you gave me."

My hand is steady and sure as I do as he has asked. He does not make a whisper of sound, nor does he twitch a muscle. As I am rounding out the curve in the last letter of my name, Aztyn grabs the knife from me.

"This is going to hurt Little Muse."

I'm not sure what to expect as he lifts my dress up exposing my right hip and thigh. The blinding pain of the sharp metal digging into the supple flesh of my bikini line is a blaring indication of what his intentions are. I watch as he sculpts his name into my skin and my body answers before I do, it is slick, ready, and traitorous. The biting sensation of the initial slice in my fresh skin and the burning fire left behind. I whimper but not in pain and Aztyn licks the blood that is beginning to drip so sensually I can feel my inner walls clench.

For a moment I almost want him to use the hilt of the knife to make me cum but I wonder if that's pushing things too far. Aztyn clearly sensing my arousal traces my clit with it instead and I wonder if I was always destined to go to hell willingly. Temptations of the flesh that's what those sexually repressed Priests call it isn't it? That's what happens when you repress feral and ancient urges. I suppose it's not much different than the opposite. I too have my fair share of perversions and I have done no repressing.

Aztyn brings me back to the moment by replacing the hilt of the dagger with his tongue. Expertly swirling circles around the small bud of my clit that is throbbing from anticipation. Aztyn lays the dagger to the side of us as he coaxes me to orgasm with his fingers and mouth in tandem chaos. I writhe beneath the hand that he has on my lower stomach, my hips bucking.

Aztyns movements slow and sensualize, this isn't feral fucking... he is making love to me. His mouth finds mine and I taste myself on his lips as he replaces his fingers with his firm erection and it finds no resistance as a slow cascade of desire drips down, marking me with need. He doesn't thrust into me with force instead he takes his time as he slides in and out. Each time sinking into me a little deeper. I moan breathily, the air in my lungs fluttering in and out as we breathe in unison. His hand caresses my face as we stare into each other's souls.

Aztyn is barely moving in or out of me at all now, and I have no idea how he's doing it but the soft and subtle movements he is making are driving me wild. I can feel every slight shift in his body and where there is usually a blur of pleasure is now a symphony of sensation. I can't help myself as I tip over the edge and only then does he resume his normal pace of fucking me, and I am pretty positive I am having the best orgasms of my life. Aztyn groans not being able to hold himself back either. It's not just release, it's a joining, a vow whispered in moans and movement. Aztyn holds me against his chest and my ears prick up at the sound of his heart beating in time with my own, our pulses synchronized. We do not wake until the dawn peeks out from behind the waterfall casting golden shadows and rainbows across the grotto. Aztyn kisses my hand where the slice I inflicted is still fresh and I smile softly as we rise and rinse off in the grotto's waters.

.

Aztyn

Sink your teeth into my soul
Rip my heart from my chest
Break me open without mercy
There is darkness here
Burn holes in my shadows
So I can let the light in
We will not be the hero's they write into stories
We will be but whispers in the shadows because there
will always be a villain in me
A villain who would sacrifice the world for you
When the clouds rain down ash upon our heads
Take me into your lungs and let me be your last
breath.

Chapter Twenty-One

Aboat is easy enough to find for my Little Muse. I'll pay a friend of mine, well more like an acquaintance. I don't have friends per se, best not to have any attachments in my line of work. I will pay a man I have paid in the past to discreetly drop a small sailboat, just big enough for two full of provisions to get us to our next port including the means to change appearances as quickly as possible. Calliope will not like saying goodbye to her blonde femme fatale appearance but I'm going to need her to channel the side of her that wants to be a fly on the wall instead of the main character. I need her to look innocent enough to trust, to give information to, to allow someone to let her walk by without thinking so much as twice about her. I am apprehensive if she has what it takes, to be for lack of a better nuance, normal. Plain Jane won't suit her, I just need her to act like it does. Underneath it all she will still be my Calliope, a succubus vixen of the underworld. She won't be able to hide the royalty in her veins but I hope she will be able to play along until we get somewhere safe, where no one knows her name.

I have thought of nothing else besides our escape since the night Calliope and I spent in the grotto almost a month ago. I was impressed by her ability to keep such a truly breathtaking place a secret. My Little Muse has always desired escape, even before she came to need one and for some reason that makes me a little hard when I think about it. I feel my skin prickling and I absentmindedly finger the vial of her blood that somehow finds its way into my hands whenever I think about her. She has bewitched me in her own deranged madness and I am felled by her. My inability to separate my obsession and love for her has crumbled me. Her surrender to me and in turn to us has become my undoing. I watch the clock tick down the hours until our departure although the 'when' part of the plan is unknown to both of us.

The little harpy says she will know when the time is right. My planner personality has never been so insulted, but the Queen gets what the Queen wants and I am powerless when it comes to her every whim and fancy. I have softened her but she has ruined me in ways that rewrote the very bones of me. I have even been pleasant with Zander despite his natural bristle towards me. A predator turned prey never takes it lying down. He didn't expect a hellhound where before there had only ever been other wolves. Poor thing. He won't handle Calliope's escape well. I wouldn't be surprised if he tossed himself onto the cliffs where she once attempted to do the same. A pity she won't let me put him out of his misery but my Little Muse has demanded a truce and a truce she shall have.

I sigh as I click through the images on my tablet. Agent Blake wouldn't be easy to kill. I recognize him from his connections to some of the souls I have condemned in my life before her. He appears as a straight -laced by the book kind of agent but I know him to be something a little different. Agent Blake has no problem sinking to a level beneath him to get the job done and Calliope infuriatingly thinks she can handle him on her own. I swipe to the footage of their exchange in her office. Zooming in on his facial expressions, watching Calliope annihilate him much to his surprise but it is his smirk at the end the one Calliope didn't see that has me on edge. See I recognize that look. He wasn't expecting to play dirty here with her but now that she has set the tone, he is more than happy to play at that level. Calliope had the upper hand when he hadn't met her face to face but now that he has felt her viper sting, he knows exactly what he's dealing with. This has thrown a hitch into our plans indefinitely. Until our little Agent problem is taken care of, we cannot leave and that alone makes me want to grind him into a pulp and chum the waters with him as Calliope and I sail away. I cannot handle him like the scum I usually contend with, people will look for answers other than the one I would stage. He's clean enough and the only people in the world who know he isn't are the criminals and unlawful he's penalized. He's a 'by whatever means necessary' kind of cop, and those are the worst kind. The men who parade as morally just, but will proceed with no morality in the name of justice. He must be eliminated and quickly or I will take matters from my sweet Calliopes hands into my own.

I am also a 'by any means necessary' kind of fellow, except I do not parade around under false pretenses, I *am* Death's right hand, and I am not ashamed to be willing to do anything to succeed, which makes me more dangerous than him. Where his false morals make him hesitate, my lack of morals at all gives me an upper edge. He is no match for my immorality or heinousness which is why Calliope has me heeled knowing she can unleash me as a weapon if all else fails. She can have her way on this one too for now anyways. Perhaps it needs a woman's touch. I tuck her vial of blood in the inside pocket of my suit jacket, and put down the tablet. We are having dinner in her garden tonight and I have invited Zander and Vivianne to witness along with a few other attendees.

Calliope will be in a dress I have designed for her. A perfect accentuation to her silhouette, black with a long and dramatic train, the embellishments and beadwork so intricate and dazzling it will almost hurt to look at her. She will glow in the candlelight just like the starlight obsidian of the night sky that will feel like it surrounds us. No one knows it quite yet, not even the guest of honor herself but Calliope will marry me this evening.

I had to plot to do something in my spare time while I wasn't plotting to take the lives of Zander or Agent Blake, and marrying Calliope seemed like a worthy enough scheme to put my mind to it as any. I saw no reason for a priest to marry us heathens, considering the circumstances this is more of a witnessed dark rite than a marriage ceremony but nonetheless I am treating it as the hallowed event it should be. I also deemed an engagement to be unimportant. Calliope has made it exceptionally clear that she is mine to do with as I wish, and I wish to marry her this evening, and I know she will oblige my desire. She's not the 'planning a wedding' type of woman anyways. Her love knows no bounds, and mine mirrors it from the shadows, quiet and consuming.

I walk down the hallway to collect her in my simple but exceptionally tailored black suit. When I open the door to her chambers she is standing against the open windows and she glows just as I imagined she would.

"What is all this for, I thought we were just going to have dinner?"

"We are going to have dinner." I respond even toned as I move towards her.

"I need *this dress* to eat dinner?" She says gesturing to the grandiose masterpiece on her body.

"I thought it would be inappropriate to have you naked while the rest of us are clothed." I chuckle softly. "By all means however, if you would rather."

She just shakes her head and I hold out my hand so that she may place hers in it. As she does, I pull her closer to me and whisper against her ear.

"You look just as I thought you would. A vision I will never be able to forget."

Calliope simpers and I see her blush. It is a rare occurrence, the pinkening of her cheeks, but I have discovered if I can catch her off guard with a poetic enough phrasing, she melts like snow meeting fire. In those moments that she is melting for me, I gripped in her gaze become water. Formless, fluid, and willing to mercilessly drown.

When we walk in through the garden doors my eyes are fixed on her expression. Rapidly shifting as she realizes what is happening. "Are we getting…"

"Married?" I finish for her. "In a sort of way, yes my love."

Her eyes roam the gardens that I have transformed into a place fit for a wedding. Hundreds of candles line the walkways in little clusters to light her path. Fairy lights are strung throughout her flowers and vines giving the garden a whimsical and magical look. I have had the altar made up of all of her favorite flowers and more lights and clustered candles placed in front of her fountains. Her eyes widen as she notices the few guests in attendance. Vivianne has tears in her eyes, beside her stands Lucy who looks at Calliope with a love that is really very enduring and even Zander is there, his vibrant anger softened. Looking back at me her face is full of bewilderment.

"Why would you do this?"

"You deserve the kind of love you read about in those books, despite your belief that kind of love is not meant for you. You are right though that kind of love is not meant for you."

I tip her chin up my hands on either side of her cheeks.

"We were never meant to be the ones love stories are written about. We are too ruined and ruthless, too soaked in sin. But I love you Calliope Veritas. I was never meant to be a hero, I am a villain through to the very depths of me, but I am yours if you'll have me."

Tears brim on her soulful blue eyes and very softly she breathes the words

"Fino alla morte il mio incubo"

"Till death, my nightmare."

I cannot help but grin radiantly. This may be the happiest moment of my life, and you can bet that being in my line of work "happy" doesn't often come into play, but I am effervescent and she is every reason. I give her a ring with a three carat teardrop stone made of our blood surrounded by diamonds. After signing some "official" paperwork I had drawn up, we all sit down and have dinner like we are ordinary people at an average wedding, and for a moment it feels as if it could stay like this forever.

In reality it was only about an hour before the inevitable. Vivianne looked down at her phone and gasped, pulling Calliope aside to tell her that an official investigation had been opened against her in regards to the disappearances and alleged murders of several missing people cases. Something I had read this morning in a report that happened to come across the desk of a certain Agent friend of ours.

Calliope waves her off in her perfunctory way, which I have realized is not actually a personal slight towards me but a defense mechanism she uses when she is caught off guard. Calliope is cunning and feral but she prefers to have a plan of attack, she never goes in blind, and this is less of a blindside and more of what she knew would be the next move in a game of chess, except she hasn't quite figured out what *her* next move is, so she is extra lackadaisical. Vivianne is emotionally distraught and excuses herself from the small party. I kiss Calliope on the cheek a few moments later and excuse myself citing a need to use the facilities. Instead, I dart into a stall and take advantage of my self-granted all access pass of Cephalonia.

Viv went straight to her office as I anticipated she would. Her next step is one I was hoping she would execute as well. Vivianne accesses the employee files officially absolving Calliope of any physical ties to Cephalonia and begins drafting what will be Calliope's exit speech. As she should, this is risky business. Currently only Calliope is under investigation. She is under no obligation to answer any questions regarding her involvement or lack thereof inside Cephalonia. Vivianne will date that she absolved her

270

position and duties before the first incident "legally" and therefore pardon any activity that would reflect badly on the company as a whole. It will take more than just a little red tape to stop our Agent friend and Viv knows that but right now she needs to focus on falsifying documents that separate their precious deity and her precious legacy. I give her an edge by sending an email from an address I just had made under a new employee. Viv won't care where it came from. I don't have time to cover my tracks and create a well-established identity of this new employee for the books but by the time Agent White Bread pieces this all together Calliope and I will be long gone. If I have anything to say about it, we will be long gone before he even gets his greasy little bureaucratic hands-on Cephalonia's books. Documents I made up last night were sent under the subject line "copies of Ms. Veritas exit files" Calliope and I being married means I cannot be called to testify against her in court. Just a little bonus of our nuptials although Agent Blake will certainly try but that is only because he hasn't met me yet. I am still a shadow here, but I won't be for long, Not with Agent Blake on the case, which means Calliope and I are running out of time much faster than we anticipated. Although everyone will use every connection, they have to keep Calliope out of trouble I may have to do something drastic to get us out in one piece.

Calliope

Agent Blake is getting on my nerves. If he's not careful I'll let my Nightmare 'take' care of things. This man should thank me... they all should for the sacrifices I've made to bring a little justice to the world. Try as he might, it will be in vain. He'll never even get close.

Cali

Chapter Twenty-Two

Lately I have been spending more time in my office than I would like. All this FBI nonsense is giving me a headache. I haven't picked up a book or been to my garden all week. It's just every day fake paperwork to sign and books to fudge. It helps that I haven't been seen in public since the first incident. Vivianne has long been rumored to have taken over my position on the internet and in gossip columns. We have been preparing for this inevitability for a very long time. My role and 'official' involvement changed when I became the deity they now worship and love. The rest of the facilities are legit, the healing centers, the amenities, the farm, all exactly what we claim to be so why should the island suffer for my misdeeds? The cult is the little bonus on the side, the extra dessert that not everyone is entitled to.

It should be seen as a separate entity altogether although they won't see that vision. All they will see is the bloodshed and the lives lost. The system talks about justice but if there was any *real* justice, this cult wouldn't exist at all. They wouldn't have notarized me for killing Aztyns brother, they would have strung me up and lit a match. I am no idol. Just a woman who wanted to live through an ordeal without any damages to the body I use to get what I want. I did what I had to do and I never asked for this hive mind religious experience but they needed me and, in a way, I needed them too. The cult gave me purpose when I had none. Provided a sense of control and an outlet for my behavior. When my insides feel like they are crumbling and the screaming gets too loud, I can always hold a Reaping. It's not about the blood and the shock value, that's just part of the show, the part that's for *them*. It's become a coping mechanism for *me*. When the chaos threatens to spill out of the wounds, I have stitched back together a million times, it calms the raging storm inside me.

Fucking married men, doing drugs, drinking on yachts, doing my best to spend my inheritance, all the reckless behavior, none of it ever felt as good as giving someone the justice they deserve and helping the victims who have suffered needlessly to heal. Society would rather lock them up and waste taxpayers' dollars to feed and house them with no hope of rehabilitation or reform, only a glorified grounding. Or worse yet, let them go with little more than a slap on the wrist because of who they are or how much money they have.

I took a *broken* system, and I *fixed* it. When justice would not rise from law it rose through me. They should be fucking thanking me, throwing a parade in my honor. Instead, they will try to make an example of me, they will vilify me and paint me as a villain. Except Aztyn and I will be long gone by then.

For the time being the show must go on, and I am to make an appearance on stage left. Aztyn sits on the edge of my desk as I press the button to answer Agent Sour face's call. Viv is patched in but Aztyn made sure no one would know that. I hear the click of the connection and heavily roll my eyes.

"Ms. Veritas"

"Agent Blake." I don't correct him on my new last name, the longer it takes him to realize I am connected to Aztyns brother, the better for both of us.

"By now you know we are investigating you."

"I have been made aware…yes."

"I hate to do this so informally but you understand. You being on that island and all. Do you care to answer a few preliminary questions before we have you brought in to your closest FBI office?"

"I mean it can't hurt, could it Agent?"

"Certainly won't hurt me, Ms. Veritas. Well, that's just swell. Do you happen to remember any of the names that I sent in that email, the list of the missing believed to be associated with you?"

He's much too cheerful and it makes me nauseous. All of this is so fake and we both know it.

"Not one sir."

"I find that strange. See there are members of your *'community'* and I use that word loosely, prominent members even who are most definitely associated with the names on the list."

"It's a small world Agent but it's not that small. Are you suggesting that I am associated with all of the associations of every member of the community here? I'm not even on the board of directors, haven't been for the last 3 years."

"That's news to me. I'd like to see some paperwork on that. Why would you continue to hold an office if you are no longer involved in Cephalonia's day to day operations?"

He's surprised by my confession as he should be.

"The office was always there. I used it for your benefit. I still have my original room in the private wing too if you'd rather be shown there next time we meet."

Aztyn grunts trying to keep in his laughter and I shoot him a look that speaks for itself. In response he slips beneath the desk, hikes my dress up and spreads my knees apart.

"That won't be necessary," Agent Blake clears his throat. "Back to what you were saying Ms. Veritas, no I don't expect you to know everyone. I am interested in how you have collected such an inner circle of people connected to the list of the missing. Seems an awful coincidence to be connected with so many, for example you have a Miss Clara Creedence connected to a Mr. Henry Mason and you're saying neither name refreshes your memory?"

"Doesn't ring a bell."

Aztyn begins to make a "come hither' motion inside me and my inner walls clench.

"That's a shame because I think you do know her. In fact, I'm pretty sure you're well acquainted with Mr. Mason as well. Why don't you tell me about the members you are more *intimately* aware of?"

I cough lightly trying to conceal my arousal and keep the upper hand in this conversation.

"There are no members that I am intimately aware of."

I match his tone but I am doing everything in my power not to moan as Aztyns tongue finds my already pulsing clit.

"I thought you might say that." The agent huffs mockingly. "See although most of the members don't have anything much to say about you one way or another, a very small percentage have nothing but heartfelt praise to say about you. One might even say they *idolize* you."

He chooses his words carefully, saying everything without saying anything is an art after all.

"I certainly wouldn't use that term but are you saying it's a crime to be popular?"

I play coy and innocent which does nothing but get under Agent White Bread's skin.

"Certainly not Ms. Veritas, what I'm saying is…"

I cut him off impatiently. Mostly because I can barely contain myself any longer and only partly because I do not care what he thinks he has deciphered.

"What you're saying is you have nothing Agent Blake. All you have is a few simps who really think I'm just the bee's knees and some missing people connected to my fanbase."

As I am speaking Aztyn emerges from beneath the desk and I push my knees back together. He moves behind me motioning for me to stand and when I do, he kicks my chair across the room and grabs me by my hair tightly causing me to arch my back, struggling to contain a welp.

"I think I've put together most of the pieces, only a matter of time before I put together the rest." Aztyn pushes my head down beside the speaker of the phone and enters me from behind slamming into me before I can think to resist him, not that any part of me wants to.

"There's nothing to put together Agent Blake, you're grasping at straws."

I struggle to articulate as I grasp my desk for purchase against Aztyns violent but lustful interruptions. For a moment I wonder if Agent Blake can hear the wet sounds Aztyn's thrusting is making in the room, but instead I discover that I am apathetic. Let him recognize how seriously I take his threats.

"Perhaps you're right. On the off chance you're wrong though, we'll be seeing each other very soon. Goodbye Ms. Veritas."

His farewell is followed by two soft clicks reminding me that Vivianne was also on the line. She will not be pleased with mine and Aztyns lack of respect for the severity of the situation.

The thought quickly passes though as Aztyn turns me around and picks me up my ass finding the desk underneath it as he resumes his harsh fucking of me. I love when he takes control and lets the monster inside him free. The angle that he's hitting as he puts my legs on his shoulders is deeply satisfying, my entire body is tingling as he pushes me over the edge gushing like a fountain. That's probably going to leave a ring. As if sensing there was a vibe to kill, Vivianne bursts into my office. Aztyn does not slow or falter.

"Will you two get some kind of grip?"

Nothing changes except I get a second wind knowing Vivianne is in the room. I always did like to be watched. I whimper as I lock eyes with Aztyn and he slows only slightly, just enough to let my orgasm take me over as I tip my head back half giggling. *Fuck.* I don't stop climaxing as Aztyn follows suit even though my eyes are fixed on Vivianne now. As much as she doesn't want to admit it, if I asked her to join, she'd fall to her knees and clean up the mess I made on Aztyns cock with her mouth. She likes to pretend she's above all this now, but there was a time she would have begged to share a man with me.

"Jesus fucking Christ this is serious and you two act like it's a circus."

I readjust myself, sliding off Aztyn and pulling down my dress as I kick his pants towards him.

"You're such a fucking buzzkill. I remember a time you would have been angry for not being invited."

"Those days are long behind us."

"I can see that," I say impatiently. "Well get on with it then."

Viv doesn't skip a beat as if she didn't just walk in on Aztyn and I ferally fucking.

"He immediately subpoenaed the exit files. Our lawyers are going over everything now making sure he will have all he needs to stay out of our books as a whole."

"So why are you here then? Could have been a fucking text Viv. You sure you didn't want to join?"

Vivianne just rolls her eyes.

"I have an informant in his branch. They're coming to extract you Calliope. They want you off this island and into their custody for questioning."

"Let them try."

Aztyn interrupts. A fire in his eyes I've never seen.

"When?" He demands, and the energy in the room changes.

"I don't have that information yet."

Viv answers like a schoolgirl being chastised by the headmaster.

"When you do, you will inform me immediately. That will be all Vivianne."

Viv turns around and leaves my office without another word.

"How did you do that?" I question.

"Do what?"

"Make her leave like that. I was expecting a lecture on my lewd and disrespectful behavior." I say smirking to myself.

Aztyn just chuckles but I can see the worry behind his eyes as he grabs my hand and sends me out of my office with a smack on the ass.

"You need a book and to sit in the garden, and I need to make a plan."

Calliope

I feel uneasy as if something waits for me in the waters, waiting to swallow me whole and eat me alive. For the first time, I'm not sure I want to meet it.

Cali

Chapter Twenty-Three

I did need a book and to sit in the garden but for the life of me I cannot settle. Something about today feels strange and I can't put my finger on it. I hate when I feel like I am waiting around for the other shoe to drop. Something is waiting to swallow me whole, and I do not want to know what it is.

I look out across the beautiful blooms. People wonder how the gardens are so nice here and here's my secret. Plants love blood meal and I've been disposing of the blood meal made from the Reaping's into the garden since they began. We needed a practical way to dispose of the mess and both the community garden and my personal garden are beautiful because of it. The bones make bone meal, the remainder of the bodies are more of a problem but less of a problem for the marine life around here. Lots of sharks feed in these waters and I've used that to my advantage. I will miss the gardens the most. I think I've been saying goodbye to my island ever since we started the cult. As much as at one time I needed the cult and it needed me, I think we have both outgrown each other. It's time for Calliope and her followers to be put to rest.

Aztyn says I'll have to choose a new name. As much as I love the name Calliope, I am almost relieved. It wouldn't really feel like starting over if I didn't become someone else entirely. I am not too keen however on having to dye my hair. I chose a deep chocolate brown. I've never seen myself with any other hair color other than blonde and the shock will probably kill me but *c'est la vie* and at least I'll die free.

I need to do some damage control with Zander and Viv…again. I seem to constantly be falling out of favor with them one way or another. Sitting down to dinner after Aztyn and I sealed the deal it almost felt like those old days in university. I think they felt the same way, until the news of course. Reality crashed down upon us all in that very moment and we went right back to being the vile people we are, forgetting the innocent people we once were.

I think changing my identity will put me back in touch with the woman I once was before this all happened. Sure, I was a maneater by nature, but honestly that's on men for being so easily beguiled. I can't tell you how many secrets have been revealed in my ears, all for the chance to impress me. As if stocks and bonds, and insider tips could ever make me horny. Maybe a leopard can't change its spots but this cult leader is leaving every ounce of her old life behind. I wonder how many people have wished for the same opportunity. To be able to leave life behind as they know it and truly start over with a blank slate. I assume some of those people were people who deserve a second chance more than I do but tough for them. Life isn't about what we *deserve*, it's about what we *create* for ourselves. I succeed because there isn't anything I am unwilling to sacrifice or do or risk for the success I want. That's the difference between someone who is a success and a failure. The lengths you're willing to go to achieve what you want.

Aztyn doesn't think I can 'rough it'. I'm not as delicate of a flower as he thinks I am but it's sweet that he's so concerned. My mom didn't raise me to be a princess, she raised me with grit. The princess life chose me but he is correct in thinking I have become quite accustomed to it. A re-roughening of my pampered edges won't kill me.

I read through a few pages of my book before a bombshell hits me. I'll have to leave all my precious books behind. It's taken me years to establish my collection and suddenly I am devastated. Some of them I haven't read yet and I don't have enough time to do so before it will be time to escape. If I could stop time to do so right now I would. I bet Aztyn doesn't have my entire collection of books concealed at his little hideaway. It's probably all poetry and classical works and a girl needs some swooning and yearning and she definitely needs smut. Some of his hidden funds will be going towards new cliterature mark my words.

I will be bringing no funds; it would be too suspicious to drain my bank accounts right before my escape. Aztyn says he has a plan to make sure that when we escape no one will know we have done it, and what we leave behind will tell the story we need to tell in order to cover our tracks. I am not privy to this information. When it happens, he says one of us needs to be surprised and since he's doing all the grunt work, he gets to be the one who knows what's going on which I concluded was fair.

◆

I am bored of waiting for Aztyn to collect me for dinner, so I retire to my chambers to wait for him. I take a quick shower, rinsing my body off and fantasize about Aztyn washing my hair. The heat from the day has seeped into my skin and I turn the shower a little colder to help regulate my temperature.

After my shower I lay in my bed, naked, waiting for Aztyn to arrive but the sun sets and one by one the stars come out to greet me. The chill of worry snakes through my ribs. Aztyn would never do this to me, he promised. Then anger fills my veins. What did I really know about the man anyways? He did come here to kill me after all. What if he decided that my best fitting punishment was to remain alive and suffer endlessly? I try reasoning with myself before coming back to anger. The storm in me rages with every breath. Hours have bled into each other, and all I've done is wear a path into the floor.

I decide to take matters into my own hands and suddenly I find myself outside the door of his personal room. A place I have never been inside of. A place that holds more secrets than I probably want to know. I knock hesitantly but there is no answer so I knock a little louder. The door moves with the force of my hand and I realize it's been slightly ajar this whole time. I take a deep breath not knowing what lies behind it.

When I enter the room I am comforted at first, nothing seems out of place. I slowly realize that nothing seems out of place because he isn't here. The drawers are empty, the shelves too. Nothing about this room links it to Aztyn except the faint smell of his cologne. The fury I feel at this realization burns me from the inside. There is very little chance Aztyn has moved rooms without telling me and more of a chance than if I look under every rock on this island I will not find him.

I rush back to my room and rip open my closet. Flicking switches as fast as I can get to them until I burst through the door to the grotto. I can still see the impression of where we laid together the night I gave him my blood. Shimmers of memories dance behind my eyes. Additionally, to that imprint I can see footprints leading toward the waterfall and suddenly it's grief instead of anger rushing through my nervous system and it feels as though I've been left to rot in the hollow of something once sacred. A crushing loneliness coils around me, heavy and inescapable.

How could he do this to me?

I break into a thousand pieces but not in a way anyone would expect. They would expect tyrannical rage but instead I sob, sharp and graceless, like a stranger inhabits my skin. I clutch my chest as my heart threatens to beat right out of my ribcage. My heart slams against my ribs like it wants out, like it's trying to follow in his footsteps without me. I feel faint and dizzy like I've been in the sun too long and my breathing is rapid and shallow. The world tilts beneath me and the ground feels distant. My heart turns to ash in my chest and I am drowning in the violent wake of my sorrow.

289

I collapse into the sand, its rocky granules biting into the skin of my knees. Time slips away as I weep, the minutes blurring into silence. I remember nothing of the walk back, only the weight I carried with me.

When I come out of my numb reverie it is because Zander is banging on my door. I do not know if it has been hours or days, just that I am exhausted and I do not want to see him. I can feel the sting in my eyes and the puffiness surrounding them. I roll over away from the door. My curtains are drawn, the room an echoless void of black. I hear Zander outside mumbling about breaking down the door, and then I hear Vivianne's voice but I do not hear what she says. Silence follows and I shut my eyes again.

Why didn't he just let me jump that day?

The next time a noise startles me, it is a bang on my floor to ceiling windows leading out onto my balcony. I rise from my coffin of a bed and draw the curtains back to investigate. A small colorful island bird has flown into my window. I open the latch and step outside. It is nearly dusk, the sun no longer blinding but changing into shades of orange and pink. I look down at the poor creature and sit beside it, the stunned bird climbs onto my outstretched hand as if recognizing that I too am disorientated and damaged.

Eventually my little companion flies away and this saddens me deeply. The tears flow again but this time the sobs that wrack my body are silent. I slowly walk myself to the shower, turning it on and sitting on the cold tiles. At first it is almost too hot to stomach but eventually it runs cold. It feels like crisp rain and I wish it could wash my memories of Aztyn right down the drain. I trace the pink scar on my palm wondering how long it will take to disappear if it ever does; some scars don't. I eventually crawl out of the shower and back into my bed.

◆

The next few days go by in a blur. I do not eat. When I sleep it is fitful and broken, sometimes I wake myself up crying or screaming depending on the dream. I let no one see me. Zander comes by every day and talks to me through the door. I listen but I say nothing and still he comes. He will always come, and he will never let me go until I am in the grave, and yet he's not the one my heart yearns for.

I know they know I'm alive but I don't feel alive. I feel like the dead, trapped in the veil between. This is the place between breath and burial, and I am its quiet inhabitant. The heaviness that holds me here is suffocating, the memory of him more so. I ache to be cleansed not just my skin, but marrow and memory but even I know that will never be possible. He will eternally swim through my very veins, our souls intertwined inexplicably. I could burn the world down and still he would remain; smoke in my lungs and a name on my tongue. The next morning it is not Zander who comes, it is Vivianne. Her soft knock startles me but still I cannot bring myself to speak.

"You can't stay in here forever Calliope, you know that." I hear her sigh before continuing. "You need to eat something too, if not for you for the love of this old door here. Zander is going to break it down and force feed you if you don't."

A single set of footsteps follows her words. I feel the faint echo of a smirk on my face. I want to open my mouth, walk across the floor and open the door but the will to execute these tasks is lost. They feel trivial. The weight of my loss makes breathing feel redundant. Grief has hollowed out meaning and everything else is just an ear-splitting interruption to my silence. I also haven't forgotten about my little FBI problem that still needs dealing with.

I can't escape on my own. What am I supposed to do? Build a fucking boat like I'm Noah? The future has blurred and with it any ounce of my desire to self-preserve. Nothing even makes one lick of sense. He hadn't even the decency to Dear John me. Everything I have ever loved has died and Aztyn may as well have died the day he left me to rot on this island without him. I have never let another being so close to my soul as I had let that man, no one had ever gotten beneath my skin or completed all the aching and hollow parts. I made room for him inside of me and now that he is gone reality feels bleak and lost. He had set fire and awakened parts inside of me I didn't know existed. I had given myself to him in ways I had never even dreamed of. I am nothing but a cathedral of empty prayer, still standing but utterly forsaken, the remnant of devotion desecrating the grounds. This heartache has no name on my lips, I have never tasted its bitter flavor and mark my words I never will again. Grief has come to swallow me whole but if I manage to rise from this wretched suffering well…

Hell hath no fury like me.

Aztyn

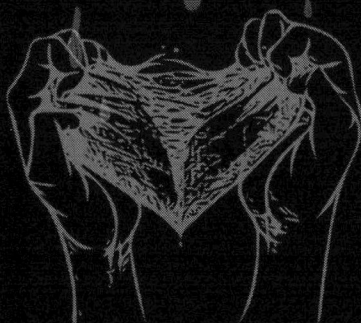

Please forgive me Little Muse,
For you know not what I've done.

Chapter Twenty-Four

May that woman have mercy on my soul for what I have just done.

Who am I kidding, she will never forgive me?

Fuck.

This might have been a mistake.

Calliope

I don't know if it's been days or weeks. Grief is funny that way. Distorting time while your world stops spinning, but it doesn't really stop spinning does it? The world keeps moving while you stand deathly still. Except I don't feel like standing still anymore.

Cali

Chapter Twenty-Five

I am dressed and presentable for the first time since I found out My Nightmare had vanished leaving only devastation in his wake. No sundress today, a crisp black pantsuit takes its place, but my big sun hat and large sunglasses are front and present. I dramatically place a black veil over the hat to complete my look. I am in mourning after all. In my hands a lit cigarillo in a long cigarette holder. I casually stroll past Zander into Vivianne's office like I haven't been catatonic and non-responsive for countless days.

"Gather the cult members in the ritual room,"

I demand while Viv's mouth opens and closes like a guppy.

"*Immediately* Vivianne."

I turn to face an equally lost for words Zander.

"There will be *no* questions."

The ritual room is soundless when I step onto the stage. I do not sit on my throne; I walk right past it to address my followers. I look around the room and everyone is unnerved. Calling a gathering like this is unorthodox and they have every reason to be nervous.

"From this day forward, the flame of our cause has officially been extinguished."

Murmurs break out from amongst the gathered and I wait until their attention has returned to me before speaking again.

"There will be no more Reaping's, no more drugs, no more gatherings and not another word of anything we have ever done here."

The room erupts with protests and questions.

"I will not be elaborating any further. If you're lucky you will leave this forsaken graveyard with your life, but anyone who speaks out against me or my ruling will be silenced, the old-fashioned way."

I snap my fingers and Ivan stands beside me on cue.

"I'll have Ivan and the boys cut out your fucking tongues."

The room falls still and the people are wordless. They know not to take my threats as idle.

"My decision is final, you may all leave and don't forget, these walls have ears. Watch how you speak, even when you think you're alone."

With that I turn on my heel, confidently pushing my way past the curtains to the back room. Vivianne and Zander follow, dumbstruck by my ruling to cull the cult. Zander is the first to break the quiet.

"What the fuck Cali."

"You can't just make decisions like that without consulting us," Viv piles on.

"Actually, I'm pretty sure I fucking can. This is my life too, in case you all have forgotten. I want the retreat shut down as well."

"That you definitely can't do without us agreeing to it," Zander comments meekly.

"Maybe not, but I can blackmail you into it. We've done plenty of shady things together. I could tell Agent Blake everything."

Viv nearly chokes on her own spit. "Are you fucking kidding me Calliope?"

"If you tell him everything you'll go to prison for life," Zander pleads with me, his eyes begging and confused.

"I don't want this anymore Zander, none of this. I don't care about going to prison."

"Well, you don't get to decide for the rest of us Calliope, just because Aztyn..."

I cut Vivianne off.

"I think I just fucking did. Say his name again and I'll have Ivan cut out your tongue too."

Ivan comes to stand behind me, right on cue for the second time this evening. His presence speaks for itself. Vivianne may fuck the boys occasionally earning her a certain favor with them, but I run this island, and it's about time she was reminded of that.

"Take your unsoiled reputation and your money, and reestablish something somewhere new Viv. Make the smart move."

"Please Cali, don't do this," Zander begs me. "We can fix all of this."

"Just let her have what she wants, Zander. She's lost to us now. You were right, he *was* the end of everything."

●

I dismiss Ivan with my instructions. In the next few days Viv will privately announce the closer of this island to the public. Those with lives to go back to will simply go back to their vapid existence. The cult members will be paid out their initial investments as hush money and then some.

The staff will be let go, or reassigned to whatever scheme Viv comes up with to give her purpose. Then she will announce the closure to the public and in about a month's time, this island will be an empty cathedral just like me. Unthreaded and unstitched from the inside, only the bones of belief will remain.

The closure of the island will tie up the investigation. Lawyers and our connections will do the rest. Viv won't leave a thing that would impute any of us to the cult, the members are rightfully terrified of my remaining power, and eventually the investigation will be dropped due to lack of evidence. I'll ask for the gardeners and kitchen staff to be the last to be let go. I will have to stay while the loose ends are tied up, but once I am no longer a person of interest, I too will leave this defiled paradise behind and I will never return. I will retain ownership and on the day I die, someone will be given my diary with my only truths written amongst the pages and they will inherit this portal to hell and do with it what they wish but at least someone will know what happened here and I will pay for my mortal sins where I belong, in the depths of hell back on my throne. Someone will know I wasn't always a monster, and someone will know that I fell in love with one too.

In my depression I had thought about throwing myself from the cliffs but I remembered a promise I made to him.

That I would *live*. His love or whatever it was and the grief of losing him changed me profoundly. He gave me things I never thought I would have, however brief. I am deeply affronted and resentful, the only man I have ever loved betrayed me but that does not make the love, or the memories cease and so I love him still. I love him enough to keep my promise. The island will be the only thing that remains as a testament to that promise.

I finger the scar on my hand, then the ring he gave me as I sit on the edge of my beloved island cliffs. I guess it won't be the only thing that remains. The wind rushing past my ears drowning out all the other sounds. I close my eyes, the darkness I find behind them disorientates me in a way that makes it feel like I am floating. I can still feel him here sometimes and part of me is waiting. The part that will *always* be waiting. The part I will leave here when I walk the grounds for the very last time. I will bury that part of me in the thick earth of the land and it will grow roots in the rubble of the past and I will finally be able to begin anew.

I open my eyes, flowers from the trees on the island are blowing through the wind and for a moment before my eyes adjust, I think I see a boat just on the sunset's horizon. When I blink the blur away, there is nothing but the line of where the shadow of the sea meets the melting sky and I sigh heavily, my heart returning to the pit of my stomach.

I don't want Vivianne and Zander to hate me, but somebody has to be the villain in their story and it's easier for everyone if it's me. It was always meant to be me. The two of them are forever bonded on a level that I can never compete with. As long as I've known them, they have not only supported but encouraged and accepted each other. Viv has always been more of his mother than his sister especially after their mother died and Zander has for the most part always listened to her.

He will follow her to whatever she thinks up next, eventually settle down with who she tells him to, and they will continue the cycle of rich kids marrying rich kids and having rich babies. It is what they were born to do after all. I'm sure they both feel cheated, like I've stolen something from them. What they do not realize is that I have actually given them a gift, one I may never have. I've given them freedom. From me, from this island, from the cult. I've given them a blank slate, and they didn't have to go to jail, lose all their money, their reputation, and have to rebuild the hard way. I've done them a favor, and one day they will see through my exterior walls, and know I loved them, even if it didn't seem like it at the time. I'm so tired of watching everything I touch turn to ash. Better I make the choice and spare them the ruin before they too begin to burn. I'm making the choice before they ever have to feel the flames.

Calliope

These decisions on the outside look like a manic episode gone terribly wrong, but I've never been thinking clearer in my entire life. There are still a few ghosts I must put to rest.

Cali

Chapter Twenty-Six

I pick up the phone receiver on my desk and dial.

"I need to speak with Agent Blake please."

"I'm sorry ma'am but he's asked not to be disturbed," a sweet southern voice on the other end of the phone tries her best.

"I'm what he wants to be disturbed by darling." I chuckle before continuing. "Tell him it's Calliope Veritas."

"Right away Ms. Veritas."

It is not long at all before I hear the click I've been waiting for.

"Ms. Veritas."

He sounds drunk, as anyone would be in his case. I imagine him in his office, blinds drawn, slumped over his desk, defeated.

"I'm calling to invite you to the island Mr. Blake, as my guest this time."

"You won Ms. Veritas. I don't know how you did it, but you won. Why on God's green earth would I set foot

305

onto that island and expect to leave alive? Do you think I'm stupid?"

He whisper-slurs into the phone, Agent White Bread is losing his composure.

"This island isn't God's earth Mr. Blake, it's mine. We're no longer enemies and as such you have my word you will leave unharmed and to answer your question no, I do not think you're stupid. The smartest of them if I were being honest. I believe you're something else cliche of your kind. *Curious.*"

"I'm supposed to believe that you'll indulge that curiosity?"

He almost sobers up right at that moment and I can hear the wheels turning in his head.

"I'm not going to lie and tell you you'll have a smoking barrel. I think we both know each other well enough to know that will never happen. You think I'm some dumb blonde?"

There is silence on the other end until a knock comes to his door. I already know what the knock means so I hang up. His plane tickets and escort have arrived. I don't take no for an answer and Agent Blake is smart enough to know that. He will pack no bags, there will be no time to sneak in a wire, no spare moment to form a plan. What I am giving him is a professional courtesy. I respect his integrity and his ability to string together practically nothing but rumors and hearsay into something *almost* tangible. The man just needed proof, he needed just one person to crack, to bend to his will but nobody would. For that I should be grateful.

From the outside it looks easy to penetrate my circle but the truth is all have failed to do so where their intentions were not pure. The ones who did make it were given a garden of the gods and because I gave them something that was stolen from them by the system, they would never betray or forsake me. I gave them a gift no one else could and their hands are just as stained with blood as mine, I created it that way. Besides my followers like their tongues in their mouths and I can attest that for a few of them, that attribute would be of a great loss to us all if they didn't. What my followers didn't silence, my connections did. I've done plenty of favors for plenty of high-profile men over the years. I was never as worried about it as Vivianne or Aztyn. I just had to decide whether I wanted to live or trade one prison for another.

●

This island feels haunted by the presence of them all. Even the many who used this place as a sanctuary and as a place to heal, what it was truly intended for in the first place.

The grounds feel soulless without them. Some of them cried saying goodbye to this island leaving little offerings in the stone walls they had erected over the years with their own hands. Little pieces of themselves they had mourned over their time here, leaving one last final prayer shoved between the cracks of stone that it wasn't just this place that made them good and whole.

Most of the staff are gone now too, just the gardeners and a few personnel left in my private kitchen who will be gone by the end of this week. When Lucy departed, I shed a few tears. She came to personally say dasvidaniya to me. She told me that she had made more than enough money years ago to build her own spa and line of products she had been developing here on the island but she had made a promise to stay as long as I needed her so she had never thought about leaving. She thanked me for giving her the opportunity to make her dreams come true and I wished her well and told her that of them all I would miss her most and not just because I actually remembered her name.

Zander came around in the end. He understands me on a level that Vivianne can't. So, when he waded through his emotions and mine, he came to the conclusion I knew he would. That we had been lucky up until now that I was giving them the only chance we all had at ever being free of this. I was giving them a sweet soft death and the chance to begin anew.

Vivianne was more stubborn, she had always had less of a soft spot for me in contrast to her brother. She left the island without saying goodbye, without so much as a glance in my direction but I know the truth that underlies *her* hard exterior. I know that she is incapable of goodbyes, and I know she cried on her way back to the cold house she had been running from her whole life. Zander followed her within the hour.

I took my third of the profits after all was bought and sold. Most of my money went to my staff. I gave nearly all of it to Ivan, the boys, and I saved a good portion as an investment into Lucy's business. I kept just enough to build a small garden house for me overlooking some water somewhere and my investment money would keep me afloat until I found what I was looking for. I no longer wanted to be a devourer of men, I just wanted the simple quiet life Aztyn had promised me and I would get it with or without him. Agent Blake will be here by morning, and a few days after the rest of the inhabitants of this island have left. I will too.

The media frenzy was short and sweet. Cephalonia closing its doors was pale news in comparison to the turmoil going on in the world. Our coverage was more about what the twin financial powerhouses would do with their money next that made anyone who cared about this place hold their breaths. Whatever they did it would have the Belmont mark on it, and they would eat it up because of that. The rumors faded with me into oblivion and obscurity. I gave one last press conference with Viv and Zander before they left. When asked what I would do with my life now that I was no longer the face of Cephalonia, I told them my ultimate goal would be to become a face that no one remembers and to fade away into the recesses of everyone's mind. Viv and Zander chatted about their future plans in an ambiguous way never truly revealing anything. I'm sure Viv has something spectacular up her sleeve likely in tech or security.

I wonder if the cult will continue to exist or if they too will fade into the void of what was once a secret that bound us all. When Ivan removed all the brands and markings tying anyone to this cult it wasn't as poetic and ceremonial as when I placed them there. Many of them cursed me for the pain and I did not blame them. This too would keep them, as much as myself, safe. Now all they were left with as a reminder was a small scar, the least of what could have transpired if you ask me.

I did not remove mine. It will serve as a reminder that things can change in an instant and that our choices in that fleeting moment shape our future.

.

Calliope

I am running through the motions, and time is running through me. After today there will be one more person in the world who knows my story. I wonder how my favorite Agent will handle his moral dilemma when he realizes I am not the wicked creature he thought he was chasing.

Cali

Chapter Twenty-Seven

When Agent Blake arrives, he looks exactly as I would have imagined a man disgraced in his career would look like. Disheveled with yesterday's suit askew, five o'clock shadow darkening his face. When he approaches me, I can smell the whiskey that he no doubt had plenty of on the flight over.

"I trust your flight was comfortable?" I say greeting him.

He looks at Ivan but Ivan is looking directly at me.

"Lurch here going to stay with us the whole time?"

I stifle a chuckle and glance at Ivan nodding my head and he turns on a dime with a grunt to go watch us on the cameras. The two men were clearly annoyed with each other.

I shrug in the Agents direction.

"Would you like a tour this time? I will let you know the facilities are empty so there's no staff to service your needs, although my private kitchen is still open."

"Do you have a bar?"

This time I don't stifle my chuckle.

"I'll have the kitchen bring us what we need to my private gardens."

I smile as I usher him through the grounds and out the doors that lead to my gardens. He is silent most of the way except when he grumbled a thank you at the man who brought him his drink.

"Keep em' coming," he mumbles and I nod in agreement.

We sit in my garden at a small table built for two where lunch welcomes us although neither of us reach for food quite yet. There is too much tension to eat.

Looking at me curiously he finally speaks.

"Why am I here Ms. Veritas."

"You have questions, and I have answers. No need for formalities anymore Agent Blake. You might as well call me Calliope."

I grab a piece of cheese from the charcuterie board in front of us motioning for him to eat and I pop it in my mouth. The only thing he's clocked more than me is the food and I assume he wants to make sure I wasn't trying to

314

poison him. Still looking at me he puts some food on his plate and before taking his first bite he asks me another question.

"What do you gain from me being here…Calliope?"

I laugh a real laugh and it surprises him.

"For once…nothing, Cedric."

He raises his eyebrows at the use of his first name but says nothing just curiously taking me in, wondering what my angle is so I begin to speak.

"I respect you and what you managed to put together before the big guys came down and told you to stop investigating these cases. If I'm correct this was going to be your big one and I stole that from you so I want to give you something back."

"But not a smoking barrel," he says, taking a swig of his Old Fashioned.

I smile softly.

"No, not that but I am willing to answer some questions you have."

He looks me up and down before responding.

"You're a very beautiful woman Calliope."

I look him up and down equally long.

"That's a statement, not a question Cedric."

"Won't your husband get the wrong idea if he sees the two of us here like this?"

315

My heart pounds in my chest as I finger my ring.

"My husband has relieved himself of those privileges. There's no one on this island but the man you called Lurch, myself, and a few staff members."

I answer calmly but I am anything but calm.

"Aztyn Diamandis, right? I suppose that would make you Mrs. Diamandis, not Miss Veritas, no?" He says casually between mouthfuls.

"Did you come here to inquire about my marital status or about this island and your former case?"

"I didn't want to come here at all…"

"Now who's lying?"

I smirk knowing he gave himself away already.

"Are you…jealous of my husband Cedric?"

"I will admit that physically you are the exact type of woman who I would normally pursue, but I'm not into murderous women with a god complex."

"That's a shame, I fuck like a minx."

"I bet you do."

Cedric swallows hard and I know he's picturing me naked. I twist in my chair a little, my black dress rouching over my body just slightly enhancing my curves.

"What about your wife? What would she think?"

"Ex wife. But you knew that." He winks in my direction breaking the fourth wall of our masquerade, "Let's stop fucking around, shall we?"

I shrug nonchalantly leaving the ball in his court and he dribbles it around before finally asking me a real question.

"How did you get them to follow you the way you did?"

I know what he means.

"I gave them something no one else could. Something that had been stolen from them."

I shift my focus behind him.

"In a world full of participation trophies and nepo babies where 'everyone is special', no one is special Cedric. They fed on the justice I handed them like it was their birthright, forgetting it was mercy, not proof of their worth. I had bestowed a gift upon them and they looked to me for…life in a world where before they had only felt lifeless."

"How did it begin?" He asks, nearly downing the remainder of his drink.

"The way all great and wicked things do I suppose. By accident."

I watch Cedric's eyes knit together in confusion before explaining myself. I tell him my story, leaving most of the details out but telling him enough that he understands. I

317

watch the way his brain comprehends that I am not quite the monster he thought I was. A monster still, yes, but a different breed than he thought he was hunting. He can justify my wickedness because he can taste its reason and logic but he can't quite come to terms with it. I still murdered people in cold blood with very little regard for their human life. I deemed other human lives, the lives of those who had suffered by their hands more valuable than the judged. He still believes all human life is equal and that the taking of any life is a crime but who is devastated if the child rapist, or woman beater, or the man who runs the child sex trafficking ring is dead? Tell me who misses the people I have snuffed out besides those that benefited from their wickedness. He chooses his words as carefully as I do not want to give away his secret too early.

"The man in the story, the one who assaulted you, he was your husband's brother…no?"

"He was Aztyns brother, yes, unbeknownst to me at the time."

Saying his name makes my stomach curdle in grief.

"Did Aztyn know you murdered his brother?"

"He did, he came here to exact his own justice for my transgression."

"But he fell in love with you instead, didn't he? Little Black Widow."

He shoots back the rest of his drink, and a staff member instantly replaces it with a new one.

"Honestly, who doesn't."

I swallow mine hard. Talking about Aztyn is making me dizzy and I'm losing my composure.

"Did you know he was an FBI agent?"

My world stops spinning and all the sound of the garden is replaced by a high pitch ringing, my face blank and staring.

"I beg your fucking pardon?"

"Did you know that Aztyn Diamandis was a former FBI agent who went rogue during an undercover operation about 6 years ago?"

"He failed to mention that before we married."

I manage to squeak this out through my gritted teeth. The anger is returning to the hollows of my bones.

"Vivianne did."

"I highly doubt that she would have never allowed me to risk the trinity like that."

"My guess is she found out shortly after he had already left, kept it from you out of pure love, not spite."

"It wasn't out of love that she kept that from me," and I scoff before continuing, "She wanted me to pull myself together for the sake of this island. It was selfishly motivated on her part if it was motivated by anything at all."

We both let the truths of the day fill in the missing pieces. Our minds racing to make the connections we hadn't seen. I break the silence first.

"He did mention to me once that he had a past with the law, I just didn't think he meant he had been the law."

"I didn't think I could agree with a fanatic's devotion, but I see why they would have walked into burning buildings willingly for you."

We both sit staring at each other. If this was one of my books this would be the part where we kiss. Instead, he breaks the silence with another question.

"If you could go back and do it all again…, would you?"

It sounds like a question wine drunk housewives ask each other after a few too many but somehow no one has ever asked it of me.

"The answer to that question is moot. I could say that I would never step foot on this island if given the second chance and that would assuage the guilt you feel right now for agreeing with me. Devotion is a small price to pay for justice. The outcome would have been the same. One way or another I would have ended up here. I believe in the premise of what we do Cedric, and if I am being honest stabbing that man felt like it had been a long time coming."

My answer settles into his brain and I watch him wrestle with his conscience. He doesn't want to agree with me outright but if anyone is going to see the vision it is the man whose justice in taking me down was stolen by a signature here and a phone call there, as if I never even existed.

"All you're really guilty of, is the murder in self-defense of Alexander Samaras, and a flimsy case for coercion. That's barely a life sentence in most states. It would have taken me years to take you down, find the truth and nail you with more than circumstantial evidence. The media would have eaten this case up. They would have made you into a messiah again."

"You won. Even though you didn't see it that way. I may have escaped your brand of justice but the cult is dead and so is Cephalonia. Death was the only way out; death has always been our only way out."

"The other side though would have crucified you for The Reaping's Calliope. So would I. That's why you haven't mentioned them."

We are interrupted by a member of my staff refreshing our drinks and taking away the scraps of food leaving a fruit tray gathered from the island between us and several pastries and desserts. I choose my words very carefully. I won't have him ruining this all now with some notion he can still give me my poetic justice. I have seen the irony of this play out a thousand times but I am not that stupid, and he is clever enough to know that.

"I think we all have things we hide even from the dark Cedric."

"You know they wouldn't tell me anything. Your devotees. It was the people who were jealous of them, they were the only ones who would let things slip here and there but even they wanted to be seen in your favor. They feared your wrath just as much as they were desperate for your love," he lights a cigar he has in his pocket filling my garden with the smell of sweet tobacco and I close my eyes drinking in the smell.

"It's really quite impressive, the pull you have," he says after some time waking me from my reverie.

"You doubted my ability to command?"

"It's my job to find the cracks. Sitting here across this table from you, I don't doubt your power even a little. It's no wonder I couldn't find any."

"You flatter me, Agent Blake."

He scoffs.

"In a different world, if we were different people, I'd take you right here in this garden until you screamed my name for everyone left on this island to hear. My intention isn't to flatter you."

"In a different world I would have eaten a man like you for breakfast and had you kissing my feet and branded by lunch."

Cedric laughs in a deep timbre.

"I have no doubt of that either."

I just shrug. The heavy truth hanging between us.

"So, what's stopping you?"

"For one, I knew Agent Diamandis. Before and after he went rogue. I like my skin on my body."

I harden at his mention the warmth evaporating from my body and my voice.

"He lost his claim to me when he left me here to rot. I have no husband."

"I think he would beg to differ."

A different kind of silence hangs between us now. The tension returns to the air, thicker this time choking the words from my mouth. We both know no matter where I go, the scent of death will always linger in my wake one way or another. I will never be free of this island, or of Aztyn, not even in eternal rest. No rest for the wicked they say.

"What will you do now Calliope Veritas?"

He interrupts my thoughts with his last question. I just smile at him giving away nothing.

I've been baptized in blood and now I must be cleansed with fire.

323

Calliope

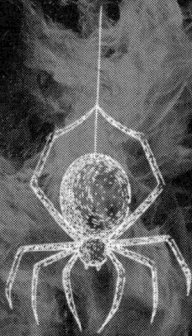

I've always loved the way fire consumes and cleanses. When a fire burns hot enough it leaves nothing behind but a scorch on the earth. Before long nature takes itself back, rewriting history to make way for an impossible future.

Cali

Chapter Twenty-Eight

I woke up from my last slumber on this island looking forward to the day for the first time since Aztyn left me here to crumble. I have chartered a helicopter to leave here tonight. The last of my belongings were shipped off to the new house today. I found a much smaller island with enough space for a garden, a small hobby farm, and my own personal library. I realized packing up my books to ship them that I have over 1000 novels in my collection. That makes me an official library and I already have the builders working on the shelves in the main area of what will become my new house. I let go of all my former staff once they had completed their final tasks and hired new staff under my new name. Two gardeners, a maid, and a personal chef. Parts of me may have changed, but that doesn't mean I want to go back to scrubbing my own toilets. I did not hire a beekeeper. I learned enough from my time in the apiary, and I have saved that therapy for myself.

The bleak unthreading of what remained here took more time and more of me than I expected. My last task taking the longest. I couldn't find the perfect location to move to. No place felt untouched enough, hidden enough or safe enough. With everybody vacated the island was sort of tolerable. No one needed me for anything and I spent my days browsing property listings and reading in the garden or the gazebo on the cliffs, occasionally sitting on the edge of those cliffs letting the wind rush past my ears for hours. I thought it might take a whole year to find what I was looking for but all of a sudden, there it was about 3 months after Cedric departed the island, everything I had been looking for in my new beginning.

I still haven't heard from Aztyn and I have stopped expecting to. It took a long time to stop looking for him around every corner. I don't see him in my peripherals but My Nightmare stalks me in his namesake. The fitful sleep I am now used to wake me at all hours of the night. In my drowsy hazes I sometimes wonder if he will just appear from the fog as he does in my dreams. Come to finish his haunting the way he started it, with the intention of taking my life and gripping my last breath from my lungs, no eternal soul to claim, just straight to damnation for me.

I reach the cliffs on my goodbye tour of the island. Sometimes I still wonder why he let me live that day, why he promised me a quiet life I did not deserve with love the likes of which I had never felt just to rip it all away. I still don't understand why he didn't just cleave the skin from my bones, rip my heart from my chest, and put me on display like another of his horrific and spine-chilling artistic exhibitions. Instead, he did something the emotional equivalent of making me feel as if he had, and additionally was just keeping the blood pumping through my veins for his own sick amusement. This is worse than death, it is invisible torture down to the very cells that make up the structure of my body and yet my body still craves his next to mine, my heart still yearns for him, and I still burn at the thought of his whisper at my ear. It was all smoke and mirrors and I don't know which outcome I prefer, but I think death would have been kinder. They lied when they said it was better to have loved and lost. I would have rather thrown myself from those cliffs than to experience this no matter how good the sex had been or how enchanting it had been to finally feel seen.

I didn't need the glimpse of real love, however twisted we were to forever stain the way I see the world. The romance novels I read at least had plausible deniability, they're fiction. Aztyn and I were real, as real as the rock beneath my feet and when that rock gave way, I became a different kind of darkness. I thought I had nothing to lose before Aztyn came along. Then he gave me everything I had never had. He accepted me for who I was deep down to my core, even the incredibly depraved and venomous parts, the ones that claw and hunger and consume. He loved me in spite of them, sometimes I wonder if he loved me because I was as equally as fucked up as he was. We were each other's perfect equals, in immorality, damage, and monstrosities. The perfect counterparts to one another. I, his muse, carved from sin and madness. Him, my ruin wrapped in reverence; my requiem in the shape of a man.

I sway in the wind letting it take me ever so slightly. My toes curl around the sharp edge. I have stopped looking for him to save me from the pain he caused, and today I will leave behind searching for reason in an unreasonable act. I don't desire to take my own life although I have thought about it. I thought leaving this place and living the quiet life he promised me would be more spiteful than throwing myself from these cliffs. I think a part of me will always wait. For a secret hidden note, a glimpse in my peripherals, that sharpness that enters my bones when I sense he is near me and the feeling of being prey in his eyes no matter how much power I wield.

I know he feels me linger in his skin like acid. Burning away whatever was left of his humanity. He was changed too, I saw it in his eyes the day I told him all my truths, the day he pretended to tell me his, the night I gave him the offering of my blood. He was metamorphosed by us, by me; just as much as I was transfigured by him. A permanent etch upon my flesh. As if the universe itself were following a script I find myself already thumbing the place on my inner thigh where he carved his name remembering every sharp slice of the knife, silently calling out to him somewhere in the ether.

♦

The next place I find myself on my goodbye tour is my beloved gardens. The only part of this island I am sad about leaving. Most of my prized flowers have been moved, my peonies and roses transplanted at great cost to me, and a heavy stress to my gardener. The rest he insisted and assured he could plant and make them thrive again, even without the 'added nutrients. I gave him the biggest bonus of all after he explained to the new gardener how I liked my blooms taken care of.

Most of my statues have been moved to the new island as well. All that remains is the fountain where I once swam to retrieve a blank letter much to the chagrin of my always watching Nightmare. I almost grin at the memory. Looking at the garden practically empty of life makes it feel even more melancholy. I realize what I loved about this island like the bees, my library, and the life that I once felt here, I am taking with me to the next one. Whatever remains will be a scorch on this land until nature takes itself back. I shut the door to the gardens for the very last time.

My second to last stop is really the beginning of the end. The control room. Since I had so much time to plan my exit from this place, I had time to think about *how* I wanted to leave this graveyard masquerading as paradise. I think the most poetic end is to cleanse the land with fire so that life might have a chance to find a way once again. I had some help from Ivan but at exactly 9:00 PM the first charge will go off and every 6 mins another charge will go off until everything has burned to the ground with just enough time for me to make my way to the rendezvous spot where without looking back, I will finally start my life over, free of all of this except what hangs on my conscience, which I'll admit is dangerously little.

I don't deserve this life I am embarking on, I know it, and anybody hearing this story would be inclined to agree. Sometimes good things happen to bad people, life isn't fair and anyone who claims otherwise is selling something. No one is lucky or special or unstained by sin. I just wear mine more proudly. It doesn't weigh on me anymore, *it just is*. I inherited rot and rebuilt it in my image tearing apart the wreckage they called order. I didn't just fix a broken system, I made it bleed, and commanded it to kneel and call me Mother.

Zander sent me a letter a while back. One I assume was a secret from Vivianne. He said she had forbidden him from speaking to me but hadn't said anything about letters and his charm shined through even in written word. I almost miss them but then I remember how all I touch withers, crumbling to dust between my fingers, and I don't. I suppose they think one day I will pop back up like nothing ever happened. Just like I always did after an internal break in my reality, but this time was different. This time I'm not coming back. This time I'm leaving what's left of Calliope Veritas in the ash and the smoke.

I check my purse for my new passport and citizenship papers, I thumb the new letters that make up my new identity. *Nyx Graves*. The primordial goddess of the night. A woman once worshipped who now only answers to herself, soft in the way that smoke rolls across the tongue but sharp like a severed bone. Death and burial of the old. I have people who can make things happen too. I didn't need him. I feel the corners of my mouth pulling into a quiet and subtle smile. It feels bittersweet and almost like a dream that this is finally happening. I haven't allowed myself to feel joy in quite some time. It feels foreign and a little unpleasant. The best I can hope for is contentment with my new life. Asking for anything else feels like asking for too much. I am already towing the line with getting to start a new life. Best not anger the gods now.

I feel the first charge go off, a little rumble beneath my feet, and my eyes flicker to the camera screens in the control room then down to my watch. Nine on the dot. Ivan is exceptional at his job. Not many people know this Vivianne included but Ivan was the first man to convince me I could run a cult. He was the bodyguard and right-hand man to a cartel boss I dated once. He kept in touch over the years despite how things between me and his former boss ended. The second that Vivianne suggested we get a security detail and some muscle; I knew who to put into the pool. The twins never even knew that he and I were acquainted. I loved that about Ivan. I never had to tell him how to act, he just knew. It was why the twins were so surprised at the end that he had sided with me instead of Vivianne. Watching her have to swallow her pride and admit defeat, to surrender to *me*, after I had allowed her to feel superior to me and 'special' humbled her on the spot and she remembered what they had both forgotten. This cult was mine, all the devotion lay with me, and that it was my world and they were just living in it.

Cedric was right when he said that the pull I had was remarkable. I've always had that way about me. I still believe it to be more of a curse than a gift. How can you tell if people really love you, or if they love the way you make them feel when they look at you, never really seeing you for anything other than what they want to see? I think that was what has changed about me most. Once someone sees you, I mean really *sees* you for the very first time, you can't go back to being unseen. Until Aztyn, I'd never known the ache of being truly seen and he didn't just see me he rearranged me. Took the parts that I was hiding in the dark and brought them into the light, and then he worshiped them. He didn't put me on a pedestal, he brought me down off the cross. I can thank him for that one thing if nothing else.

I see the second charge on the screen but it's too far away to feel, I know if I start walking now, I'll have just

333

enough time to stand outside my cathedral and watch it burn before having to scamper to the rendezvous point. As though summoned by my pure thought alone, Ivan comes in on the radio I have in my hand.

This is Lurch to Black Widow, do you read me?

Loud and clear Lurch what's your eta?

35 out, there's a storm coming make sure you blast those extra charges yeah?

Copy Lurch, Black Widow out.

I already cut all communications except by radio and this island has been a dead zone for weeks. The deafening silence was peaceful to me, with only Ivan to speak to. I have mostly been alone in my thoughts or immersed in other worlds within the pages of my books. This final scene was crafted with one purpose, to leave no trace of me worth hoping for. I click the button for the extra charges before I leave the control room. Slipping from behind the door I briskly walk in the direction of my cathedral, knowing that it will be engulfed in flames by the time I arrive but that I must see it before I leave this island forsaken by any god who answers in the light of day.

♦

The cathedral is the true testament of my dedication to my craft. If I was going to have a cult, I was going to do it the right way. The stained glass is already broken and most of one side of the cathedral has been burned away, the stone floors remaining, the seal I had repoured blank shining in the flickering flames around it. The air was thick with the stench of ruin. Acrid smoke clawing down my throat like burnt metal and memory. Salt from the sea tangled with scorched timber, blistered paint, and the sickly-sweet reek of something unnatural. It wasn't just buildings burning, it was every secret the walls of that room held and every sin we thought we could keep buried. I hear more charges going off in the public area of the island and know my time here is coming to a quick end. If I am going to make the rendezvous point and not actually burn to a crisp, I need to move.

As I turn towards my escape route, the same one I would have used with Aztyn I can't help but yearn for him, for the ghost of a future that died before it could begin. A part of me wants to live out of more than just spite, a part

335

of me dares to hope that somewhere in the wreckage and blight of my sins there is another part of me that *does* deserve a happy ending. Redemption is for all sinners, isn't that what they say? Maybe there is no redemption for me, but perhaps there can be peace until I reclaim my rightful place in hell.

Calliope

Death is the only way, it has always been the only way.

Cali

Chapter Twenty-Nine

I walk through the gaping hole the church door left in my bedroom's entranceway. I wasn't about to give up my best ground score. It will greet me at my new home. Something in my chambers is amiss besides the fact that there is a corpse in my bed. I check to make sure it's still there, that it hasn't walked off like a living nightmare and she is still exactly where Ivan placed her. She even kind of looks like me, not that it will matter much. There won't be much left of her by the time this is all through. The fire should burn so hot it consumes any trace of any of us being here at all but in case there is anything left to remain this has to look real. When I asked where the body came from Ivan told me she died of natural causes.

He nonchalantly told me he had a few friends in a few places. I didn't bother asking any more questions. The truth is I didn't care. I cared more about getting the security systems offline than I did about where my body double came from. What's one more final sin in the grand scheme of things?

My bedroom is the only place on the compound that hasn't been gutted completely. I really only took my books and a few of my favorite dresses. It's almost as if time has stood still here. Like I am walking through the pages of my past. Thoughtfully putting the book down in favor of a new story. One where I can be free.

I don't have time to be sentimental. I take one last look at myself in the mirror. I'm still not used to the dark hair that now frames my face or how I sometimes look like a porcelain doll, my eyes impossibly large. I am dressed in black head to toe, a satchel bag at the ready on my arm like I'm going on some kind of spy mission. How much work does a girl got to do to get a new identity around here? I take one last look around my chambers and through the smoke that has begun to trickle in as more of the compound burns around me, I see a figment of my imagination. Except the figment of my imagination speaks.

"I like you as a brunette, it suits you...*Nyx.*"

He says this as if he hadn't left me here to wither away without him. I stare at Aztyn in disbelief. My teeth clenched and my stomach grinding. The urge to run and jump into his arms is stifled by the swift anger rising from my gut.

"What are you doing here?" I shriek with all the venom I can muster.

"The better question is, how did you not know I was coming?"

My eyes dart around the room looking desperately for something to throw at him. They settle on a crystal bowl left on the coffee table and I grab it, raising it above my head before throwing it in his direction. He dodges it of course and it smashes against the wall behind him.

"Pretty good arm you got there. Surprising for a princess."

"I don't have time for this. You can burn too for all I care."

I turn to leave but he rushes to my side holding me back.

"*We* don't have much time actually. I can see you're upset so..."

"Oh, you can see I'm upset? What gave you that fucking impression?" I say breaking free of his grasp and clocking him in the mouth with my first.

"I deserve that Little Muse but can we get going?" He says lightly, wiping the blood from his mouth with the back of his hand grinning like a fool.

"You don't get to come with me Aztyn."

The room is steadily increasing in temperature and more and more smoke begins to fill the air.

"Of course I do, I'm your husband."

He smirks in my direction gesturing towards my safe room. This exchange reminds me of our first encounter on the cliffs. Instead of intriguing me like he did then he's infuriating me further.

"I can explain everything while Ivan holds a gun to my head if you wish Calliope, but right now we need to get out of here."

Another charge goes off too close for comfort. The glass in my chambers breaks from the vibration knocking us both to the ground. I feel the crunch of the radio beneath my body. I was supposed to be gone by now. Aztyn is by my side in an instant holding his hand out which I refuse to take. I stand on my own accord staring him down the entire time.

"You don't get to walk back in here after destroying me, and demand I take you back and listen to more of your lies."

"I demand you listen to my explanation. I never asked you to take me back," he says calmly dodging something my hand made purchase with as it clashes to the ground.

"Besides, we never broke up."

I'm sweating now, from the adrenaline, from the fires licking the walls, from seeing Aztyn again. It's all almost too much to bear. I have to hold it together.

"At the risk of us both dying here in vain of the preparations I've made to have a new beginning I have a few things to say."

My hand clasps around a flower vase still full of flowers.

"Throw another thing at me and mark my words Little Muse I'll give you twice the punishment I gave you for fucking Zander. I'm a patient man, but not that patient."

I tilt my head and cock my arm the vase front and center. Aztyns eyes burn as if nothing would please him more than getting to punish me for something he very clearly deserves. Aztyn shifts his weight and suddenly he's beside me again, his hand on my wrist squeezing hard until I let go of the vase and it crashes to the floor beside us. I can smell him over the fire that's burning around us, his mahogany and tobacco scent invading my lungs. I soften against my will as tears fill my eyes.

"You broke me Aztyn, not with the manipulation or the lies, or the borderline abusive style of punishment you have for my offences."

He smiles wickedly at this point in my speech and my pussy clenches in response even though I feel my cheeks are wet with tears.

"You broke me when you abandoned me, without a trace in the middle of the night. Then you come waltzing in here at the Cinderella midnight hour as if I'm supposed to just forgive you?"

I raise my hand to his face connecting with his cheek and his eyes burn holes right through mine. My fight or flight kicks in and I get the urge to kick and run just like the prey he makes me feel like.

I should have been long gone by now, who knows if Ivan is even still waiting for me. We both look up as a loud cracking sound rips through the air, sharp and sudden as if the ceiling is about to crack in two at any moment.

"I broke you because I knew you would do what needed to be done, and you had to be motivated naturally to do it because death was the only way-out Calliope, death has always been our only way out."

He pulls me close to him in the thick smoke that's filling the air. It's entirely too warm and I feel my legs start to go wobbly at the knee. I feel his arms bearing my weight and I let them. My only way out now is cradled against his chest either that or we both die in the flames. I make one last plea for my own sanity in this moment where I am forced to surrender to the assistance of this man, just like the day he saved me from myself

"And if when all this is over, I still want to escape even if it means escaping from you, is that still on the table?"

"You can never escape me Calliope. I will always find you because I was always meant to find you. You could run forever, and I would be but steps behind you to hunt you into the afterlife. You run through my veins now. You're a part of me just like I am a part of you. I'll never let you out of my sight again."

Then he kissed me, and I felt the desperation within it, the longing, the ache he had felt all this time without me as the storm that Ivan had warned me about fills the room, still not strong enough to douse the flames. I still have my questions but I knew the moment I saw him he would always have the answers and I would grasp at their reality even if I knew they were flat out lies. The only thing I feel now is truth so I take it for what it's worth, even if it is just an *illusion of lust*. It's the closest I'll ever get to salvation and he and I both know it.

"I promise if you let me explain, it will all make sense. I bent time and cheated fate to be here this evening. Trust me, just one second more. I'm not asking you to forgive me, just hear me out."

"I forgave you the second I saw your face. Ivan has a helicopter outside the grotto, if he's even still here."

When the second crack rang out the ceiling did crumble, crushing us beneath the weight of the rubble. The smoke choking both our lungs. The last thing I remember is Aztyns body flexing against me as we were tossed to the ground trying to shield me from the inevitable. I wonder if we'll look like the Lovers of Valdaro when they unearth our bodies from this tomb.

Death is the only way; it has always been the only way.

Nyx

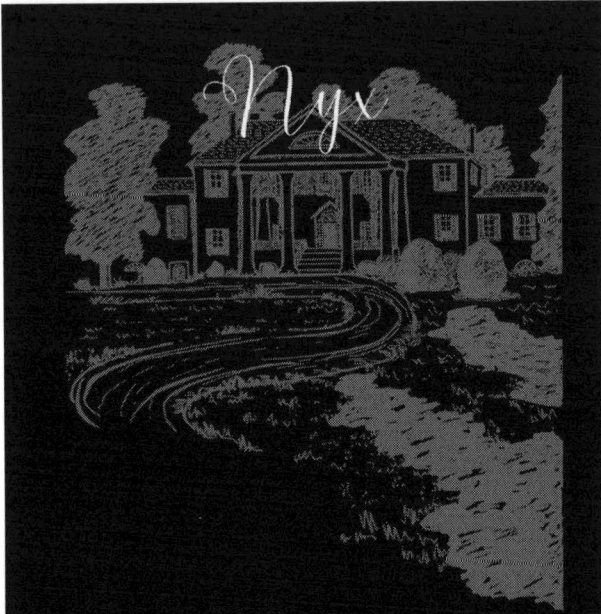

Calliope only knew death. Let me tell you about <u>living</u>.

Nyx

Chapter Thirty

I don't remember much from those early days. I
know Ivan pulled me from the wreckage, having
finally found the switches in the secret
passageways. He watched the ceiling collapse on us from the
safe room. He reluctantly saved Aztyns life, as a favor to me
and for no other reason. He took us on the helicopter to the
island. He gleefully held a gun to Aztyns head while he
explained himself just like Aztyn said he could and I let him
hang there at the end of it all wondering if I would let Ivan
pull the trigger. I didn't.

Aztyn explained that he knew me well enough to know
that I would do the next most logical thing when escape was
no longer an option. That I would burn everything to the
ground. Although he wasn't expecting me to be so literal,
but I am nothing if not thorough. When I didn't search for
him, he accessed my computer and concluded through my
internet history that I was instead searching for a new place
to start my life over.

He sent a fake ad to my account. Within 24 hours a private party had sent a bid for that particular piece of property in which he already owned. When the last of my books, the bees and the staff showed up, he knew it was only a matter of time before I did. Something in him sensed the dangerous edge I was walking on, the tightrope between life and death, and he came for me. When I asked him why I should forgive him for abandoning me in the first place, he said I shouldn't. That what he did was unforgivable, but that he hoped one day I would come to understand it was the only way we could ever have a future.

Then I stabbed him with a fork.

He commended me on being quick enough to do so and I smiled at him for the first time since we were rescued. I couldn't believe how he had manipulated me into buying this island. The same island Aztyn had prepared for his retirement. The one he had told me every detail about before falling asleep at night. The one I had unconsciously looked for when I searched for a new life.

When I remembered what Cedric had said about him being a former FBI agent and confronted him about it, he told me that he may not have told me directly but he didn't *not* tell me either.

I grabbed Ivan's gun and shot him in the foot.

When he said 'you shot me' in disbelief I told him I thought I'd save him the trouble of shooting himself in the foot and he laughed which made me want to shoot him again but I didn't do that either.

Actually, we made up quite loudly that evening when I finally let him back into my bedroom if I recall correctly, all bloodied and war wounded. The echo of my former self once thought about trying to slip away into the night without him, but I knew his threat to hunt me into the afterlife was a real one albeit finding it quite romantic at the time. I still think it could have been really great foreplay to play Carmen Sandiego for a while, chasing each other all over the world. With Ivan as my bodyguard, I might have actually stood a chance. In the end I decided it wasn't worth the punishment when he finally caught me and crawled back into bed instead.

I watched my former self be declared dead by authorities on the news which was pretty surreal. A tragedy the newscaster called it. I laughed when he said it. My estate was awarded to my surviving husband of course. The townsfolk at the closest port think Aztyn and I are just eccentric rich people who made their money in stocks and bonds just trying to 'get away from it all'. They know us as Nyx and Silas Graves. We associate with who we need to in town and they know only what we tell them. They have no reason to suspect we have entire previous lives to hide.

Ivan stayed with us for a while to make sure we didn't kill each other, or to make sure I had help to dispose of Aztyns body. I'm not sure which. I asked him to retire as a man for hire and to be my personal bodyguard, but he said I didn't need him anymore, and he never did learn how to sit still. When he was confident I wasn't going to inflict any more damage on Aztyn, he left knowing he would always have a place with me. In the end, he had been my most loyal friend. He still keeps in touch.

Zander went on to marry an AI tech guru's daughter and lives in Japan, he has a little boy and seems really happy. I almost sent him a letter once. A version of me long since buried wanted him to know I was alive but ultimately, I decided it was best if he continued to think I was dead. Vivianne runs the US branch of that family's AI tech company and has been rumored to have eloped just recently to a US Marine. From the leaked gossip photos, she looks like she married for love after all. Both the twins got endings they never would have gotten if I hadn't made the choices I made in the end. I hold no guilt, but I wish they could see me as the woman I have become. I think Zander would be proud, but Viv would be the most surprised.

I'll never be a trad wife, but I look pretty different in my apron baking honey cakes with our raw honey, and chasing after the ducks I've affectionately named. I'm not all born-again though, I had to adapt. You can't fake your death and still expect to lean on the living. I still have my staff of course and occasionally Aztyn and I run harmless little hustles on the tourists when we get bored, but mostly we eat the fruit from our garden, have coffee together every morning, cook dinner together every evening. It's the quiet simple life he promised me and I've never been happier.

When Aztyn makes love to me at night he calls out my real name and he still calls me his Little Muse. He spends his days writing poetry while I read, sometimes when it rains he reads his poems to me, and sometimes we just dance on the porch to the sound of the rain thrumming against the roof. He is still as forceful and dominant as ever, but it's different. Not in a lousy way but in a way that is contrasting. We no longer fight for our lives and the soft easy life has affected us both. We breathe deeper and easier every day that passes. I have no doubt that the monsters deep inside us both wouldn't hesitate to come out if circumstances called for it but nowadays they mostly slumber. Except on the occasions that I need my Nightmare to fuck me loud enough to drown out the surviving traces of my past.

A fragment of me will always be ravenous and he will always be the cure. Taking control, breaking me apart, and putting my pieces back together. It is the alchemy of us. He loves the surrender, and I love the chase. Our pasts almost don't seem real somedays and other days this life feels like the whispers of smoke. Like if I move too fast it will all just dissipate into nothing. Those are the nights I panic and my dreams are filled with rivers of blood and endless fire. Still, he holds me steadfast. Never faltering. Not even on the nights I still have the urge to run away. When I wake up from those seemingly endless nights of restless sleep we travel to the nearest airport and he takes me somewhere new. Somewhere the threads of my past cannot catch up to us and we stay until I am ready to go home.

I may not have deserved a happy ending but I got one all the same. I do not take a moment of our life for granted. I know what chains await me in the afterlife. What sins I must carry with me into the ether and beyond. I also know that Aztyn will be right behind me come hell or high water. I know I will never be free of him, not even when death calls us home.

The End.

About the Author

Kylie Doyle is a Canadian author, content creator, and gothic forest fairy living in a cozy off-grid tiny home in Alberta. She's the writer behind the darkly enchanting Hunt For Magic series and her newest novel, Illusions of Lust, a cult-themed dark romance dripping in obsession and vengeance.

Kylie has been immersed in the publishing world for quite some time and is the founder of Author Alchemy Consulting, where she mentor's writers and entrepreneurs through branding, storytelling, and soulful strategy. She also curate's immersive bookish experiences and events that feel like stepping into a living fairytale—often dark, always unforgettable.

When she's not plotting deliciously twisted tales or reading tarot by candlelight, she's creating moody, magical content that inspires others to live their most authentic, unapologetic lives.

Trusted by indie authors and readers alike, Kylie is a force of transformation on and off the page.

Follow her @write.by.moonlight to step into the shadows of her worlds.

Acknowledgments

To everyone who believed in the magic of this story... thank you. I know this one took me a long time to spit out and I hope it was worth the wait. I went through the craziest life transformations in the two years that it took to get this book written, and I just need to thank the readers who never gave up on me, and even re-read Hunt For Magic just to have something from me to read. I promise the last two books for the series are coming in 2026. I couldn't have done it without your never-ending support.

L-This book wouldn't have ever begun if it hadn't been for you. Everyone owes you a special thank you, but especially me. Thanks for making me your favorite author. You make me proud to me a big sister. I love you.

The Inkwell Guild- You guys pushed me through the end, when I was craving a community, I reached out and there you were. You are my favorite pack of weirdo's, my coven of literary witches, and just the best people on the planet. Who said you shouldn't be friends with strangers on the internet? I can't thank you enough.

Manufactured by Amazon.ca
Bolton, ON